David Sharrock, Ireland correspondent, The Times

'Brilliantly inventive and original. An immediate and hilarious classic.'

Richard English, author of *Armed Struggle*

'Brutally funny about academics and paramilitaries... made me laugh out loud on a Ryanair flight.'

Ruth Dudley Edwards, author of *Newspapermen*

'The funniest book I have read for years... a threat to human dignity.'

Malachi O'Doherty, author of *Empty pulpits*

'An unprecedented voice, unparalleled sense of humour, unequalled insight. Christopher Marsh has it all.'

Felipe Fernandez-Armesto, author of *Pathfinders: a global history of exploration*

'A daring debut novel... a hilarious take on Belfast life.'

The Irish World

'Witty, engaging, joyous: a real pleasure.'

Paul Bew

A YEAR IN
THE PROVINCE

A YEAR IN THE PROVINCE

Being the memoir of Jesús Sánchez Ventura

Christopher Marsh

**Beautiful
Books**

Beautiful Books Limited
36-38 Glasshouse Street
London W1B 5DL

ISBN 9781905636679

9 8 7 6 5 4 3 2 1

Jacket design by Ian Pickard.
Printed and bound in the UK by CPI Mackays, Chatham ME5 8TD.

For Katie and Lucy

Prologue

In which a peculiar decision is made.

My name is Jesús Sánchez Ventura, and this is the story of my quest for a better life. I will speak to you in English for the very simple reason that I am more than competent so to do. Perhaps you will from time to time find my language almost diabolically fluent. You must understand that it is learned from the classics of your literature rather than from the old man in your dingy northern pub or, worse still, from your televisual celebrities (I spit out the words with scorn). Every night, I go to bed with better men than they, with Shakespeare or Dickens or Wilde, and I know what I am doing. I have slept with most of your literary giants, and they have infected me in a thousand ways. I therefore make no apologies for lashing you with your own mother's tongue. Dare I say, gentle reader, that my English is probably superior to your own? Climb my linguistic tree and search its boughs for diseased fruit, if you must, but please do not be downcast if you throw up nothing. Instead, take heart from this pledge: my memoir will present you with almost everything that you could wish for in such a narrative. It has orgasms, phantasms, fanaticism, witticism, ostracism, osteopathy, empathy, energy, synergy, misery, mystery, history, hysteria, wisteria, wisdom, condoms, cordons, organs and, last but not least, orgasms. It also has the kind of circularity that brings wholeness to life even if it never really advances one's cause. As if this were not enough, it has natural scenery that can only be described as – how do you say? – picaresque. Are you with me? *Bueno*.

My strange tale first began to twitch on a sultry evening in southern Spain . . .

Begoña and I sit together in the shade of a vivid orange tree, sipping the first of the new wine from my dead grandfather's finest earthenware goblets while a golden oriole flutes melodiously from my nearby bush. Blue and yellow butterflies flit aimlessly around us and the fruit ripens silently in the boughs overhead. Andalusia has never seemed more tranquil. Down by the wall, one of the goats emits a loud hissing sound, as if punctured, and, seconds later, a more than pungent odour visits our hospitable nostrils on the softest of zephyrs. After a moment, Begoña lifts her head, fixing me with that large and mesmeric green eye. Her question catches me in the unawares, just below the belt.

'Do you think we will always live here, Jesús?'

I deliver an automatic response.

'My ancestors grew these olive trees with their bare hands, and I am but a steward.'

'No, but think about it. Do you really believe that we shall die in this house?'

This time, I hesitate.

'Why do you ask these questions, *chiquita*?'

'Oh, I don't know. I was wondering. I mean, we're happy here, aren't we? This is our home.'

I am about to reply in soothing affirmation, when something lands on my head with a dull thump. It is an orange, but no ordinary orange. No, this is a symbolic orange, and by no means the last that you will encounter in this story.[1] It comes to rest on the dry ground beside me, and I feel momentarily decomposed. I stare at it but, just for a second, completely fail to recognise it as any kind of orange at all. It could be anything. I experience the strangest sensation. My answer, when it eventually emerges, is utterly unexpected in its passion and power.

'I am so damnably happy that I might as well be dead already.'

She could say any number of things in response, but Begoña being Begoña, she seeks no further clarification. She is so delectably intuitive, and can feel my intentions throbbing in the hot air between us. After watching me in silence for several seconds, she says calmly and decisively, 'Then we must move somewhere else.'

You will surely be craving further information on my personal passage to this extraordinary moment, and I fear that we must therefore cast some light into the dark hole that is my background. Let me fill you in.

My father – may he blow his own trumpet with the saints and angels in heaven – was at one time an olive magnet, and the richest man in our pueblo. As young boys, my

---

[1]   Where we are going, all the oranges are symbolic.

3

brother and I were accorded great respect as the progeny of Alejandro Sánchez, and we strutted the streets of Picazón del Moro (The Moor's Itch) with our heads held high in the clouds. Over time, lamentably, this changed. The olive business was hard and the fruits of our labour were small and difficult to place. Global warming has not been kind to Andalusia. Our father lost his nerve, and spent far too much of his money and time in the company of the Dutch exiles whose domination of Andalusian culture was then only in its infancy. He would sit in their progressive pancake bars in Granada, frittering away the Sánchez inheritance and listening with prickly ears to fantastic northern stories of overcrowded cities and cool climatic conditions. Quickly he lost his mind, and, as we say in Spain, 'where the mind goes, the body will soon follow'. And so it proved. With body and mind both lost, there was no hope for my dear father and, reluctantly, we buried him.

My brother grew dull and sullen in the wake of Papá's demise, and we will have no need to speak any more of him. He left Andalusia to study engineering and, nowadays, he builds light aircraft for the wealthy playboys of Madrid, like some servile fool. I, on the other hand, decided to fill my dead father's tempting void with my bubbling precocity. Though I was younger than my brother, I was always my father's favourite, and his chosen successor. Permit me to share a precious memory. One day, some time before he died, we two stood together on the slope amongst the olive trees. The sun baked our heads, and the vultures soared patiently above us, carried high on their thermal blankets. Papá put his arm around me, enveloping me in his agricultural charisma, and

4

said, 'My boy, you must promise me something. Well, one of two things. Your first option is this: swear to me on your honour that when I am gone you will cherish and nourish what remains of our land.'

Of course, I was flattered.

'Yes, Papá, I promise.'

'Good boy, but hold your horses. You must hear the second option: promise me that you will get the hell out of here before it is all gone.'

Now I was confused.

'Must I make my choice now, Papá?'

'No, a firm commitment to fulfil either one of the two promises will be quite sufficient at this point in time.'

'Then, Papá, you have my word.'

He nodded.

In that moment, that happy moment, the revolutions of the world seemed to cease, and all the planet's creatures heard for one short second the cosmic harmony of the spheres. Papá's feet, however, remained firmly on the hard, dry ground: he looked down at it, and expressed his desire to enrich the earth with some fertiliser or, better still, a little cow manure ('*un poco de caca de vaca*'). This last phrase became hooked like a trout in my mind, and I began chanting it rhythmically while I danced frenetically between the trees. For a moment, Papá forgot his cares, and he too began to skip and shout. Eventually, exhausted, we ground to a halt, and leant on one another like a pair of rakes, still consumed by mirth. We laughed and laughed, sending raucous guffaws echoing through the mountains all the way down to the shimmering blue Mediterranean.

I first came across Begoña on the eve of her seventeenth birthday, and was immediately struck by the sultry, seductive beauty and exotic mannerisms of her companion and best friend, the delectably diminutive María de la Contorsión (as we say in Spain, 'Where women and sardines are concerned, little ones are best'). We were drinking in one of the many bars in Picazón del Moro, and my eyes followed this spell-binding creature for the entire evening. I knew she knew I was watching her from the way in which she seemed not to, and I interpreted her studied disinterest as an unequivocal sign of arousal. When she prepared to leave, I bade my companions farewell and strutted straight through the heavy wooden door in a mood of ascending *expectación*. As I had anticipated, she was waiting outside and she met my gaze without flinching. I moved closer. 'Don't touch me,' she said with a deliberately sharpened tongue, 'I am not a guitar.' Then she took one final puff from her cigar, and said to me, 'Your olives are too little and I have no taste for them, but I imagine that you can make love to my friend.' From that moment on, I knew that Begoña was the only girl for me. And when I examined her closely, I soon saw that she was rather beautiful – most pleasantly constructed, and a wonderful sight when in full flower. I noted her sturdy stems, and her lovely complexion, sometimes yellowy-orange, sometimes orangey-pink, and occasionally, in moments of unbridled passion, pinky-purple. 'This one will blossom miraculously,' I muttered to myself, 'provided that I keep her compost moist.'

We met, married and mated within the space of five exhilarating years, settling into an easy, almost telepathic compatibility and operating as a formidable team (particularly me). Our happiness was always grounded in a shared predilection for acts of love committed outdoors, *al aire libre* (you would probably say 'in the air freshener'). This was somewhat seasonal, and we usually interpreted *Semana Santa* (Holy Week) as our signal to 'let loose the juice'. Begoña would drift into a mystical trance in order to select the most stimulating of locations. I still feel a certain twinge of physical discomfort as I recall the punishing schedule we followed during the spring of our first active year. In one typical week, we made rhythmic, even poetic love in no fewer than forty-two different places (if you read the list aloud, your pleasure will be buttressed beyond belief): in the courtyard, up a mountain, down in the village beside a fountain, in the fields, beneath the stars, outside shops, on moving cars, in amongst a herd of goats, dressed as saints on carnival floats, up against rough bricks and mortar, over the rainbow, underwater, on the pavement, down a well, up a cork tree, inside a bell, after lightning but prior to thunder, on top of gravestones (one time, under), twice or thrice on sandy beaches, under olives, lemons, peaches, almonds, cherries, figs and grapes, on ancient rocks of improbable shapes, watched by cattle, wolves and eagles, vultures, otters, tourists, seagulls, neighbours, hermits, nuns and priests, beneath the table at village feasts, and – probably the best of all – while tumbling over a waterfall. On this last occasion, Begoña sustained a compound fracture of her right wrist, and she opens jam jars with a curious, jerky movement to this day.

Our courtship was interrupted only by my decision to

attend university in far-flung Salamanca. I studied English and literature, developing a taste for academic pursuits that quite dumbfounded me. Under the tutelage of the imminent Professor Polvo, I obtained a first-class degree in record time (it took me five weeks in total, but during one of these Begoña was visiting and we were busy 'sight-seeing'). I then suffered something akin to what I think you call 'burn-out', but managed to rekindle my flame in order to complete a highly commended doctoral thesis six months later. This piece of work duly became that published masterpiece of literary criticism, *Playing With (S)words in Renaissance Europe: Vocabulary and Violence*, a work with which I imagine you are already familiar.

When I had completed this innovative study, I gathered my notes and returned home to Andalusia. Begoña and I resumed our outdoor pursuits until and beyond the point at which she found herself with child, and we hurriedly decided to make our vows before God got wind of us. Her parents, for their own unfathomable reasons, did not regard me as a suitable matchstick for their eldest daughter, and they spent a number of days chasing us through the ancient cork forests on horseback and clad in light antique armour, wielding pitchforks and voicing their misgivings with a distressing combination of syllables and decibels. We, in contrast, were naked and mounted only on a shared mule (also naked), and it therefore came as no surprise when we were eventually encircled in a clearing. At this moment, Begoña began to sob, her breasts and buttocks wobbling in captivating unison. This sad sight would have cracked and crushed a heart of stone, and in an instant her parents were overcome with love. I too succumbed, and so we two were wed.

During the next five years, we overtook the family farm, inadvertently catapulting my mother into oblivion, and produced three children of our own, all of them daughters. We named them Concepción, Purificación and Dilatación, and we took pride in the fact that they had known no other life. They were healthy, happy, and completely organic by default. If anything, they seemed to develop more quickly than urban children and we smiled inwardly as we watched them out in the orchard, skipping barefoot amongst the snakes and scorpions and treading only occasionally in the wrong place. I loved each one, and I dotted on them from a suitably manly distance. It was a simple life that we led. We had neither television nor internet, but my word how we glowed! In contrast, my brother's children in Madrid seemed simply to be taking up valuable space on a shrivelling planet. To judge from the photographs, they had the appearance of battery-operated chickens, and each Christmas we would chuckle outwardly to see their dumb, vacant faces staring blankly out at us from the glossy prints. I would not like to say that we were smug, but we were unbelievably pleased with ourselves.

We performed quite a forward roll in the life of the pueblo, and considered ourselves content. Begoña was one of the leading lights in the annual 'Concurso de los Roedores' (Contest of the Rodents). This extraordinary spectacle takes place every July in Picazón del Moro, and obsesses the minds of all local wives for at least twelve months beforehand. Each woman selects a pet rat, and names it after a local saint or matador. The señoras then feed and pamper their animals, invariably neglecting their menfolk in the process. The rats are trained meticulously for the day on which they will all career insanely through the narrow streets, decked out in gay ribbons and pursued by their excited mistresses, who shriek and scream in encouragement, each one hoping that her beloved creature will reach the plaza first. The woman who trains the victor is crowned '*La Reina del Verano*' (Queen of the Summer) and permitted to skewer the first rat – by custom, not her own – in preparation for the barbecue that marks the festival of St. Roland, who was of course gnawed by assorted small animals until only his pelvis remained (it is now in the cathedral at Seville). In those happy times, those years without tears, I loved such occasions with a passion, never imagining a day upon which I, and even my beloved Begoña, would grow weary of the rat race and crave something different.

Then, out of a burning blue Andalusian sky, came that fateful bombshell of realisation. I will put it simply for you: we were too happy, our air was too clean and our produce too fresh. Without realising it, I had come to feel that a life without change and challenge was no life at all. In the weeks that followed, I found myself craving unfamiliar metropolitan things that had somehow infiltrated my consciousness without my knowledge: litter, cinemas, neon lighting, ladies of the night, umbrellas, pooper-scoopers (we call them *caca-cans*), baseball caps, bubble gum, shiny magazines, cocaine, hooligans, beefy burgers, cotton wool balls, riot police, and so forth. We purchased a small television set, and huddled around it to watch the advertisements for modern material goods. We also installed a computer, thus plugging ourselves into contemporary culture once and for all. Begoña bought her first bra, and discarded the contraption made from large seashells and fencing wire with which she had somehow supported herself for many years. We ordered our first DVD, and Concepción and I had great sport spinning it to each other across the courtyard before, eventually, it was lost in the undergrowth. The knowledge that we could simply purchase another one was truly liberating. For the first time in my life, I began throwing things away, sometimes just for the sheer fun of it. I was a little embarrassed, creeping out in the night to toss perfectly good tractor batteries or items of furniture onto the rough ground just above our land. Then I would scurry back to bed, snuggling up against Begoña as if nothing had happened. My secret sense of disquiet eased, however, when I skulked up to my private dump one night, only to find that my wife was already there, hurling tasteful little statuettes of the Blessed Virgin over the fence!

Even fresh oranges lost their appeal. In earlier times, I had taken primitive rustic delight in being able to pick them straight from the tree, as and when we needed them for cooking or throwing at foreign cyclists. I would stand beneath the branches in the cool heat of early evening, simply absorbing the scene for a few minutes before making advances towards my chosen specimen. The oranges suspended there looked to me for all the world like little balls of sunshine, tiny offspring of that great citrus fruit in the sky. I would grope them, one by one, on the tree, carefully selecting those that – at this single moment in time – were utterly perfect. Then I would pick the best, carrying them purpose-fully into the house with a benign but slightly demented half-grin on my face. The oranges would sit on the chopping board, awaiting their destiny, and I loved the fact that an hour later they still held so much of the sun's heat within their dimpled skins. I would lift them up, cradling each in the palm of my hand and marvelling at its warmth.

This childish ecstasy came to a rude end when we watched an advertisement for an international chain of supermarkets on television. We saw row upon row of fruit so bright and colourful that – may God be merciful – I felt an excited trifle. Concepción put the thoughts of us all into words.

'Papá, why aren't our oranges big, shiny and beautiful like those?'

Begoña said something about wax, but I was already on my way through the door. I went directly to our trees. It was true: our oranges were dull and small. They looked like the malformed country cousins of those modern super-fruit, and they shamed me (shame is very important in Mediterranean societies).

But if we were to move, then where were we to go? It was a question with which we grappled for days. We needed a location that was the very opposite of our current home. Begoña and I agreed that our existence in Picazón del Moro was warm, dry, relaxed, easy to comprehend, secure and integrated. Logically, therefore, we were looking for somewhere to build a life that was cold, wet, tense, incomprehensible, insecure and disintegrated. We searched the virtual globe, but could find few places that met all of our exacting criteria. Amongst my father's personal belongings, his pitiful collection of special effects, we found a box full of cheap paperback books written by dried-up Spaniards who had fled north in search of *agua* and *aventura*. Such forward-looking literature was already fashionable at the time, and remains so to this day. Poor Papá had evidently been dreaming. We read his books avidly, and learnt all about *El Esquimal de Extremadura* and many other brave characters.[2] We waited for inspiration, but none came. Each session ended ignominiously with me drifting off to fondle some of the heavily processed and imported chicken nuggets that graced our new freezer. Was it not a veritable wonder that creatures reared on a diet of God-knows-what and killed on the other side of the world, possibly as many as five years previously, could be transformed into these unrecognizable pieces and brought to my home, where they provided me and my family with food that was so much cheaper and more convenient than the real live chickens that pecked idiotically in the dust outside our house?

Then, one day, I returned to the kitchen and found Begoña stimulating herself in front of a television programme that drew comparisons between the Basque separatists and the Republicans of a mysterious land called Ulster.[3] They were broadcasting an interview with a very old and very angry man of the cloth. He was standing on the steps of a church, and the wettest-looking rain we had ever seen was thrashing his face. His idiosyncratic white eyebrows grew straight out

---

[2] This was a man who left one of Spain's poorest regions to begin a new life in the far north of Canada.

[3] The Basques, according to experts, are directly descended from Cro-Magnon man. I will say no more.

from his face, forming a natural umbrella that protected his eyes from the onslaught. Unblinkingly he continued to shout, and I feel sure that his head would have ignited but for the cooling effect of the rain. He was, as we say in Spain, 'climbing up the grapevine'.[4] With the aid of the subtitles, we were able to learn that this man was no lover of the Irish republicans. Without the aid of the subtitles, we would have been completely bemused and not a little troubled, *como un cerdito en un acuario de tiburones*.[5] My English – you will now concede – is formidable, but this strange pale-faced anti-priest filled me with bafflement. I looked at Begoña and Begoña looked at me. At last, we knew where we were going.

---

[4] I think you would say 'going up the wall'.
[5] 'Like a piglet in a shark tank'.

PART I

Summer into Autumn

Chapter 1

In which Jesús prepares for adventure and is perplexed, bemused and confuddled in strict rotation.

Strange though it may seem, we both felt that destiny was at work. Belfast sounded perfect with its anagrammatical possibilities (Stab Elf, Flab Set, Stable F) and its shiny ring of menace. If our goal was to escape from cosy sun-dried contentment by seeking renaissance in a challenging drizzle-drenched urban environment, then surely there was nowhere more suitable. Our relatives in Spain were incredulous, and their reactions formed a set of jangling variations around a simple theme. A single example will therefore be sufficient. One day, I returned home to find Begoña's father feeding a large bonfire in my own courtyard. As I drew closer, I realised that he was burning my father's collection of escapist books and chanting 'Pernicious! Pernicious! Into the flames they go!' I affected a quizzical expression, and he addressed me thus: 'I will kill you, you goat, you lizard, you snake! I should have forked you in the forest when I had the chance. I always knew that you would bring madness to my daughter, but now you are leading her from Herod to Pilate.[6] Many

---

[6] You would surely say 'out of the frying pan into the friar'.

17

people, you know, go looking for wool and come back shorn. It will not happen, it cannot be. You can embark on your voyage to hell, if you want – in fact, I will pay you to go – but you will not uproot my Begoña. She stays.' I listened carefully, but did not panic, sensing that this was nothing that could not be resolved over a bottle of fine wine and some *chorizo de erizo*.[7]

He was dumping his anxieties on me, but I soldiered on underturd. Begoña and I commenced a vigorous campaign of research, making full and inventive use of our new computer. Our electricity supply was intermittent, but we nevertheless learned all that we could about our promised land. We decorated the house with hand-written and informative reminders. Our fridge bore the following message: 'The people of Northern Ireland consume more tranquillisers than anyone else in Western Europe.' The nearby cupboard, in contrast, sounded a more optimistic note: 'According to surveys, Northern Irish men and women actually feel safer as they go about their daily lives than most other Europeans.' I wondered whether the reason for this might be that everyone was under such heavy sedation. Begoña was not so sure, and directed my attention towards the note that she had fixed imaginatively to our magnificent toaster: 'If sectarian killings and punishment attacks are excluded from the statistics, then Belfast has for many years enjoyed one of the lowest crime rates of all modern cities.' We were much reassured by this. And every time I visited the lavatory, I was reminded that 'A quantity of rain equal to

---

[7] Hedgehog sausage, a speciality of our pueblo.

the average annual deposit for the whole of Andalusia falls every lunchtime in Northern Ireland.'

Little by little, we were making the acquaintance of the people of Belfast, even before we enjoyed them in the flesh. Begoña had attached a historical note to the inside of our ancient front door: 'The roots of today's conflict go back at least as far as the Protestant plantations of James I's reign.' This intrigued us. We did not know any Protestants in Spain, and we were astounded to discover that they could actually be grown from seed. I knew that this was precisely the kind of detail that I would have to master if I were to find employment in Northern Ireland's mainly learned seat, The Royal University of Belfast (RUB). We were not rich and we knew that one of us would have to save some bacon. We further reasoned that the global success of *Playing With (S)words* might stand me in good stead with the academics.

Once again, the hand of fate beckoned me. Half of something called a 'job-share' was advertised on the internet:

'*The Royal University of Belfast seeks a lecturer in early modern history (to share duties with Dr. Connor McCann). The successful candidate is likely to specialise in the history of England and/or Ireland in the period 1500-1700. S/he will be research active and will join a department rated 10* in the most recent RAPE.*'

The final sentence smelled a little fishy. It had a cryptical dimension, and we soon realised that it was written in some sort of secret cod. The 'RAPE' was presumably a terrorist organisation (perhaps the 'Republican Army of Patriotic

Eire'), and the expectation that the person appointed would be 'active' sounded rather ominous.[8] Was it all part of some subterranean drive to recruit an informative mole? Despite these misgivings, we decided that I should submit an application, regardless of the fact that I had no training as a historian. So, I duly drafted a fantastical *curriculum vitae*. Begoña had learned from an American magazine article ('How to get what you want right now') that, in the modern age, an ability to fabricate an impressive 'résumé' was all part of the employment game. 98% of leading US directors had apparently said that they would much rather employ someone with an excellent but massively deceitful CV than someone whose potted career was solid but honest. The most highly rated job applicants in corporate America were those who could not only manufacture a fine life history from thin air, but who could then persuade a 'lie detector' machine that they were telling the truth.[9] All this seemed strange to me, but I knew that I would have to adjust my instincts if I were to survive in a competitive urban environment. So I took the statistics seriously and really went to town. By the time I had finished, I had even convinced myself that I was the man for the job, and one of my old professors at Salamanca graciously produced a reference that ended, as I recall, with the fulsome tribute, 'Dr. Sánchez

---

[8] Many weeks later, I learned that 'RAPE' stood for 'Research Activity and Productivity Evaluation', the intrusive monitoring system that dominates the lives of British academics and inhibits their appreciation of even the most basic pleasures of life.

[9] In Andalusia, we have 'lie detectors' too, but we call them priests (and half of them, I must concede, are broken).

Ventura is, by his own admission, an historian of profound significance, and I urge you to consider his plausible application with reasonable though not exhaustive thoroughness.'

I was interviewed by 'video link' in Granada, and managed to skip through this minefield without loss of face. I assured the inquisitors that any number of groundbreaking academic articles were 'in the pipeline' (for Spaniards, this means 'stuck' and 'causing an impassable blockage', but to English speakers – most fortunately for me – it apparently conveys the more optimistic sense that something is well on its way). I was delighted to receive a letter the following week advising me that the job was mine. Months later, I learned that I had in fact been the only candidate. Four others were called to Belfast for interview, but their plane from England was hijacked by the members of a tiny organisation called PIRATE (the Pure Irish Republican Army True and Everlasting, itself a 'splinter group' of BRAIN, the Best Republican Army of Ireland Nowadays) and forced to make a landing in the sea. Two of the four survived the impact, but found themselves in no condition for interview. Clearly, the saints were smiling on me.

At home in Picazón del Moro, the entire village joined us to celebrate our news in a spontaneous festival of hysterical cackling. Only our children seemed uncertain, and they took to sleeping out in the shed with our hard-working old nag, Señor Polifacético.[10] They spent their nights

---

[10] You would without doubt have called the beast 'Mr. Multi-faceted'.

huddled against his flea-bitten flanks, sobbing like orphans. They also fell into the unpleasant habit of mumbling incomprehensibly rather than enunciating their words with clarity and confidence, as we had always taught them to do. Such was our single-mindedness, however, that we managed to fight off the infection of their dejection. We believed that our course of action would benefit them in the end, and that they would one day come to salute both our visionary rigour and our missionary vigour.

I assumed responsibility for buying a house in Belfast, and spent many hours on the telephone to a variety of your so-called estate agents. Our conversations were frank and honest. I would explain our situation and hint at our nervous excitement regarding the prospect of moving to such a famously dysfunctional city. Typically, they would reply, 'So yous're looking for a safe area?' I would then ask if they actually had clients who were seeking property in 'unsafe' areas? To this, they would say something like, 'Och, yud be surprised, so yur wud.' Here, I usually scratched my Latinate stubble before asking what 'safe' signified. They replied, 'Well, you know, *mixed*.' The first time I heard this, I asked in all innocence how readily a somewhat handsome Spanish man called Jesús would be accepted in female-only districts of their cold northern city. At this, the agent hung up the phone without making any attempt to satisfy me. Begoña suggested that 'mixed' might refer to the combination of Catholics and Protestants. In my view this seemed unlikely, given that everything we had so far learnt of Belfast seemed to demonstrate that the 'mixing' of Protestants and Catholics was a bad idea and hardly 'safe' at all. I therefore telephoned my new colleague, Dr. Connor McCann, and was advised that an area in the south of the city would almost certainly be the most suitable. We had little option but to take his advice on trust. Begoña and I were both anxious that our new address should reflect in some way the boldness of our decision and the radical change that was about to occur in our lives. Our first choice was the marvellously evocative 'Chlorine Gardens', but the house there fell through just before we signed on the dotty line. And so we settled for a substantial property on the purposefully named 'New Forge Lane'. In order to seal the deal, we had to sell a little of Papá's land, but the rest – along with our old house – was leased to José Antonio Rivera 'Morante de la Puebla', one of my many bull-fighting cousins.

Chapter 2

Which recounts the story of Jesús' first face-to-face interactions with the curious people of Ulster, as well as his unprecedented astonishment at the greenness of their fields.

We arrived in Belfast on a rainy Thursday evening in the first week of August. In a mood of intense optimism, we resolved that, thenceforward, we would communicate only in English, even among ourselves, in order to advance the integrating process. We had secured the services of a local family-based transportation company called 'Movers and Shakers' and, the following morning, six members of the McFadden clan drew up in their ramshackle van and began to unload our worldly goods. We cast our beady eye over them, and Begoña scurried back and forth in excitement as stocky men with dark hair and pale skin sweated and grunted in her immediate vicinity. We did not find them easy to understand, and Begoña said, 'How exciting! I think they must be speaking Irish.' Sure enough, one of these remarkable urban peasants gestured towards her and said, 'Shay's a fockin' crarker, soshay is.' The others nodded and said 'I.' Somebody added, 'An ays apoof, fit fer the Parliament.' Grasping at the one word I recognized, I attempted to infiltrate their intercourse by asking them for their opinions regarding Northern Ireland's elected assembly. They all laughed with hearty glee, and one said, 'The Parliament wazanold bar, natafockin' Sembly mayet.' Another said, 'Sagay nockin shap, natafockin' talkin shap.'[11] They all chuckled once more, but the conversation lapsed after the oldest of all the McFaddens came upon the scene and said to his boys, 'Will ye stap takin the hand out of him? Ay's a dacent spud.' One of them answered, 'Shiramoanlycoddin, so I am,' and they all returned to work. Of course, I did not follow all the intricate twists and turns of the dialogue – I was flying by the seat of my linguistic pants – but I am proud to say that I did not besmirch my honourable self.

We were so exhausted by the time the McFadden wagon trundled off along the lane that we simply could not face the prospect of unpacking. The girls were squabbling *como buitres alrededor de un cuerpo* (like vultures around a carcass), and we resolved that a weekend trip out of the city might be beneficial. We unfolded our pristine map and wondered whether to travel up into Antrim or down into Down. We reasoned that a southward journey might be best avoided, lest little Dilatación imagine that we were bound for Andalusia. This endearing toddler possessed an acute sense of direction and would smile in hope whenever we travelled south, even if it were simply to pass from the bedroom to the bathroom in our new house. Her geographical sensitivity was, I presume, the product of an early childhood spent in

---

[11] Eventually, I learned that in Belfast there was once a homosexual pub called 'The Parliament'. Some of the strange expressions used by local people on this and other occasions can be pursued fruitfully in the small glossary that I have positioned at the back end of this modest volume.

rural Spain, during which she had regularly displayed an ability to find her own way home from distances of up to thirty miles away. It was only after settling in the city that we realised how remarkable were such walking feats. Of course, she soon lost her navigational facility and began bumping into furniture just like everyone else.

The next morning, we drove north through County Antrim in a hired car. Its bright green colour helped to awaken our senses, but was as nothing compared to the violent verdancy of the countryside around Belfast. It was utterly bewildering to people who had previously known only the parched dull brownness of most of the ground in Andalusia. As I drove, I glanced over my shoulder and saw that all three girls had instinctively raised their arms to their eyes in order to defend themselves against the grotesque green glare of the fields. Even on an overcast day, the grass emitted a sinister fluorescent glow, as if enlightened by aliens. Then, at 11.07, the sun punched a hole in the grey sky and the rich green of the landscape became literally dazzling. We all screamed, and the little arms of Concepción, Purificación and Dilatación flailed wildly in the back of the car. My watch stopped, and Begoña complained that strange lights were dancing in her head whenever she closed her eyes.[12] It was only with the utmost effort that I managed to keep the car on the road, and we stopped at the next petrol station to purchase five pairs of sunglasses. By this time, the gap in the clouds had closed again, and the shop assistant said, with a jaunty smile,

---

[12] Back in Belfast, a doctor diagnosed something he called 'my grain'. (In Andalusia, we do not bother with such afflictions.)

'Yous'll not be needing those today, sure you won't?' Eager to engage, I explained our predicament to him, but he looked at me as if I had requested that he chop his own grandmother into bite-sized pieces.

We proceeded towards a wild place called Glenariff. Here, we parked the car and walked down the spectacular gorge, through which the river crashes and splashes in its unnecessary haste to reach the coastal plain below. With our sunglasses installed on our nut-brown noses, we began to appreciate the beauty of our new homeland. We climbed down the ingenious wooden walkway, our collective sense of anticipation stimulated by the potent roar of Mother Ulster's passing water. This sound grew more insistent as we descended, and soon we reached the first of the dramatic waterfalls. Our eyes bulged against their protective shields to see such a volume of water in August, of all months. In Andalusia, many of the mountain streams are completely dry at this time of year – visible only as dry pathways of rocks in depressed channels that wind their way through the pine and cork forests. At Glenariff, a seemingly inexhaustible ejaculation of excited creamy-white water tumbled and rumbled its way through the richly wooded ravine, sending up clouds of spray to merge with the water vapour that hangs permanently and menacingly in the Irish air. The steep sides of the gorge were covered in damp mosses and drippy ferns, together with a variety of resourceful trees, many of which grew horizontally from cracks in the rock before twisting upwards towards the sky. We gazed at the scene for many minutes, and then we continued our descent.

While the river did some quieter stretches, we watched a handsome little bird plunging into the brown water in search of small aquatic buggers and other fast food. From our guidebook, we learned that this was called a 'dipper'. Dilatación looked fascinated, and I saw the chance to begin working on the enhancement and advancement of her broken spoken English.

'Can you see the bird, *chiquita*?'

'Why he jump in water?'

'He's looking for a meal, I think. What do you suppose he will eat for his lunch?'

She thought for a long while, then answered decisively, 'Chorizo, bread and some peaches.'

My word, how we laughed at her!

During the remains of the weekend, we saw for the first time some of the rich scenic wonders of Antrim. We drove up towards Ballycastle, taking the stomach-churning Torr Head road. This winding and undulating route was as steep as anything we had ever seen in Andalusia, and the view across the grey-blue sea to the so-called Mull of Kintyre was inspiring. Naturally, I began to hum your infamous Paul McCartney song, which is well known even in the remotest corners of Spain. Its tune, I think, has the almost cancerous ability to infest the minds even of those most determined to resist it. I still have not quite shaken it off, if the truth be known.

With our spirits dampened only a little by my involuntary music, we drove on, stopping at Murlough Bay and Fair Head, which together form the north-eastern corner of Ireland. Murlough faces Scotland and we found it a beautiful and uplifting place. Its wooded slopes led gently down to the sea, and were peopled largely by wild goats. Fair Head was still more of an imposition. The stone on this promontory was granite (and still is, to the very best of my knowledge), and the vertical cliffs towered two hundred metres above the water. Out to sea, we could discern the curious shape of Rathlin Island through the softly wafting mist. Atop the cliffs, the pink heather was in full bloom, but nothing softened the starkness of the drop. The five of us crept towards the cliff edge on our stomachs, and peered down at a million monstrous boulders, strewn at random by the elements around the cliff's bottom. Simultaneously, four pairs of sunglasses dropped from our noses (only Dila had the good sense to secure hers), and a few seconds later we could just hear the curious clatter of modern plastic on ancient rock.

The walk back to the car was harrowing, and we had to ration the use of our one remaining pair of glasses. Predictably enough, Dilatación was dissatisfied with the arrangement, and this normally sturdy little creature actually begged me to transport her upon my shoulders. To my astonishment, Purificación also asked to be carried. We were completely unfamiliar with such behaviour, and, at first, I was a little angry. But then it dawned on me. Here we were, beginning to fabricate a new urban lifestyle for ourselves, and was it not possible that the morning's new sensations and reactions were actually the first grapes of our grapeless harvest? I for one had never marvelled at rural scenery in quite such a sentimental manner, nor had I ever driven around with no other purpose than to admire it. We had purchased modern consumable eye-wear, then discarded it, and soon we would simply buy some more. We had eaten sandwiches filled with meat from animals whom we had never met. And now, to capitalise it all, OUR CHILDREN WERE CLAIMING AN INABILITY TO WALK EVEN SHORT DISTANCES! Surely, this amounted in sum to classic *urban* behaviour. Begoña and I smiled at one another, sharing an unspoken realisation, and we each bent down to lift a child while Conchi brought up her rear. Admittedly, we still could not really see where we were going, on account of the obscene Irish grass, but we were quite definitely on our way.

On Sunday, before returning to Belfast, we visited the Giant's Causeway along with hundreds of other urbanites and tourists. Begoña asked one of them why it was so named. Neither of us could truly comprehend the reply, which seemed to involve an individual named 'Finn McCool', whom we presumed to be an Irish-American pop star of some description. The basalt rock formations were certainly arresting, but may I say that we have always found it difficult to understand why the Causeway is regarded as the jewel in County Antrim's crown when so much of the coastline is so bewitching? I put this question to an obese man with an ice cream as he prepared to board the tourist bus that carries visitors the short distance from the café to the Causeway itself. His answer unsettled me.

'What dya mean, yer daft eejit? When I come here from Belfast, I can stay on me arse all the time. Then I can drive round to Ballintoy harbour and have something else to eat, so I can. It's tiring, you know, all this sea air. Good for the head, but.'

This last expression sounded like some sort of threat, and I tried to defuse the time-bomb of his anger with another question.

'What about the famous rope bridge at Carrick-a-Rede? Do you go there?'

'Lord, no!' he replied, 'that's far too strenuous, so it is – you have to walk miles from the car park.'

At this moment, Purificación appeared by my side and said, 'Papá, I no go on bridge with fat man.'

I prepared to don my flax jacket and take one of your Belfast bullets for her, but, to my surprise, my heavyweight companion laughed out loud and said something like, 'Och, yer wee darrrrrrrlin!'

We stopped for a meal in the Bushmills Inn early that evening. Afterwards, Begoña and I drank something called Irish coffee beside an open fire in the lounge while the children crawled under the tables in the adjacent restaurant and masqueraded as Spanish farm animals. Purificación's impression of old Señor Polifacético was uncanny. Eventually, we were gently encouraged to leave, and we tottered out into the street to find our car. As we walked along the road, which was merrily decorated with little flags of red, white and blue, Conchi demonstrated to us that her spoken English had improved immeasurably during the course of just one afternoon.

'Papá, how do you spell "udder", like on a cow?'

When I spelt it out, Conchi said, 'I think they write it differently here, and they've drawn it upside-down too. Look at that sign.'

On a telegraph pole, three metres up, there was indeed

a faded metal sign crudely depicting an inverted udder (in truth, it looked more like a scarlet glove) and labelled 'UDA'.[13]

As we pondered the significance of this, we also became aware of the shrill sounds of some sort of musical ensemble, evidently comprising flutes and drums. It approached us from an invisible location. We climbed into our car, and drove towards the village's central *plaza*. In excitement, we rolled the windows down and parked by the roadside. The music was rough, and some of the players were clearly inebriated, but it all had an uncooked energy and the rhythms were tight and irresistible. Our girls clapped in time, and smiled their captive smiles. As the band passed us, we noticed that some of its more toxic members were gesturing in our direction and shouting strange things at us. I thought I heard the words 'Paddy-wagon' and 'Fenian scum-truck', but I could not be sure.

---

[13] I have since come to understand that the symbol was the 'red hand of Ulster', while the sign was the work of the loyalist Ulster Defence Association.

Chapter 3

Regarding an episode in which Jesús is tempted to disgorge his food upon a motley gathering of his new colleagues.

In the weeks that followed, we unpacked and spread out. This helped us to find our feet, and soon we were ready to put the best one forward. Steadily, we translated a house into a home. The girls attached themselves to other children in the neighbourhood, and they gave every appearance of enjoying their fresh experiences. They immediately began to acquire local accents and expressions, displaying an effortless capacity for integration of which I was mildly resentful. When Purificación suffered a catastrophic accident in the toilet, for example, I overheard Conchi say to her, 'You'rre a querr mingerr, so you arrrrrre.'[14] We further discovered that, at the bottom of New Forge Lane, we had convenient access to an extensive network of pathways along the banks of the River Lagan, superb for urban recreations such as cycling, jogging and flashing (all new to me, but highly rewarding). I also ventured into my new place of work up at RUB, where the friendly departmental

---

[14] I requested and obtained the following translation: 'You are an unusually messy and repulsive person, and that is certain.'

secretaries, Miss Place and Miss Pelling, introduced me to the office that I was to share with Connor McCann. They were exceedingly apologetic, and it was indeed a peculiar room. Once upon a time, the building had been a domestic dwelling, and our office, though now fitted with bookcases, sported a rusty antique bathtub in the corner. 'Is that where I must wash my students?' I quipped. The secretaries swapped their looks, and I could tell that they were entranced by my humorous sense.

Gradually, Begoña and I began to extend our tentacles, fixing powerful suckers on anybody who strayed within range. We were invited, one evening, to dine at the home of my head of department, Professor Norman Boyle. He had lived all his life in Belfast, but surprised us by distributing glasses of a very fine *jerez*. As we sipped, we also grasped the opportunity to enquire about some of the little difficulties we had so far encountered in our attempts to interact with the local people. We learned, for example, that 'Fenian scum truck' was an improvised term, used by animated loyalists, for any green automobile. Begoña also asked about regional accents, prefacing her enquiry by kindly commending the other guests on their comparative comprehensibility. 'But we find some of your *compatriotas* confusing,' she added. A tidal wave of laughter broke over the table as it was explained to us that more than half the guests were, in fact, English themselves. 'RUB is full of English academics,' said one of them. 'The students have a rhyme that runs, "A few came over and chose to stay, the rest were just left here and can't get away".'

Instruction was also offered on the appropriate

terminology to use when referring to the surrounding region. This began when Begoña asked how far it was from Derry to Londonderry. Professor Boyle said, 'No distance at all, and about a million miles', which clarified matters admirably. Everybody chortled merrily at Begoña's expense (I added my voice to the chorus, for the sake of politeness), after which the geographical scope of our discussion broadened somewhat. We were bombarded with advice from all sides, and I watched as the expression on Begoña's face passed from bewilderment to boredom *via* fear, severity, anger, amusement, irreverence, ambivalence and serenity. When you read the lines that follow, you will understand how she felt.

'Protestants are happy to speak of "Northern Ireland", but many Catholics prefer to use "the north of Ireland".' (The speaker here is Professor Archibald Briton, a wrinkled anthropologist.)

'It is possible for citizens of the Republic, living in parts of County Donegal, to drive due south in order to arrive at 'the north', by which they mean our own dear statelet.' (Dr. Mark Down, a small and gleamingly pink historian of hygiene.)

'But more committed republicans and nationalists speak of 'the six counties' that were, in their view, unfairly detached from Ireland's other twenty-six in 1921.' (This from Connor McCann.)

'In theory, "Ulster" can be used by Catholics and Protestants alike.' (Professor Boyle himself.)

'Yes, but Catholics take the term to refer to the ancient province of Ulster, which includes the six counties of

Northern Ireland plus three others that are now part of the Republic, while Protestants speak of "Ulster" as if it were coterminous with Northern Ireland.' (Dr. Phyllis Stein, another of my colleagues from the history department.)

'In a pub in Portadown, I once heard a fascinating argument in which two individuals from opposing traditions just shouted "Ulster!" at one another, over and over again.' (Professor Briton.)

'Oh, and Protestants use "the mainland" with reference to what they see as the rest of Britain, and "the province" as a short-hand for Northern Ireland, but Catholics generally eschew both terms, though they occasionally use "the province" to identify the ancient jurisdiction of nine, not six, counties.' (Dr. Dudley Backle, another historian, in a mostly unpleasant greenish jacket.)

'I was once doing fieldwork on Rathlin Island, and I witnessed a remarkable interpersonal confrontation. Two islanders, one a Protestant and the other a Catholic, came to grief as they attempted to voyage to "the mainland". Thinking that they were bound for the same destination, they arranged to share a boat. When they set off, however, it became clear that the Catholic wanted to go to Ballycastle in Ireland while the Protestant was hoping to visit a cousin in the Scottish port of Campbeltown. Relatives watched aghast from the cliffs as the two grappled for control of the rudder, which swung this way and that. Neither of the bodies was ever recovered from the ocean. Extraordinary!' (Professor Briton, back by popular demand.)

After sixty-seven minutes of this, I felt nauseous and had to deposit myself in the lavatory. When I regained the table,

Professor Boyle – may St. Roland watch over him – was dragging the conversation to a close.

'In general,' he advised, 'call this land "here", call the Republic "the south", and call Britain "over the water".' He added, 'Never ask individuals to tell you their religious denomination. Instead, if you wish to play our game, listen carefully to their names and see if you can work out where they come from. A girl called Abbey Newton who lives in Newtownabbey is likely to be a Protestant, but Gerry Donnelly from Derrygonnelly is almost certainly a Catholic. You'll soon get the hang of it. It's quite simple really. In any case, outsiders tend to be given a wee bit of leeway because they don't know any better, poor things.'

At the end of the evening, we walked home with the immensely personable Connor McCann, who offered us kind and valuable advice on buying a car of our own in Belfast (he said we should avoid green and orange). Within a few days, we were the delightful owners of a very comfortable and unnecessarily capacious white 'people carrier', and I learned by observing the other male members of my neighbourhood how to exhibit a healthy measure of urban car lust. Before long, I was waxing, polishing and sponging with the best of them. I joined the disjointed community of masculine vehicle-lovers, and every Sunday I would proudly wash my car, transforming our sloping driveway into a torrent of detergent. The other men of New Forge Lane did the same, and each tributary joined the majestic river of foam that flowed down towards the sea. It was like being back at Glenariff! Occasionally, we would grunt at one another, but actual words were rarely exchanged.

Nevertheless, there was something strangely unifying about our individualistic rituals. I had arrived, and I now thought very little of Picazón del Moro. The orange groves had lost their ZING, and seemed a long way off in time and outer space.

Chapter 4

In which Jesús makes love in the presence of badgers and is accosted by a small but purposeful hound.

As the dank dreariness of summer gave way to the dismal dampness of autumn, something began to change in my relationship with Begoña. At the time, it did not seem that we were drifting in opposite directions, and the bondage between us still seemed robust.[15] Indeed, we spent many happy evenings cuddling and snuggling on our new sofa, watching the local television stations in our shared effort to get a lid with a handle on the bubbling saucepan of Ulster culture. Some of what we saw was unquestionably distressing. Although the 'troubles' were supposed to be almost at an end, we heard again and again of riots, feuds, beatings, arson attacks, sectarian assaults, and violence against the police from Catholics and Protestants alike. More occasionally, there were political killings and explosions. We were grateful for the newsreaders' valiant attempts to alleviate the misery somewhat with quirky tales about odd characters from the

---

[15] It is, of course, perfectly possible for two individuals to drift in opposite directions while actually becoming closer together, but our progress, regrettably, was otherwise.

bogs or the glens or the mountains. In this way, we flew with the hang-gliding vicar from Stranocum, swam with the sleep-disordered boy from Kinnahalla who one night made it all the way across the sea to Scotland without waking up, and received particular pleasure at the hands of the white witch from Ahoghill who could cure all manner of bowel conditions using only a charming carrot.

We were also rather bemused by one of the so-called continuity announcers. He was called Keith McClief, and he would appear on the screen in between programmes, sitting behind an important grey desk, eager to inform us of what was about to pass through his channel. His hair was glossy and black like that of a virile young stallion but his skin was old, wrinkled and a curious mixture of the colours purple and grey. He tried always to be optimistic, but his smile had patently been nailed onto his face. Every few seconds, the studio lighting would rebound off one or other of his unnaturally white front teeth, illuminating our living room like a flash of Mediterranean lightning. The extreme cordiality of this man had a threatening quality, and he gave us some of your heebie-jeebies. Naturally, we discouraged the girls from exposing themselves to him. No man could be truly so happy all the time, unless of course he had something extraordinary going on *debajo de la mesa*.[16] We simply did not believe in his enthusiasm, and we suspected that his shiny shield concealed a life of bitterness and misery. We sensed the truth behind the tooth.

One night, we put Mr. McClief out of his misery a little

---

[16] Beneath the table.

early and wandered out into the garden. It was an unchar-
acteristically warm and barmy evening, and we were therefore able to sally forth wearing only thick jeans and a
combination of your 'wellies', 'sweaters' and 'fleeces' (in
Spain, only sheep wear such things). The children were all
aslumber, and the stars were even visible in the sky. Of
course, it was not Andalusia, and the artificial glow of the
24-hour clock prevented us from viewing the more retiring
of constellations, but there was romance in the air, none-
theless. Something stirred deep within me, and I took Begoña
by the hand. After a moment, she turned to face me and
stuck a soft kiss onto my rugged lips. Then she whispered,
'I have interested your prick and now you must prick my
interest.' Oh dear! I commended her for attempting to deploy
an English idiom, but explained as gently as I could that
this one simply did not stack up in the circumstances.
Sometimes, I generously forget that she is not quite my
equal in matters linguistic, a fact that will acquire additional
clarity in the sentence that follows this one. She reached for
the zip of my fleece and pulled me close to her before
whispering, slowly and deliberately, 'Then I must disembowel
you?' I explained what this meant, and she said, 'I know,
you imbecile.' Our eyes met in a moment of mutual distrust,
and each of us started to turn away from the other. At this
point, I suddenly saw her funny side and she saw mine.
Now, we giggled like two love-stricken teenagers on the
cusp of *primera penetración*, and began the complex business
of undressing. After some twenty minutes, we stood naked,
man and woman, gazing on one another in the cooling air.
'Hell, eez cold!' complained Begoña. For less ardent couples,

this might have siphoned off the petroleum of romance from their love-tank, but I was ready with a restorative question: 'Would you like me to install my central heating mechanism?' Bego did not demur, so I commenced (and swiftly completed) the simple procedure.

At the point of climax (mine, of course), Begoña whispered, 'We are being watched.' I rolled off her with the kind of slurpy-squelchy sound that is not normally audible in great literature. We lay still, and listened. There were curious snuffling noises close at hand, together with the occasional excited squeak. We peered in the direction of the sound, and gasped as we saw three small ghostly shapes moving across the lawn. Bego reverted to her native Spanish, and implored St. Agnes (the patron saint of repentant gardeners) to gather us up in the folds of her cloak. 'No need to panic,' I hissed, 'they are only badgers.' The three creatures, hearing my voice, waddled off through the hedge into our neighbours' garden. We followed them through the interstice, moved by some primitive hunting instinct and temporarily oblivious to our nakedness. The badgers were circumnavigating the house, bound for the immaculate front lawn, and like a pair of lunatics we followed. We watched as they began to dig energetically into the grass in search of grubs or worms. At this moment, the whole experience took a turn for the worse and we suddenly felt that home was far away. A dazzlingly bright security light clicked into action, eclipsing the moon completely, and a door in the house opened just wide enough to release the most ferocious dog I have ever seen. It was one of your so-called 'Jack Russels', and in the disorientating glare of the electric light it seemed to me like some nightmarish, salivating monster from a Gothic novel. This beast paid no heed to the badgers and advanced towards us at an alarming velocity. Now, Begoña and I are both athletic, but fortunately I am more so. Adrenalin pumped through my bloodstream, and I established an early lead that I was never to relinquish. I impressed myself with my ability to sprint, despite the fact that my *media-errección* was swinging violently from side to side like an untethered industrial crane. I reached our house in a matter of seconds, instinctively slamming the door behind me. Begoña did not fare quite so creditably, and suffered a serious bite wound to her right ankle during the brief but crucial interval between her arrival at our back door and my decision to re-open it. There was a certain amount of permanent damage to her muscles, and – even today – she sometimes walks with an almost imperceptible limpet.

Chapter 5

Which explains how Jesús found his first friend, and also how he watched Mr. Keith McClief giving pleasure to some housewives in a coffee shop.

My wife and I remained physically compatible, even combustible, but this was only one side of the conjugal coin. By day, Begoña and I often had little intercourse, for we no longer seemed to spin in the same circles. She spent a great deal of time shopping, either 'down town' or 'on-line'. I was frantically busy preparing for my first semester at RUB, but cultivating a public air of serenity so that nobody would realise that I was out of my normal element *como una cabra en una astronave*.[17] I put in the hours (no time for the flowers) and strove to keep panic out in the bay by buying very expensive history books, virtually at random. In just a few weeks, I consumed more historical 'companions', monographs and scholarly articles than I had managed in all my previous years on the planet. The worst of these was an essay on the history of population levels, entitled 'Paternal fecundity, mortality variables, and the timing of marriage in urban England, 1520-1780: some previously unremarked

---

[17] You would say, 'like a goat in a star-ship'.

44

feedback loops'. Now, you will have gathered, gallant reader, that I am a man of buoyant disposition. I float like a light white ding-dong ball on the murky green cesspool of life. This article that I read, however, drove me right to the brink of suicide. It was only eleven pages long, but to me they were eleven long pages. The essay took me five full days to read and, somewhere around the midway point, I actually attempted to drown myself in the bathtub in my office. I was thwarted only by the subtle interaction of two contradictory factors: the presence of Connor McCann and the absence of a plug.

During this period, I was also learning to recognise my new colleagues. They were as strange a collection of your so-called outcasts, misfits, drop-outs, odd-balls, cast-offs, outfits, throw-backs, drop-kicks, half-wits, back-ups, mis-casts, half-backs and out-and-out cough-drops as one is ever likely to meet.[18] Only Connor, a thoroughly engaging 'fella', could conceivably have blended into orthodox European society (though I was also slowly fondling myself towards Professor Boyle). When I asked Connor to proffer me some guidance concerning the nature of our fellow history lec-turers, he said, 'Och, I think it's better that you make up your own mind, Jayzus – I don't want to be influencing you with my personal prejudices now.' I was grateful for this prudent response, but my thanks grew still deeper when, the following day, he inserted into my pigeon's hole a hand-written sheet of paper bearing the following remarks:

'*Dave Grainger*: English, but has lived here for 30 years

---

18 Note how cleverly I use your curious composite colloquialisms!

or more. Paranoid about paramilitaries, hence nervous demeanour. Students call him 'Grave Danger'.

Norman Boyle: sound as a pound but mad as a hatter. Intellectually sharp. He can do that professorial thing where you sleep through a seminar, then awaken at the end to ask a series of penetratingly perceptive questions. They say he *dozed* his way to the top.

Dudley Backle: earnest, ambitious, sleekit.[19] Has no self-knowledge and always wears that jacket. Talks crap. Stands too close. Make up your own mind.

Mark Down: English toff, rather mean-spirited. Clearly gay, but doesn't know it or won't admit it. Likes to make students feel small, in public if possible. Anally retentive – a man of few turds. Born with a silver spoon up his arse. Strangely pink.

Phyllis Stein: not as grim as Backle, but hard work. Young and pretty, but small and seriously wound up. Seems to have 7000 volts running through her continuously. Unnervingly bright, very up-tight. Visiting from England.

Ivar Orr: indecisive Galway man. Don't get caught talking to him in the corridor.

Ardal McCardell: largely anonymous, strangely lifeless. May be a hologram.

Grainne Toal: middle-aged, a bit run down. Shagging the dean, and spends a lot of time at the Faculty Office (abbreviation: Fac Off).

Hamish Vickery: most lecherous of lecturers, and they all know about it. Students call him Professor Caresser.

Connor McCann: good judge of character, recognises

---

[19] A local word meaning sly, slippery and slimy.

quality. Incredibly popular. A friend of the weak and feck-less. Handsome raker. Doesn't always tell the truth (just joking).'

Luckily, I spent minimalist time with most of these people. With one or two exceptions, they kept me at arm's length, and on occasion I had to brush off their cold shoulders. In fact, only Professor Boyle and Connor McCann would feature extensively in a film of my life (the rest could all be played by one of your versatile character actors). Connor and I got on like a famous ton of bricks on fire. I enjoyed him right from the start, and he continued to grow on me like some large and luxurious fungus of the forest. I drank litres of coffee with him every morning, and we spent the afternoons urinating happily into our bathtub. I liked his tall, bespectacled, toothy, hairy, slightly cross-eyed, shuffling, anaemic appearance because it made me look particularly dashing when I stood beside him. Connor guided me around the library and taught me all about the more obscure local sports such as 'whirlyball', a rural game in which competitors are spun around several times, then challenged to throw a small metal sphere as hard as they can at a tethered cow. This is entirely quaint and charming, but it is nevertheless banned by the myopic governments of Ireland and Northern Ireland alike because of the alleged cruelty. Nowadays, the game is only played underground.[20]

Concepción and Purificación, my two eldest girls, shared my affection for Connor, and they understood far more of what he said than I did. They loved him, and he could

---

[20] This is presumably why I never heard another person mention it.

reduce them to hysterical giggles with his fine facility for comic accents from all corners of the planet and his strange range of facial expressions. In fact they rather tended to hog him, displaying the unmitigated selfishness of the young. Conchi and Puri liked nothing more than to meet up with Connor in one of Belfast's many so-called 'caffee shaps' for what they seemed to call 'a bit of crack and a wee blather.' On one occasion, we all assembled at a pre-arranged location beside the Waterfront Hall, and wended our way into town. Connor kindly bought for each of the girls a dense, sticky, chocolate slab coated in fluorescent green icing (called 'A slice of Ulster.') They adopted solemn expressions as their plates were placed before them, and began to eat in silence. Mildly embarrassed by this conduct, I asked, 'What do you say, girls?' Conchi's upper and lower jaws were already welded fast, but she eventually separated them with a series of violent jaw movements and gagging sounds. 'Och, sorry Connor,' she said, 'thanks for these, they're delicious. You're a wee dote.' Before she could elaborate on this, something or someone over by the door arrested her attention, and she whispered excitedly, 'Check out yer marn!'

A most unusual customer had entered the premises. He wore a purple suit with a green shirt and blue tie. He also sported dark sunglasses, despite the almost inevitable greyness of another overcast Belfast morning. In he breezed with his erected head, and wished a 'good morning' to the crowded room, as if its inhabitants must have been expecting him. The implausibly black hair and the immobile smile gave the game away. Puri nudged Conchi and said, 'It's that fella, you know, the scary one from the telly! But he's awful small, is he nat?' As so often, she was right, for the surprisingly runtish Keith McClief was among us! To my amazement, an awful hush fell over the room, and groups of middle-aged women sniggered like schoolgirls and glanced surreptitiously in his direction. It was almost as if a being of universal stature – perhaps the Archangel Gabriel – had touched down in earthly space. Dumbfounded, I turned to Connor.

'Has he accomplished something in his life of which I am ignorant? Did he, for example, negotiate the first of all the ceasefires, or play football for Manchester United?'

Connor laughed. 'No, no. He's just the wee man from the telly.'

'But look at them all,' I said. 'There must be more to him than this?'

'See Northern Ireland?' replied Connor, 'It's a small and introverted place. Sometimes, apparent non-entities or absolute blethercumskites can be feted like superstars. In a way, it's a good thing. We set the threshold for fame and success quite low so that everyone can have some kind of a chance. At the end of our road when I was a wain they put up a sign that said, "Best-kept medium-sized working-class Catholic housing estate in Northern Ireland 1987". It's still there today. I suppose such things are a kind of compensation for our other troubles.'

As if to illustrate his point, a tableful of hefty housewives rose to their feet after some considerable exertion. They gathered together their plastic bags, from the tops of which protruded a selection of cheap romantic paperbacks, bottled cosmetics, flowery garments, antiperspirant sticks, dieting magazines and chocolate bars. With shuffling, creaking precision, they moved like some giant military convoy across the floor, plotting a course towards the door *via* the table at which Mr. McClief, the man with the teeth, was seated, in all his pomp. As they approached this crucial intermediate destination, I noticed that each of them carried one of the café's paper table napkins in her hot hand. For one blindingly vivid moment, it occurred to me that they were going to smother him. I was sadly mistaken. Keith McClief looked up, grinned atrociously, and said, 'Hello ladies! And haven't yuus been busy!' The women glanced proudly at their bulging bags, before one of them summoned up the courage to speak. From our position, we could not hear the details of their fluid exchange, but it clearly related to the napkins. With well-greased charm, the pint-sized Mr. McClief produced a silver pen from his pocket jacket and began to sign them, one by one. In this moment, the napkins out-manoeuvred their ephemeral destiny and reached for eternity (throwaway goods that would never be thrown away!)

My increasing familiarity with the ways of the strange city in which I now lived was founded upon the observation of such episodes, and upon the expert commentary provided by Connor. Little by little, I and my family were settling into our new lives and learning to understand a region whose schizophrenic personality is beautifully reflected in its varied gifts to the world: the Titanic, the poet Seamus Heaney, the Ulster Fry, pneumatic tyres, controlled explosions, Bushmills whiskey, coffee jar bombs, the Giant's Causeway, kneecappings, various forms of specialist surgical expertise, unprovoked gang attacks on ambulances and fire engines, wiry little boxers with soppy tattoos, the Ulster-Scots dialect (in which 'Exit' becomes 'Wae Oot' and dyslexic children are 'wee dafties'), the deafening Lambeg drum, bogus insurance claims for falling over in the street, and idiosyncratic memorial inscriptions. This is one that I found in an old graveyard near the Ulster Museum:

'Here lie the bones of Patrick O'Connor,
Once a goer, now a gonner.'

Chapter 6

Concerning what befell when Jesús applied his offensive charm to his new neighbours.

Our progress towards total absorption continued apace, despite a moderately unsettling encounter with the people who lived next door. They fetched themselves up on the doorstep two days after our act of nocturnal trespass. The name of the evil dog, we now discovered, was Carson. This creature accompanied Irving and Edith Naughtie on their visit, and watched us knowingly through a thin veil of contempt during the exchange. Needless to say, Begoña and I were more than a little nervous as we sought to establish whether this was truly a hospitality call from our neighbours, or rather their attempt to confirm, prior to informing the police, that we were indeed the people who had been spotted prancing naked through their garden in a state of considerable ardour. The first minute went surprisingly smoothly, and we learned one another's names. I then explained that I was an academic, and Irving identified himself as a judge. This nutritious morsel of information rather discombobulated me, for I have never been at my most composed in the company of magistrates or monks. I managed to say, 'It is surely a pleasure to meet you, Judge Naughtie,' but I could go no further. Other nice-ties were clustered on the tip of my tongue, but I was quite unable to spit them in his direction. Driplets of sweat gathered around my temples like rosary beads, and my manful efforts to suppress my nervous giggles resulted only in an obscene farmboy smirk which I failed to erase during the remainder of the conversation.

Judge Naughtie appeared a rifle truffled by my behav-iour, and I dug myself deeper into his hole by committing a cardinal sin. Professor Boyle and Connor McCann had both warned me of the danger, but I nevertheless slid inexorably into a stinking pool of it. Here is what I fool-ishly asked:

'And are you Protestants or Catholics?'

Now he bristled a little, like a large brush.

'We don't ask one another questions like that.'

My crest must have fallen visibly upon receiving such a slap, and Judge Naughtie, to his credit, found a little com-passion in his heart.

'Don't worry — no offence taken. I'll not answer your question directly, but perhaps my dog, *Carson*, will offer you a little clue.'

Now I was truly lost. I looked uncertainly at the dog and the dog looked angrily at me. What was I supposed to do?

'*Hola*, little dog,' I said, 'would you mind telling me whether your master hangs to the left or the right?' (Connor had taught me this useful expression.)

I was as friendly as could be, but the rude animal said nothing in response (I was not altogether surprised).

Instead, it sniffed at my trouser leg and released an unnerving growl.[21]

Begoña and the girls were faring a little better with Edith, at least until the point at which she asked them all, 'Did you see the badgers last night?' Conchi and Puri purchased for their mother a moment of thinking time by squealing 'Badgers! Are there badgers?' and throwing themselves onto Edith's lap with their little teeth gnashing in misguided imitation of the animals concerned.

'Jeepers Creepers!' said Edith Naughtie. 'Aren't you fearsome little beasties?'

She then looked enquiringly at Begoña, as if to say, 'Answer my question, lascivious lady of the darkness!'

Bego was evasive.

'No, we saw nothing. But we did hear a bit of noise, around eleven o'clock I think.'

'Yes,' said Edith, 'It was the strangest thing. Carson chased some intruders. Irving caught a glimpse of them, and swears not only that the man was naked but that he was carrying some sort of a large stick. I can't think what they were up to.'

I smiled contentedly. We were in the clearing, and Irving steered the conversation back over the badgers.

'Nudists are undesirable, of course, but at least they don't dig up your lawn. Those wretched beasts are the sworn enemies of the devoted gardener, and much hated along this lane.'

---

[21] I have since learned that a certain Edward Carson was one of the founding fathers of modern Irish unionism. The dog was therefore a Protestant.

Begoña was deliberately egging on him. 'The holes in our front lawn – is that what those are? I had been wondering. I thought it must be the children. Can't we fence them out – the badgers, I mean – in some way?'

'They'll just dig their way in again. Incredible diggers with powerful paws. They just keep coming back at you. You should see my parsnips!'

'In Spain,' I said, 'we simply shoot any animal that gets on our nerves (though sometimes we play games with it first). These creatures are truly stupid. Did you know that they follow the same pathways across the land for generations upon end, regardless of changing circumstances? They do not really deserve to live. Why not poison them, or bung them in their burrows, or explode them? There are many options.'

Bego was frowning at me, almost as if I had spoken out of turn. And Judge Naughtie was not looking particularly benevolent either.

'No, no, no,' he said, 'we can't possibly do that – it's against the law. I'm afraid you have one or two things to learn about the British way of life. All we can do is try to scare them off – Carson does his bit here. Or perhaps we could *change* the law. But anything else is out of the question.'

He was patronising me, and I knew it. Fortunately, I was feeling thick-skinned and I therefore bit my lip. Somehow, we managed to draw the encounter to a close, but Begoña harangued me mercilessly immediately we were alone. She said I had showered shame upon her. I do find the memory of it a little embarrassing, and I would not have mentioned it at all but for the fact that, as it transpired, our discourse concerning the habits of the badger was of very considerable significance in the history of Northern Ireland and, by extension, the world beyond.

Chapter 7

In which Jesús finds fulfilment in football after discovering that nobody runs in the 'school run' nor rushes in the 'rush hour'.

Roots, shoots and fruits: we had to make our progress one step at a time. Having integrated ourselves into the neighbourhood with such a plum, we undertook the task of settling the girls into their new and alien educational establishments. Concepción and Purificación were thrilled at the prospect of wearing the uniforms of Lagan Meadows Primary, situated in the Stranmillis district of Belfast. They seemed to espouse the creed of metropolitan conformity with some relish, and both girls demonstrated an eagerness to please their new teachers. Poor Conchi, however, backfired like an old tractor when, in the first week of school, Mrs. Murray invited volunteers to tell the class 'Something They Don't Already Know'. She panicked, reaching inadvisedly into her memory bank for a piece of information that was distinctively her own. She next launched into a fifteen-minute monologue entitled, 'How to kill a chicken with your bare hands', during which a little boy named Barney evidently passed over on the floor. As Conchi reported it to us, 'He just fell off his chair and lay there, so he did.

Flump! Everyone jumped up, but I think he was just tired. I didn't stop my story till it was finished.' After this debut, it took her quite a few weeks to make any friends, but everything settled down when her classmates and teacher realised that she was not, after all, in league with the Prince of Darkness. Puri was digested more readily by her new companions, perhaps because she joined school at the start of P1 (as the first year is affectionately known), and so was among fellow novices. Initially, she thought she was to live at school, and appeared disappointed when we came to collect her. Once she had come to terms with this, however, she sailed through her first weeks like a knife through butter and made five or six good friends, all of whom were called Hannah McSomething-or-other.

We could easily have walked to school along the so-called toe-path beside the river in approximately twenty minutes, but we feared being regarded as odd-fits or miss-balls if we chose to arrive on foot. Begoña and I well understood that the 'school run' was one of the defining features of city parenthood, and we addressed the issue with our customary enthusiasm. Just like all the other mums and dads, we packed our uniformed children into the car each morning and joined the vehicular procession as it crawled along the Malone Road like a gargantuan metal serpent. The girls peered curiously out of the windows, and Purificación asked, 'Why is it called the "*rush* hour"?' Day by day, Begoña and I learnt the rules of the road and the habits of the highway. At times, solitary drivers would behave as if they were sealed hermetically within an opaque bubble of individualism, and would do things that nobody in a crowded city would dream of doing at the window of their living room while hundreds of people passed in the street outside. Bego had already persuaded me to abandon some of my more rustic personal habits, and I was therefore relieved to discover that many of the urban peasantry had somehow managed to preserve the finest of these, if only within the confines of their cars. Some of them picked their noses, consuming the contents with a vacant, dreamy look in their eyes. Some excavated their ears, using matchsticks or ballpoint pens which they then wiped on the upholstery. And one individual, whom I took from behind to be a businessman, was clearly reading one of your disgusting pornographic magazines as he waited for his cue to move. What was it about being alone in a car that made some people think themselves invisible?

In other moments, individuals interacted and even seemed to draw pleasure from their encounters. Drivers in the main stream would pause and flutter their headlights suggestively in order to allow cars approaching from the side roads to join the linear throng. But in darker mood, the same drivers would virtually nudge their noses up the backsides of those in front (again suggestively) in order to prevent any intrusion from the flanks. Clearly, it was important to be unpredictable and inconsistent. According to Begoña, 'They keep each other guessing. Nobody knows whom to trust. It is sexual, no?' I was intrigued by the predominantly masculine behaviour of cursing with the voice while testiculating with the arms. I took to this like a duck to cherry sauce, and surprised myself with the range and passion of my ejaculations. It was only when little Dilatación, aged three, stuck her middle finger up at another vehicle and said, 'Avaunt,

59

you whoreson dog,' that I realised – as always with a jolt – that the story of my life is not all about me.

It is never easy, even for those of an essentially positive disposition, to come to grips all at once with such a wealth of new places and new faces. My coping strategy involved some gardening and also some sexual fantasy (pardon my candour), but both of these recreations fell into the pail of insignificance when considered alongside football. I watched live matches on satellite television from various leagues around the world, concentrating on Spain, England, Italy, Holland, Germany and Denmark. Naturally, there were times at which the pressure of work made it impossible for me to maintain such scope, and during these phases I tended to hone in on topless female beach soccer from Brazil (this, for me, was a real eye-opener). In conversation with Connor and others, I also found time to reflect on the status of football in Northern Ireland. It was a picture of some considerable complexity, and I struggled to wrap my head around it. The local teams were described in educated circles as 'complete crap', but they attracted a devoted if numerically unimpressive following. Each team was either Protestant (like Coleraine) or Catholic (like Cliftonville), and many of the chants were sectarian in nature. For a spell in the late twentieth century, there had been a thoroughly 'mixed' team – Moira Ecumenicals – but its members had failed to score a single goal in three seasons of striving and its middle-class fans were derided for their anti-sectarian chant, 'Every game's a friendly!'

The 'national' team of Northern Ireland generally fared only a little better in sporting terms. Occasionally, they enjoyed a 'night of nights', beating England or even Spain, but they invariably followed this up on the following Wednesday by losing 3-nil to the so-called Pharaoh Islands. They attracted a local following that was overwhelmingly Protestant, and, if ever a Catholic were selected to play for Northern Ireland, he faced the prospect of an evening's floodlit sectarian abuse from supporters of his *own* team! There were regular occasions upon which visiting squads were bemused to find the home crowd literally sledge-hammering its own players. Fortunately, the visitors' confusion rarely prevented them from 'finding the back of the net' on multiple occasions. One local player, Eoin Donnelly, withdrew from international soccer after he missed a 'sitter' as a result of having been hit in the eye with another of those symbolic oranges, thrown from the home crowd just as he cocked his shooting leg right by the goalpost. The goal would have taken the team through to the World Cup, but the fans nevertheless went home whooping for joy. Northern Ireland's supporters were therefore unique within professional sport for refusing to accept the modern view that 'winning is everything', but their alternative creed emphasised not the pleasures of participation but the primacy of Protestantism.

In any case, most of Belfast's football fans seemed to ally themselves not to the local clubs or national side but to the big teams from the Scottish and English leagues. Many were drawn to the sectarianism of the beautiful game in Glasgow, and followed the fortunes of Celtic and Rangers. Others opted out by supporting Liverpool and Manchester United. These clubs had the dual advantage of being reasonably good and comparatively neutral in religious terms. As always, however, the situation vomited fresh contradictions. I watched one match between England and Holland in a rather cramped speciality football pub called 'The Six-Yard Box'. I noticed that the man standing next to me at the bar was a fervent Dutch supporter (as, surprisingly, were all the other patrons). So, at half-time I addressed him in my halting Dutch to ask how long he had lived in Belfast. He looked at me quizzically, then asked, 'Wurr the fock arre yuuu fram, mishter?' It emerged that he was not so much Dutch as pro-Dutch on account of being anti-English. When he told me that he supported Manchester United, I observed that several members of the England team played for the aforementioned club. He said, 'White shirts – wankers. Red shirts – saints.' I was not put off, and asked whether there was not some inconsistency in his decision to support Holland, given that its players were mostly of Calvinist stock and that William of Orange had been a Dutchman. This time, his response was short, sharp and probably to the point, but I have to admit that I was unable to grasp it as it flew by my ears.

I was not only an anthropological observer of the planet's favourite sport, but an active participant too. Every Friday evening, I indulged in an hour of five-a-side football with a group of postgraduates and fellow lecturers up at RUBIE (the Royal University of Belfast Institute of Exertion). I discovered in myself an instinct and a talent for competitive sport that had rarely found an outlet in Andalusia. There were, in my life, only two pursuits that enabled me to forget completely about the pressures of the forthcoming university term. I am sure you can guess the first one, but as the weeks wore on there was less and less of this on the table. Football was the other. During that hour, nothing else impinged. It was as if the rest of the universe simply did not exist. Although I had never before played in a team, I had developed a bewildering galaxy of individual skills as a boy growing up in Andalusia. Once upon a time, I was in the habit of taking my 'ball' (usually a juicy water melon or some such) and dribbling it up through the cork forests, sometimes disappearing for days on end. Trees, of course, lack mobility and sheer pace, but when they tackle you they can really hit you hard. I was therefore tough, both physically and mentally, and I found a real football so much easier to control than a large and terminally compromised fruit.

I sought solace in soccer, losing myself utterly in the ecstasy of dancing through a crowd of ageing sociologists before slamming the ball imperiously past an overweight academic lawyer. I deployed the full range of tricks: reverse passes, back-heels, step-overs, double pull-backs and, of course, my celebrated 'butt of Zidane'. Admittedly, I was not truly a team player, and I delivered only one or two token passes per session. Most of my team-mates treated me with respect, even awe, but one in particular – a madman from London – sometimes grew frustrated. Off the pitch, he was a charming and fragrant zoologist, specialising in the study of Atlantic grey seals and their diet. This involved him in the collection and analysis of droppings from around the Irish coast (he told me that he had a good memory for faeces, and I believed him). In the football hall, however, there was something psychotic in his manner. He would buzz around me, screaming hysterically for the ball. He yelled, 'Give us a facking brike, mite,' whatever that meant, and other choice phrases. 'Wide on the left, mite!' he would cry, and 'With yer, mite!' Most alarmingly, he would sometimes shout 'Big Rod's inside you!' at the tippy-top of his voice. These four words introduced a simultaneously psychic and sexual element to our games, and it was one that I could well have done without.

Chapter 8

In which Begoña proves herself to be exceedingly neglectful and Jesús discovers that his Achilles' heel is precisely where one might expect it to be.

Begoña and I had become so self-absorbent that each of us had only the vaguest awareness of what the other was doing. Tension was building within the relationship, but we had both been protected from the need to confront it by our failure to allow it space for expression. Matters came to a sticky head one Friday evening, early in October. I had just attempted to bluff my way through my first full week of teaching, and it had been – I say it with frankness – a catalogue of calamities. In a variety of conversations with students, it had emerged that I did not know where Munster was (in Germany, I thought), nor what the relationship was between Robert and Horace Walpole (presumably a gay northern couple). In a session on the so-called Reformation, I tried to pose questions that I knew must be close to their hearts. But when I asked, 'Was Martin Luther a good egg?' nobody would say anything at all.

My worst performance came on the Friday morning in a seminar devoted to 'gender relations in early modern England' (this was not my choice, I hasten to add). I was not at my most effervescent, but I nevertheless endeavoured to ferment a jovial atmosphere by basing our discussion around a collection of seventeenth-century songs (on a compact disc that I had skilfully felched from a colleague when he was looking the other way). The idea had good prospects, but I was swiftly and comprehensively undone by a lovely lady-student *con mucho pecho*.[22] I tried not to stare, but the Andalusian villager inside me proved momentarily stronger than the sophisticated academic. My eyes oggled and my mind boggled. In an effort to salvage the seminar, I vowed to say nothing that might be deemed in any way offensive, but the reticence of the group placed me under such enormous pressure that I had little alternative but to keep talking, talking, talking. In desperation, I inadvertently introduced them to the old Spanish saying, '*la cabra con las ubres más llenas tiene más leche*', at which the student in the limelight promptly assumed many of the characteristics of a beetroot.[23] Of course, I quickly retracted my sharp point, but I could see that I had made a small hole in her already. Her fellow students might have offered me some assistance, but instead they all looked uncomfortable and unsympathetic. To my sadness, they unceremoniously gave me the raspberry and sent me to Coventry with it.

Towards the end of Fateful Friday, I dragged myself along to the Institute of Exertion, hoping for transportation to another place on a magic football. For fifty minutes, I played

---

[22] 'With lots of chest'.
[23] I will translate: 'The goat with the fullest udders has the most milk.'

with my usual panache and recorded yet another of your triple 'hat tricks'. Then, out of the blue, something traumatic happened. I sprinted back into defence, purloined the ball from the enemy striker, played a delicate little 'one-two' off the wall, rotated out of a crowd of players and accelerated like a rocket into space. The next moment, something went ¡*pum*! at the back of my foot and I fell to the floor with my long head first.[24] At first, I assumed that some jealous soul had stamped on my behind, but there was nobody there. Next, I wondered whether one of my new students – perhaps the chested one – had shot me from the balcony with an undecommissioned rifle, but there was no sign of blood. I had a burning sensation at the back of my foot, and I did not even attempt to stand, so convinced was I that something serious had happened. Big Rod drove me to the hospital, where an Eastern European doctor whose testicles were not yet down eventually confirmed my own diagnostic suggestion: the Achilles' tendon on my right leg had snapped in twain. The nurses constructed a half-plaster around my lower leg, instructed me to attend a 'fractures clinic' in the morning, and sent me home.

Begoña's reaction was an unpleasant revelation. Her sympathy was so superficial and so rapidly exhausted that it reminded me most painfully of my knowledge of your Tudor history. Admittedly, for a moment or two she affected a pitiful frown and called me her little *albaricoque* (apricot), but no sooner had I laid my crutches aside and collapsed on to the sofa than she announced, 'Actually, there is

---

[24] Where we go ¡*pum*! you go 'pop!' or, in extreme cases, 'bang!'

something I've been meaning to talk to you about.' I listened in anguish, and experienced a strange sensation that her words were simply bouncing off me like some of your wretched northern hailstones. This rendered meaningful intercourse problematic. I also noticed that she was exaggerating her funny Spanish accent: a sure sign that she was intending to manipulate me into some new and pleasing shape.

Bego asked, "Ave you been wondering what I 'ave been doing during the last few weeks?'

'I've been so busy. You have been shopping, I expect, or attending to the girls?'

'Some of the time, 'ees true. But there's more. I have been building a new shelf, and planning some initiatives of my own.'

'A new shelf? What for?'

'No, no! Not a 'shelf' – a 'self'. You know – a new *me*. There are many opportunities, and a modern urban woman 'ees not supposed to be only a wife and a mother, you know.'

'Did Achilles mention that he has hurt his foot? Could we perhaps talk about how he is going to reach the hospital tomorrow morning?'

No, we could not.

'Actually, some of my ideas are looking extremely promising.'

'OK. Such as?'

'I have set up a website and I am developing a new dieting system for all the fat urban women. They always want new ways to lose their weight.'

'Dieting? You have never been interested in that before.'

'Jesús, we are living in a new world. Of course we must have new interests. Think of your football!'

I listened with divine patience. Begoña had already earned a substantial sum of money, and she was becoming a 'hot property'. I was shocked and unsettled by the news. No man likes to watch his wife succeed, for it emasculates him. In Spain we say this: '*Detrás de cada mujer de negocios, hay un hombre plácido y flácido.*'[25] I had to admit, however, that her diet idea was a clever one. She called it the 'Shrinking Violet' diet, and had managed to suggest something new and original by concentrating her attention not on the food consumed by large ladies of the town but on the tableware deployed during its consumption. The premise was simple, and inspired by the fact that if one returns to one's very first school twenty years after leaving it one feels extraordinarily big. The chairs seem tiny, the assembly hall looks like a rabbit hutch, and the hugely imposing headmaster turns out to have been only one metre tall all along. Bego therefore reasoned that aspirant waifs could deceive themselves into gobbling less food by serving it on plates that became progressively and imperceptibly smaller during a six-month period. Customers therefore purchased a package containing tasteful mauve table settings of twelve different sizes, and instructions to the effect that a close friend should be appointed to swap each size for the next one down at carefully planned intervals. By the end of the course, formerly fat people would be greatly reduced in size and would, without realising it, be eating minuscule meals off half-sized

---

[25] Behind every woman of business, there is a placid and flaccid man.

plates. Of course, it only worked on imbeciles but it was a raging success amongst the fanatical dieters of the world.

When Begoña had concluded her exposition, I asked, 'So, why are you telling me about this now, when for many weeks you have left me to grow stale in the cupboard of ignorance?'

'Because it will obviously have *implicaciones* for you and the girls. I will need you to take over most of the fetching and carrying, at least while I organise my launch.'

I felt rough and gruff. She had really got my goat excited, and now he was at the end of his tether. Together, we descended into sarcasm.

'Very well. I will use my one working leg for all three pedals in the car, or perhaps I could hobble the girls to school along the toe-path?'

Begoña interjected, 'They will love it! I'm so pleased that you understand me. I thought you might behave like an old Andalusian farmer and command me to suppress my urges. You are finding a new shelf too, and I'm sorry about your poor foot. Truly I am.'

And with that, she made tracks towards her bed, leaving me all alone with my crutches and my half-baked plaster-cast. Had I perhaps been too soft and gentle in my reaction, more like pink toilet paper than the master of my mansion? Should I have given her some serious sticks instead? I had no answers, and I could no longer see the woods for the trees. I felt, in alphabetical order, deflated, dejected, dependent, depleted, depressed and deracinated.

Next morning, I took a taxi to the hospital, where the consultant and his nurses presented themselves to me in very different ways. Mr. Morrison was cold, arrogant and, like my Achilles' tendon, completely detached. He dealt briskly with my foot, but treated the accompanying presence of my personality as an irritating inconvenience. Once he had established that my doctorate was in literature rather than in medicine, he felt able to address me as if I were a small dog. He explained that my lower leg would be placed in a cast, with my toe pointing downwards 'like a ballerina' for four weeks. I would then be issued with a special plastic boot for a further month. After this, I could begin to walk again. If I disobeyed his instructions at any point, I would probably re-rupture my tendon and have to begin the whole course of treatment afresh. I tried to ask a question, but he wandered off muttering importantly into a curious device called a 'dick-phone'.

The two nurses tried to reassure me. They, too, treated me a bit like a puppy, but where Mr. Morrison had given the impression that he wished to put the puppy down as quickly as possible, they made it clear that they loved the puppy dearly and wanted to pick it up, cuddle it against their warm bosoms and feed it titbits. They agreed that the consultant was rather forbidding, but they attributed this to his brilliance and his punishing schedule rather than to his obnoxious conceit. They gently washed and massaged my leg, cooing all the while, and gradually I subsided into a state of foetal innocence and security. The nurses next invited me to choose from a range of coloured coverings for my new lightweight cast. I gurgled and giggled at the dizzying selection. There is so much choice in city life, and I found it quite extraordinary. They had green ones, red ones, plain ones and stripy ones. Some were decorated with football motifs, while others displayed skulls and crossbones. Eventually, I opted for a bright and cheery chequered cover, with squares coloured cream, turquoise and scarlet. 'My girls will like this one,' I said. For some reason, the nurses encouraged me to reconsider ('Once it's on, it's on. Are you sure now?'), but my mind was made up.

Chapter 9

Regarding the salty tears that Jesús shed when he contemplated a dead sailor's ear.

The next weeks were extremely trying, though not without rewards. Begoña, out of the kindness of her heart, did undertake some of the driving. More often, I relied for assistance on the good ladies of Stranmillis, many of whom volunteered for service when they saw me struggling across the playground with five bags, two pink lunch boxes, one guitar, three daughters and a couple of crutches. I cannot commend them warmly enough. Where Bego now seemed reluctant to mother even her own children, these lovely and affectionate creatures were even prepared to extend their maternal instincts to me. I pointed out to my wife that it was possible to be a contented urban lady without abandoning the softer side of one's nature, but she was far too busy to listen. Many members of my new female support staff were also equipped with enormous troop-transporting vehicles, bigger even than ours, and it was never a problem to accommodate an extra three or four passengers. Of course, in happier times I might have interpreted all the attention as in some way romantically motivated, but even I found it hard to believe that all these luscious ladies wanted to make sweet love to a crumpled man whose leg was in plaster and whose hands were blistered and bruised by his crutches. Reluctantly, I had to acknowledge that they were offering to care for me.

My most loyal female *facilitadora* was the delightful Audrey, with whom I struck up a pleasant platonic relationship. She was a few years younger than I, but already had two children of her own. I made Audrey's acquaintance because one of these, Laura, had recently dislodged the six Hannahs to become Puri's 'best friend' at school. Audrey, a Protestant, was married to Sean, a Catholic (this is called a 'mixed marriage.') He was a solicitor who worked from dawn until dusk, and Audrey said that he found it difficult to distinguish between his own children and those of other couples. She told me with delight that he had once attempted the school run on his own when she was 'full of a cold', but he had deposited his offspring at the wrong establishment. In this respect, he was 'useless', yet she obviously loved him, and the generous sums of money he brought home enabled her to drive around in a tank and meet her friends for lunch in the best of Belfast's bistros. Audrey worked on two mornings of the week, as an alternative therapist specialising in Scandinavian body massage. It was a measure of my depressed state that this delightful nugget of news failed completely to activate my masculine equipment. Objectively, I could also see that Audrey was somewhat sexy – a little worn down and plumped up by motherhood, perhaps, but tall, shapely, auburn-haired, pretty and extremely vivacious. To my mind, she was like some beautiful Renaissance nude, neglected in an attic for centuries but eminently restorable with a bit of touching up at the hands of an expert. And yet, nothing stirred. This was a low point, but at least I had a friend.

My teaching did not improve much. Half of the students insisted on glancing nervously at my wounded leg as if it were some kind of weapon. I forgave them for this (in rural Spain, after all, we frequently stare at disabled people and nobody minds at all). My magnanimity did not, however, produce any reciprocal generosity. In fact, when I took one group into the Ulster Museum to examine the artefacts from a Spanish shipwreck called the *Girona*, the students began laughing at me. This ship was part of the ill-fated Armada of 1588, and it sank off the north coast of Ireland with the loss of many hundred men.[26] As we gathered around the glass cases, I became somewhat emotional. The first tear rolled down my cheek when we considered a beautiful fragment from a guitar. I heard music in my head, and was almost overcome. At this point, I noticed that one or two of the students were smirking at me. Next, we looked at a silver ear-pick that had once been used to remove waxy bits from the orifices of some Spanish nobleman. When I thought of this, I began to weep more plentifully, and the sound of giggling escalated proportionately. Through my tears, I said, 'This pick is pointed, as you can see, and may actually have done more harm than good. In Spain, we have an old proverb: "It is not an exact science to go fishing with a crossbow." But even this was not the worst thing that could

---

[26] In Spain, we do not talk about this armada, but northern Protestants seem to do so almost incessantly.

happen to a Spaniard's ear.' I hobbled over to the next case, and the chuckling horde followed me at a disrespectful distance. 'Look here,' I sobbed, 'this is a beautiful and elaborate golden earring that was ripped violently from the head of a noble Spanish knight as he lay dying on a beach. Oh, it is enough to move a man of stone!' I pronounced a long and mournful 'Ay!' By now, the students were howling derisively in my face, and the only comment any of them made was to describe the earring as 'so *totally* gay'.

Furthermore, Begoña's business activities combined with my injury to push me into closer and closer companionship with my little girls, Conchi, Puri and Dila. In Andalusia, I had managed to keep them at arm's length, most of the time at least. They were, of course, delightful to look at and generally well-behaved. I was more than happy, at the end of a long day spent working the land, to dangle one or two of them on my knee for a while, but naturally I sent them to their mother as soon as they began to cry or smell. It is not good for a man to become too involved with his daughters. Now, however, under the grey skies of Ulster, I suddenly found myself without a choice. The three of them were completely unruffled by my injured state, and even regarded it as an exciting novelty. They were no more sympathetic than their mother, and one of them wrote 'Never too late to amputate!' on my cast. They soon discovered that they could immobilise me simply by stealing my crutches. They would then play a variety of games, in which the crutches featured as guns, fishing rods, high jump bars, cattle prods, vaulting poles, flying horses, witches' broomsticks, huge drinking straws, lances, giants' pens and loyalist flutes ('Like the ones we saw at Bushmills, Papá.')

I also had to watch as Begoña grew and grew, continually shooting out new sprouts all over the shop. The critics gobbled up her diet, and she even appeared on local television. She was lucky enough to meet Keith McClief, and he asked *her* to sign his BBC canteen napkin! I was not competing effectively, and the one scholarly publication I produced during this phase even turned to my disadvantage. I had for some time been very mildly interested in the relationship between art and philosophy, particularly during the Enlightenment. I therefore penned a short and bombastic book entitled *Paint and Reason*. Initially, this was hailed as a minor masterpiece of art scholarship, but I became one of your international laughing-stocks when, due to a translator's error over which I had no control, it appeared in French as *Pain aux Raisins*.

Chapter 10

In which Jesús, like a cat whose nine lives are all used up, lands on his head.

One Saturday morning, I took the venturesome decision to visit one of Belfast's more forbidding quarters. I awoke to the news that the previous night had witnessed ugly tripartite confrontations between the police, the loyalists of Glenbryn and the nationalists of Ardoyne.[27] For once, Begoña had graciously agreed to spend some time with the girls, so I collected my crutches, hopped onto a bus, and headed west along the Crumlin Road after changing course in the town centre. Here was my chance to raise my plummeting pecker and to jump-start the tractor of my innate enthusiasm by engaging face-to-face with the dark side of the city. I decided not to consult Connor, for I knew in my heart of bones what he would have said. You should have seen the frown he wore some days before when he saw my injured leg in its colourful cast! It was as if I myself had done something silly. I said, 'What is wrong, *amigo*? This is not my fault, you know.' And he

---

[27] 'Ardoyne' sounds somewhat like 'Dordogne' but here the similarity ends.

said, 'Surely you don't need me to tell you why that thing [and here he pointed rudely at my limb] is a liability?' This had made me cross, and so now I would act alone. This was my idea, my trip, my scenic drive towards understanding.

I decided to alight close to the suitably rough-looking Ballysillan Road, in which an inverted and blackened car was smouldering like some glamorous 1950s starlet made famous by cellulite. I ignored the bus-driver's impregnable query – 'Thass really wurrr yuu wanna be, big fella?' – and took to the streets. For an hour or two, I wandered lonely as a daffodil, studying and photographing the murals that adorned gable-ends of loyalist and republican streets alike. These artworks of the urban peasantry are actually rather impressive in their vivacity and belligerence. Colourful images of King Billy, the Blessed Virgin Mary and other paramilitary heroes haunted my head for weeks to come. I saw houses that had been burned out, houses that had been bashed in and houses that had been bricked up. A few were remarkably well-kept, with ceramic dwarves beaming incongruously in their tiny front gardens, as unconvincing as the hopeful 'For Sale' signs that were displayed in many others.

I also saw sports teams boarding buses at two different schools. At the first, a group of girls carried sturdy, well-made sticks with curious little bends at their ends. We do not play much hockey in Spain, but after some consideration I realised that this must have been the game for which such implements were intended. At the second school, however, the girls had sticks with curiously deformed ends, straighter and flatter. I asked one of them what mishap had misshaped her stick, to which she said, 'What's wrang with yurr leg, apart fram the colours?' At this, her team-mates laughed, and a slightly older girl added, 'The sticks arre fur camogie. Yuu know, like fur hurling.' This sounded like yet another of those quirky Ulster threats, so I hobbled off none the wiser as a menacingly masculine games teacher propelled herself efficiently in my direction.

I had passed through loyalist Glenbryn into Alliance Avenue, a Catholic street to judge by the roaming herds of children. The boundary between the two was marked by a gigantic metal fence, presumably designed to minimize cross-breeding and other forms of interaction. I explored the labyrinthine redbrick terraces of Ardoyne: Strathroy Park, Eskdale Gardens, Velsheda Way, and so on. On one street corner, I paused to examine a mural depicting an emaciated figure, draped in an Irish tricolour of green, white and gold while being crucified upon the diagonal bands of a British flag. The picture also bore the message, 'Though we move on, we shall not forget', and a litany of Christian names: Bobby, Patsy, Ciaran, Joe and nine or ten others. As I stood there, I became aware that a substantial group of skinny and spotty young men had gathered around me like adolescent bees. They seemed to smell not of honey but of glue, and I wondered whether they had perhaps been making something nice at school. I greeted them amicably, but they only scowled at me in return. I overheard a good deal of guttural muttering, but the only word I could discern with any certainty was "fockin", evidently a staple that held many a local sentence together. I tried once more to engage these youths in conversation saying, 'Tell me, young men of Ulster, what does this painting mean to you?' They answered with a series of their own questions, all delivered with a rather unseemly snarl.

'Huu the fock arre yuu?' asked one.

Another affected a silly voice and said, "Ay's a fockin' reporter from the Wap Weekly, so he is. Am I right, mishter?'

Before I could answer, a third asked, 'If ay's a wap, why is he dragging that bit of loyalist prapaganda aroynd?'

For some reason, he looked at my injured leg.

'See that thurr, mishter?' said one of his friends. 'That's a very pravacative plaster. Up here, you're lucky you haven't been shat.'

I glanced at my foot, and it dawned on me that – to the uncouth observer – the subtle shades of my cast-cover could appear rather like the red, white and blue of the Union Jack. I began to explain, but was rudely interrupted.

'Ay's nat a fockin' reporter. Where's his press card? Ay's a singer and a dancer, aren't you mishter? Go orrn, give us a turn. Lift our spirits with a wee sang.'

One of them kicked my crutches away, spat at my injured leg, and said, 'Don't be shy noiy. Entertain us.'

My mind went blank, or *almost* blank. I did not want to sing in Spanish, and the only English-language song I knew was one that I had recently made use of in my teaching. It was a seventeenth-century London ballad called 'Courageous Betty of Chick Lane', set to a tune with the strange name, 'Lilliburlero'. With no alternative, I launched into this in my rich and fruity baritone voice:

'Boys, let us sing the glory and fame,
Of a young lass, courageous and stout.
Mistress Betty, this was her name,
She with true courage valiantly fought
With two thumping lusty tailors,
Taking away their bodkin and shears,
But Betty was nimble and made them to tremble,
So sweetly she lugg'd the Rogues by the Ears.'

A surprising quietude had fallen over the group, and I prepared optimistically to begin the second verse. Was I to be famed as the Orpheus of Ardoyne, the resourceful visitor who had soothed and caressed the savage breast with his melodious strains?

The answer was no.

'Gat him,' shouted the tallest boy, and before I could call upon St. Iago I had been jostled to the ground for a meaty pasting. I was beginning to regret my decision to tour the wild west, when all of a sudden a large and much older man appeared from nowhere like an angel on one of your away-days from heaven. He shouted angrily at my attackers – 'Leave him be! Fock away off and play in the traffic, the lot of yuus' – and the group dissolved immediately like an aspirin. He picked up my crutches and helped me to my foot with one of his thick arms. 'Come with me,' he said in a kindly growl, 'We'll get yuu sorted oiyt.'

Fifteen minutes later, I was sitting in the gloomy fumey back room of a bar with my saviour and five or so of his life-gnarled disciples. Nearby, two men played a funny game called 'shnooker', but the smoke in the room was so dense that they had to walk from one end of the table to the other after each shot in order to ascertain whether or not a particular ball had accidentally fallen down one of the holes. On the table before me, a large glass of whiskey exuded its quietly confident amber glow. The walls were decorated with photographs from as far back as the 1970s: pale-skinned, dark-haired people with fire in their eyes (they looked like Spaniards who had been raised in darkness under the supervision of some deranged scientist). On a table in the corner stood a rather fine piece of wooden sculpture. From a single twisted branch, one metre high, the artist had fashioned a representation of two lithe lovers embracing. They were conjoined at foot and head, but there was open air between their torsos. Above them, an Irish tricolour hung on the wall, flanked by two weathered old drums, each decorated with a violent scene from some distant past. One of the mighty vanquishing giants depicted on the still somewhat hairy goatskin of the drum bore an uncanny resemblance to the man who had just rescued me, and I wondered if this was in some sense a family portrait. He pointed at the whiskey with his finger, catching my eye in the process. 'Black bush, single malt – enjoy.'

'Thank you,' I said. 'It will help me get my ball-bearings.'

I took a healthy swig, and allowed a thin golden snake of liquid to slither corrosively down the back of my throat. I looked again at the sculpture, and he said, 'Beautiful, isn't it?' I nodded appreciatively, and, remembering something Connor had said, I asked, 'Is it bog oak?' 'Bog yew,' said my companion, and everybody laughed in mysterious unison.

I spent the rest of the day in that room, and consumed a vicious variety of local beverages. I sampled 'poteen', a spirit made from illegal potatoes and reputedly potent enough on occasion to blind its consumers (I was careful not to get any in my eyes). I would have tried sulphuric acid had any been offered. The more I drank, the better I understood the accents of my companions, though it is conceivable that I grew marginally less fluent myself. The conversation flowed as smoothly as the obnoxicating liquids, and I developed a deep and drunken respect for my new *amigo*. He first did me the service of pointing out more clearly than anybody else had done that I had made a poor choice of colours for the cover on my leg. He also felt critical of my selected tune, observing that 'Lilliburlero' was a treasured loyalist marching melody, and therefore unlikely to earn a generous reception when sung to disaffected young republicans in their own decaying neighbourhood by a foreigner with a red, white and blue leg. 'Let me guess,' he added as an afterthought, 'you're an academic, aren't you?'

His name was Seamus, and he had spent most of his fifty years 'fighting the Brits, one way and another'. He did not divulge much detail regarding his life before the cease-fires, but I sensed that he had not been a lady's hairdresser. He became rather serious, and I could only maintain the semblance of consciousness by discreetly using my little pinkies in order to prop open my eyes. Nowadays, he explained, his resistance was more 'polatical', and he concentrated on ensuring that 'the voice of our people' was heard whenever decisions were taken over government funding, external investment and the arrangements for controversial marches. He claimed that, despite the end of his own armed struggle, the political war went on and would continue until the money available for public toilets and other recreational facilities in Catholic areas matched that offered to Protestant neighbourhoods. He said discrepancies in the figures had been identified by the government's own watchdog.

'That is a very clever dog,' I interjected.

Seamus also held fast to the view that 'our day will come', though he conceded that the victory might eventually be demographic rather than purely political.[28] He predicted that within the lifetime of his son Catholics would out-number Protestants in the north, and a democratic majority would vote for union with the rest of Ireland. He also said that some of those in the room favoured a return to full-scale violence against their enemies. This woke me up by tickling my fancy until it was pink. I could only giggle.

'What do you mean?' I said. 'That is an idea very silly. Nowadays, terrorists blow themselves up at the flick of a hat. They splattering themselves all over the shop. If you do your thing again, people will simply laugh. From what I hear, you give the police codewords, no? And you make warnings to the newspapers? And you run away before the bomb goes off? This is like a picnic by the fountain. You make yourselves quaint and – how do you say – *anticuado*, old-fashioned.'

He was now looking a cross trifle, so I hit the ball firmly

---

[28] The Irish version of this nationalist slogan is 'Tiocfaidh Ar La', which Seamus kindly wrote on the back of my hand in indelible green ink.

into his court with just a hint of backspin by asking him what he thought of Northern Ireland's Protestants. He said they were up-tight, scrawny and annoyingly punctual. They always had biros of different colours neatly arranged on the table before them at meetings. And they didn't drink much because they couldn't hold it.

'They are not all so dull,' I countered. 'I know one Protestant lady called Audrey who can do Scandinavian full-body massage.'

Seamus looked suitably impressed, and three of his companions disappeared hurriedly in the direction of the lavatory.

Next, he told me a joke that he had learnt from his father: 'How do you know that E.T. is a Pratestant? Because he fockin' looks like one.' I had to laugh. Truly, I did. He then shrugged his massive shoulders and said, 'Prods have their way of looking at the world, and we have ours.'

'But within your way of looking at the world, what would you have them to do?'

'They should all fock away off to England and Scotland if they insist on being Brattish. They shud go back wurr they came fram.'

'But you talk about their ancestors, do you not? Surely, their families have lived in this part of the world for many generations. Would you say that all people of Irish extrapolation should leave America, to heal the wounds of the natives?'

'That's dafferent,' Seamus growled, and I decided not to pursue it.

I next enquired how he felt about all the violence that persisted despite the supposed end of the troubles.

'I don't like it,' Seamus answered, 'and I don't participate. But what am I to duu? Our people have reasons for feeling angry, and they need to defend thamsalves against loyalist pravacation.'

'So you'll endure it?'

'We have to, until the causes arre removed.'

'But it looks to me,' I ventured, 'as if you're all stuck-up at a rather sticky sticking point on the so-called peace process. Nobody's prepared to diminish the violence any further, to take the next step down the ladder towards what we in Spain call *convivencia*, or co-existence.'

Seamus was a little irritated, and slurped his poteen as if he had a mind to squirt it at my eye. As a precaution, I closed it.

'OK, wise-arse,' he said, 'What wud yuu do aboiyt it?'

I was by now completely boozled, and I accidentally disturbed a glass, thus lacing my shoes with whiskey. In an instant, there was another drink in my hand and it persuaded me to make a suggestion.

'Well, why not imagine for one second that the logjam could be broken by tackling the violence itself, rather than by addressing its underlying causes, which look so different to those on either side of the divide?'

This talk of logjams reminded me that I had to visit the toilet to do that thing that nobody else could do for me. In the stinking lavatory, I not only concluded this pressing business, but also took the opportunity to vomit voluminously into the bowl. When I returned to the table, I was amazed to find that most of the other men in the room had pulled up chairs.

'As I was saying, you must start with the violence – because everyone agrees it is a problem, no? In my view, you just have to be more creative about imagining this down-down ladder towards peace. The first step was taken years ago, from regular multiple murders down to petrol bombs, mutual intimidation and riotous confrontations, with the occasional sectarian lynching thrown in for the sake of old Father Time. That was most commendable, but now you're stuck. There are no more rungs on your ladder, and you're still wobbling near the top.'

I looked around at a pond of attentive yet sceptical faces, and wondered whether I was destined for another beating. It did not seem so, and somebody asked, 'So hoiy do we mend the fockin' ladder?'

'Well, I think you need to dream up a hierarchy of actions in descending order of brutality. These could then be used by people on both sides as a way of gradually down-scaling the violence. Then, one day, when the violence is minimal, everything else will fall into place. Foreign visitors will come to this freakishly green land, spending their money on goods that you yourselves purchase cheaply from China. Eco-tourism will go boom-boom. Perhaps a decision will be taken to join the rest of Ireland, but perhaps it will not. Minds will at last be open to the possibility of a rational choice, and all will be well in the garden. Things can be different. Did you know that, in Andalusia, we only recently taught ourselves to put up with the Moorish savages who still live among us? You too can change.'

One man, admittedly, had curled up on the shnooker table for his *siesta*, but the others were still listening. 'Yuu keep talking about that thurr ladder,' said Seamus, 'but yuu naver say what these creative staps might be.'

I threw this bone to the dogs.

'If you want to annoy your enemies, what do you do?'

A variety of options emerged: 'Throw stones', 'Beat people with baseball bats', 'Petrol bomb their homes' and 'Throw more stones'.

'It is a bit limited,' I said. 'Surely, there must be many other ways of victimising people without actually maiming or killing them. Hard, loyalist men love their pets, yes? I must have seen a dozen of those so-called "Rottweilers" around Glenbryn. Why not start by assassinating one another's dogs? It would be a challenge. In Spain, you know, we have a saying: "It is no easy matter to blow up a dog." Then, after a while, you could all graduate on to pet muti-lation instead. Then, when that starts to feel unacceptable or risible, why not paint one another's houses in a variety of feminine colours? Don't just splash it all over – do it carefully and with professional pride. How humiliated would you feel if you got up one morning to find that your entire house had been painted *de color de cereza* overnight?'

'I thought that was "beer". Do you mean like lager or stout?'

'No,' I said, 'it is a pinky colour.'

'Och, he means *cerise*.'

They agreed that this would be a bad colour for a man's house. Now, at last, some of them started producing sug-gestions of their own.

'We could put snakes through their letterboxes, so we could.'

'Bats doiyn their chimneys.'

'Or introduce aggrassive alien plant species into their fockin' front gardens.'

'Yes, yes, yes,' I enthused, 'and you can call this *eco-terrorism*. The pissibolities are endless, so they are.'

Sadly, my capacity to drink spirits while philosophising was now exhausted, and I slumped unconscious onto the table. The last thing I saw was a whiskey glass rising aggressively towards my face. When I revived, I was in my own bed with an imperial headache. The whole world throbbed, and Begoña was not looking at her most therapeutic.

'What in the name of all the saints have you been doing?' she asked. 'Who was the gorilla who carried you in? And what has happened to your head?'

I looked quizzical, so she passed me a small mirror. There, in the centre of my forehead, was one of your zig-zag Harry Potter scars that had been crudely stitched using surgical thread coloured green, white and gold.

PART II

Autumn into Winter

Chapter 11

Which begins with a thousand bangs and ends with 'Mrs. Mop' quite distracted.

On the eve of the Feast of All Saints, our house shook with the force of multiple explosions from across the city. Begoña and I were putrefied, and latent fears concerning the return of the troubles oozed out of us. We considered our options for departing immediately, and had just begun packing when the girls burst in upon us, screaming, 'Come and see the fireworks!' We went out on to the balcony at the back of our house, and were stunned to find the sky illuminated by a multitude of rocket trails and glittering cascades. Some of the explosions, particularly those from the west of the city, were enormously powerful. None of your childish little sparkle-sticks there! I tried to imagine happy family groups gathered in communal open spaces, chattering excitedly as their menfolk detonated these warheads. The incendiary concert went on through much of the night, and was instrumental in the *perforación* of one of Begoña's ear-drums. Ever since, she has held her head at a slight tilt during conversations, like a bird targeting a worm.

I learned, after speaking to Connor the following morning, that fireworks had been outlawed in Belfast throughout the period of the troubles, and had only quite recently been inlawed again. There had, he said, been one earlier attempt at legalisation, but it had ended in disaster as rival working-class estates simply trained their rockets to shoot at one another or, failing that, at passing ambulances. The upright members of the Assembly had high hopes that a more responsible attitude would prevail on this occasion. A strict system of regulation was in place, and licences were now issued only for the last night of October.

'It's as if we can't do without our explosions,' Connor added. 'They're like the pulse of this city, and we need them like the Spanish need the sound of . . . I don't know – what's a quintessentially Spanish sound?'

'That,' I replied, 'would undoubtedly be the high-pitched whining of a young man – very much in love with himself – riding his little motorbike through the narrow streets of a village set on a mountainside, sounding for all the world like a giant mosquito.'

'Och, that's lovely,' said Connor. 'You see, with us, it's explosions. An unhealthy dependence, of course, even an addiction. Outsiders can't really be expected to understand. When I was a wee fella, our French teacher tried to set up an exchange with a school in Brittany. We were all instructed to send our pen-friends reassuring letters about the joys of life in the north of Ireland. Then it all went wrong when Colette Carrol sent hers a photo of a burnt-out building, decorated with the message "Having a blast in Belfast!" She meant it nicely, but they took it all wrong.'

'It must have been terrible for you,' I commented sympathetically, 'when the cease-fires were announced.'

Connor chuckled. 'Och aye, it was hellish – until they gave us fireworks, that is. See last night? That was a grand reunion of people and powder. If you were to compare the volume of explosive material that went up last night with that detonated in a bad month during the troubles, I bet you'd see a rough parity. We're still desperate to blow things up, but we're learning to spread it around a bit. It's decommissioning by the back door.'

'But some of the bangs out of west Belfast – were those really merely fireworks?'

'Home-made, I'd say. Don't forget – there's a great deal of expertise out there, and no shortage of equipment. And there's competition for the biggest blast. It's like the old days, but without quite as many severed limbs.'

I made a joke about the 'one-armed struggle' and my good friend chuckled in perfectly genuine amusement.

I was still propelling myself up one of your steep learning curves, with Connor McCann as my mentor, my squire and my mule all rolling over on top of one another. One morning, three students came to see me to complain about something I had said in a lecture on 'The place of ladies in Christian thought during the Renaissance.' They all addressed me as 'Dr Sánchez Ventura' (which I liked) but they were intent on calling into question my intellectual integrity (which I did not). I had prepared the lecture with obsessive assiduity, shutting myself in the Bible for minutes on end. I had, moreover, given an electrical performance, during the course of which I had burst at the seams with bravura and panache. I was therefore more than a little disappointed to attract hostile reviews. The situation brought to mind an old Spanish saying – 'The cockerel who sings is the one that ends up in the oven' – and slowly I began to cook. I can no longer recall the students' names, but let us call them Sam (short for 'So I am'), Sid ('So I did') and Sue ('So I do'). They introduced themselves as committable Christians, by which, according to Connor, they meant card-carrying evangelical Protestants, and they took issue with me for having described the Bible as 'in a sense, the first textbook on female history'. In saying this, I was of course thinking of a wide range of formidable scriptural ladies, including those of exemplary virtue and those of exemplary vice, but my three critics felt that I had 'brought the word of God into disrepute'. The accusation made me cross and I bristled somewhat. I would have left the room in order to marshal my arguments, but my passageway was blocked. I was like a stuck pig.

I attempted to explain myself, speaking to them at deliberately inordinate length of Eve, Mary Magdalene, Salome, Delilah, Rachel and Lot's wife who looked back from behind him and became a pillar of salt. I was persuasive, and I hammered away until I was black and blue in the face. My little audience was clearly struck by my efforts, and I therefore sought to develop my advantage by magnanimously inviting them to call me by my first name.

'We are all labourers in the same vineyard,' I said. 'You must call me Jesús.'

Sid was unsettled, and said, 'Och, no we couldn't!'

'Be not afraid!' I said. 'My bark is louder than my bite.'

'It's not that. It's just that we'd prefer to use your surname.'

'And my title,' I reminded them. 'Don't forget about that!'

Now they all looked a little embarrassed, so I smiled compassionately upon them.

'You mustn't get yourselves out of proportion,' I said. 'I'm sure we can still these troubled waters and become friends. In Spain, we say this: 'Yesterday, prostitutes. Today, neighbours'.'

In more relaxed mood, we commenced a detailed conversation about the sensibilities of Ulster's Protestants. I asked them how they viewed the Catholic population. They looked awkward, but the girl said, 'They drink too much, so they do. They're late for everything, and they're always looking to borrow pens in the middle of seminars.' One of her friends shrugged, and said, 'I'm a wee bit more tolerant, so I am. They have their way of looking at the world, and we have ours.'

'But within your way of looking at the world,' I wondered, 'what would you have them do?'

The third student now chipped in, so he did.

'They should all go and live in Dublin if they insist on being Irish.'

For a moment, I wobbled on my plinth, momentarily disorientated by a powerful feeling of what the people on the continent call *already seen*. Then, it dawned on me: these people were spitting mirror images of Seamus and his friends up in Ardoyne. Their accents were different, their hair was neater, and they had an air of tee-totalitarianism, but they felt things in much the same way.

We were on a well-trodden track, but I did manage to contribute one rather dazzling new idea in my discussion with this clutch of fledgling unionists. With your permission, I will share it. My suggestion was that the Orangemen of Ulster resembled badgers in their devotion to 'traditional routes' (I withheld my opinions regarding the low intelligence of the latter species). I went on to tell them about an experiment that had been reported on the news. In England, one of the soft-headed local councils had paid for the construction of special underground tunnels after grubby environmentalists with names like Boggo and Oakie protested against a major new road that traversed the badgers' ancient pathways. Apparently, the badgers had been converted to the idea just in the time of Nick, and the inhabitants of an entire system of holes were saved from certain death (but a month later, if I understood correctly, they were all exterminated by government agents for allegedly spreading rumours about tuberculosis). I assured my visitors that I was, as an outsider, reluctant to intervene in the functioning of their internal organs, but I wondered whether some of the Protestant anger generated in Belfast by official marching bans might be assuaged by some similar initiative. It was difficult to tell whether my audience appreciated my insight, but they left the room in moderately high spirits, their wounds scabbing over quite nicely.

By this stage, my own injury was also beginning to lose its power over me as the two ends of my ruptured tendon knitted themselves magically together like a couple of your lovely old clickety-click northern grannies. I returned to the hospital to be fitted with my plastic boot or 'pneumatic walker'. It was a remarkable and ingenious device. It came in two parts for easy removal, and the inside of the boot contained a series of small airbags. I was shown how to inflate these with a blue pump, until they achieved a pressure that would provide my damaged leg with the optimum degree of support. Amazingly, I could then walk around without it being necessary, as Mr. Morrison put it, for my bodyweight to 'pass through the tendon'. This seemed nothing short of miraculous, and on the virtual dance-floor of my mind I executed an arresting *fandango*.

My physiotherapist taught me a range of exercises designed to rehabilitate my foot within wider society and also to improve its bloody supply. I approached these in serious vein, being militantly determined to recover more swiftly than all the other ruptured persons whom I had surreptitiously scanned in the treatment room. I had to be whole again, and I allowed my newly developed streak of urban competitive vanity to work on my behalf. I exercised my foot devoutly whenever I was watching television or reading or polishing my pearls of wisdom before sceptical students. I rotated it in both directions, I moved it with increasing confidence from side to side, and I built up its sense of self-worth by pushing and pulling on a broad band made of flexible pink rubber. I am ashamed to say that I found the process of recovery, and particularly my contact with this stretchable device, not only invigorating but more than a little erogenous. Our cleaning lady took leave of us (and, sadly, her senses) after she found me busying myself with it in the bedroom one grey morning.

Chapter 12

Which describes how Begoña's selfishness forced Jesús to engage with his children, against all natural justice.

Begoña had all but withdrawn from the emotional life of the family, and she focused her attentions almost exclusively on her commercial concerns. She even added another string to her guitar. During one of our increasingly rare conversations, she mentioned the matter almost casually.

'Did I tell you I have a new enterprise?'

'No, you did not.'

'Let me first ask you a question: have you seen that sandwich bar in town – "O'Flynn's Irish Sandwiches"? It does very well.'

'Yes,' I replied. 'I was in there with Conchi last week. I bought her a sandwich filled with ham and something called "dulse". She did not like it. She said the dulse was disgusting and tasted like seaweed.[29] What about it?'

'Well, don't you think it's peculiar that, in Belfast of all places, there is an Irish sandwich shop, but no outlet marketing *British* sandwiches? You know, *rosbif* and things like this.'

---

[29] Imagine my delight when I later realised that she had identified it correctly!

This was, I knew, precisely the sort of issue about which Ulster people blew off hot air, and with a marked reluctance I therefore had to concede the desirability of what Connor called 'parity of steam' between the two sandwich traditions. Bego went on.

'So, I am renting a premises in the centre of the city – with the money from "Shrinking Violet" – and next week we open a shop called "The Earl of Sandwich". My marketing people came up with the title. It has a good ring to it, no?'

I tried to sound encouraging, but secretly I hoped that my wife was about to spread herself too widely. Initially, the sandwich shop proved controversial, and my uncharitable hopes seemed justified. The building was petrol-bombed by dissident members of PIRATE on its second night, but even this disaster worked to Begoña's benefit. The sprinkler system performed admirably and the police arrived to find that the leader of this banned republican grouping, Charlie 'The Fish Kettle' McAtackney, had managed to get his charred hand stuck fast in the letterbox. The authorities were overjoyed with Bego's burnt offering, having pursued him for some months. They placed McAtackney under arrest, and also recovered a wealth of his incriminating paraffinalia. The media covered the story from morning until night for two whole days, and thousands of God-fearing unionists and loyalists turned up devotedly to purchase their so-called 'coronation chicken' sandwiches. Begoña's shop was *una sensación internacional*.

Shamefully, I had to spend more and more of my time with our daughters, and if you wish to skate over the little pen-portraits that follow, I will not reproach you (I have been advised that some readers – ladies, I suppose – may find this material charming). In this period, there was room for little else in between my work, my exercises and my children. I tried to kill two of these three birds with one stone by persuading my children to do my work, thus leaving me free to attach myself to my flexible pink *concubina* around the clock. Concepción was irritatingly precocious, and an extremely advanced reader. She devoured *Harry Potter and the Advance of the Six Figures* in a matter of hours. Upon my request, she also fought her way conscientiously through V. G. Broadbrush's *Malice in Sunderland* (a monumental 1000-page tomb on the history of hatred in a northern English town) and presented me with a passable synopsis written on a piece of her 'Sexy Lexy' writing paper. But when I gave her a much shorter book called *Foreskin and country: circumcision and patriotism in England during the 1930s*, she became frustratingly withdrawn, leaving me in the unenviable position of having to read it myself. I admit freely that I wanted to exploit her talents, but I had never aimed to upset her rotten apple cart (not consciously, at least). Conchi's vocabulary was unnervingly extensive, and she soaked up words as if she were made of blotting paper. She, more than any other member of the family, combined an enviable fluency in 'Ulsterese' with a parallel capacity for absorbing and deploying the new language of urban consumerism. She flaunted both, invariably peeving my spleen in the process. I, in contrast, still felt a little self-conscious when I tried to toss local or current expressions into the ears of my conversational companions, and I once had to climb into my dark wardrobe for a time after I heard Conchi say, in a heated discussion with two visiting friends, 'Ackaway with yuu, yuu pair of sponges, it's the cuulest product on the market, a right canty wee thing, so it is, and yuus'll not find better specifications or a keener image if yuu surf till ye burf, sure ye won't.'

Purificación was different. She annoyed me in two ways: firstly by dancing through life like some kind of ethereal wooden nymph; and secondly by her apparent immunity to the charms of metropolitan materialism. Connor described her as 'through–other', a local word apparently signifying some degree of vacancy and a tendency to make others want to wallop one. She was just as clubbable as her big sister, but Puri's interaction was not grounded in language to the same degree. When her friends came to play, she would lead them into the garden or down to the river in search of fox footprints and otter poopies. Learning to read was, in her case, proving a most painful chore, and the only words she could spell with any firm consistency were 'crap', 'bugger' and 'wedding tackle'. Puri, like her mother, rarely took advice, as the following touching anecdote will reveal to you. She arrived home from school one day, only to find the limp and tiny body of a goldcrest – the smallest and now also the unluckiest bird in Ireland – lying on our doorstep. Externally, it appeared perfect: impossibly delicate, its nondescript body plumage serving to highlight by contrast the dazzling and rather seductive stripe of orange across the top of its minute head. Presumably, it had flown into the glass window and kicked one of your buckets on the way down. For a while, I tolerated Purificación's interest in the bird, and even found her an old ornithological book from which she extracted certain information concerning its diet and personal habits. But as the afternoon progressed, I became somewhat decomposed by aspects of her behaviour. She first examined the body in intricate detail, stretching out the wings, spreading the claws and attempting to open the beak. This was acceptable. She also insisted, however, that her bird had not expired but was merely unconscious, and that she would be able, given time, to revive it. She attempted mouth-to-beak resuscitation, and, when this failed, proceeded undaunted with elementary flying lessons. Puri demonstrated the basic technique to her little charge, then launched it out of an upstairs window to the cry of 'Fly, little one, fly!' I was by now anxious to draw the whole experiment to a close before Begoña came home, knowing what a dim gloss she would apply to her wayward daughter. I thought I had accomplished this objective by staging an exhibition of chocolate and cash, but three weeks later the goldcrest, now richly malodorous, bubbled to the surface in Puri's underwear drawer, lovingly wrapped in a piece of tissue paper upon which she had, with some considerable effort, written 'Mi bd is *not ded.*'

The two of them were like your chalk and cheese, and they found it maddeningly difficult to play together without fireworks. Many of their arguments involved that centrepiece of the modern household, the little channel-changing black box for shooting at the remote television. These were not even battles over which programme or DVD was to be viewed, merely over who had control of the 'zappy'. Conchi and Puri were perfectly capable of missing an entire episode of one of their favourite programmes while they struggled for possession. Most of the violence was verbal rather than physical, but their shrill voices operated on the same frequency as one of those novelty rape alarms and had a similarly disturbing impact on everyone but the girls themselves. They called one another all manner of local names in their turbulent exchanges: binlid, dirtbird, blirt, girney gub, scut, skite-the-gutter, galeeried gunter-pace, thundergrub, spoon and sponge. I tried to block the sound by concentrating, for example, on what appeared to me to be a rather charming three-way circuit of sexual electricity between the presenters of your marvellously erotic *Blue Peter* programme, two of whom were delicious vest-clad young women (and I forget about the other one). With shame I must tell you that, while my daughters bit metaphorical chunks out of one another, I would sit there enraptured, day-dreaming of a scenario in which Ruth and Olivia used my excited body ('Here's one I prepared earlier') to demonstrate to the boys and girls some basic penetrative techniques.

This produced in me a state of arousal, but never quite a productive solution. Sometimes, I tried to persuade Conchi and Puri to fight physically rather than mentally, but they always hijacked and side-tracked my expressive train of thought.

'You know, girls,' I said, 'sometimes violence is the only answer.'

'That's not what my teacher says,' replied Puri. 'She says violence is never the answer, and I believe her.'

Conchi never liked it if her sisters spoke before her, and

now she positioned herself like an American football player hoping to score a put-down.

'Sorry, Puri, I didn't catch that,' she said sweetly. '*What* is never the answer?'

'Violence,' replied Puri.

'Ha! So it is sometimes the answer, because I asked you a question, and your answer was "violence". Sucker!'

There was now a tear in Puri's eye, but she managed to say, 'Don't be clever, you big bully. You know how it upsets Papá.'

One afternoon I even tried arming them with a range of suitable items lifted at random from the kitchen: assorted root vegetables, a bowl, a block of cold butter, a bag of flour, a wooden spoon, a selection of fruit, a rolling pin, a packet of sugar and a frying pan. I retired upstairs, anticipating a tension-releasing episode of extreme and messy violence. I nodded in self-congratulation as muffled sounds emerged from the kitchen – but when I descended again an hour later, I found to my discomfiture that they had concocted a delicious-looking plate of classic Irish potato-apple cakes, and were still bickering like cats. They clearly felt at home in Ulster, but not, maddeningly, in one another's company.

Little Dilatación was more like Conchi than Puri, but the sheer force of her personality set her on a distinctive pedestal of her own. She really irked me, being as stubborn as your proverbial mule, and more clever by approximately 50%. Dila clearly felt that other runners in the human race had a responsibility to accommodate themselves to her vision of the universe, rather than *vice versa*. In this characteristic, she bore an uncanny resemblance to the local politicians who glared out of our television while explaining angrily that 'campromise is nat an aption'. In her own distinctive way, then, she too was stamping her footprint on Northern Ireland and developing an appropriate personality to boot.

Dila ruled the household with an instinctive combination of regular intimidation and occasional benevolence. She was impervious to all the reforming tictacs of adults. My attempts to buy her a one-way ticket on the so-called potty-train came to nought, and she made it perfectly clear that she had no intention of abandoning her fabulous modern nappies. In Spain, we had not thought twice about our primitive reliance on the old knotted towels which we washed by hand until, one by one, they went to pieces under the strain. On arrival in Belfast, however, we gleefully pulled our heads back from this endlessly tedious loop of laundry and equipped Dila with throwaway 'Dumpers', the latest brand of commercial nappies. For children above the age of three, these were officially labelled 'training pants' by the marketing men, presumably to help parents come to terms with the stigmata of eternal nappyhood. But nappies they quite clearly were. I was frankly flummoxed by their capacity to have and to hold, in sickness and in health, bucketloads of this, that and the other without imposing any discomfort on their wearer, beyond the scientifically unavoidable weight gain. These 'Dumpers' seemed to us implausibly effective, and the subject of their evident defiance of the laws of nature was one which I found endlessly absorbing.

Chapter 13

Which recounts Jesús' adventures with a spell-checker and the unfortunate episode in which he was almost given a sack in which to place his post.

Up at RUB, November was truly a can of fish and Connor and I came perilously close to blowing our jobs. It is one thing for a Spanish *hidalgo* to assimilate himself into a rabidly materialist modern city, or for a foreigner from a hot Catholic background to blend into a society that is awash with cool northern Protestants. It is quite another for an essentially well-hinged individual who generally goes with a swing to find happiness and harmony among a group of academics. I had not realised, when I perused my contract, that the United Kingdom's universities were so intensively monitored and assessed. In the attic of my mind, I had anticipated complete freedom to think, write and recreate myself. I had imagined that I would be able to publish and teach whatever I wished, provided that it all had some vague connection with the infinitely elasticated concept of 'history'. Instead, I waded into a toxic swamp of government 'benchmark' documents, 'programme specifications', 'self-evaluation' summaries, 'student tracking', 'reflexivity', 'transferable skills', 'research footprints', 'intended learning outcomes', departmental 'emission statements', 'scholarly skidmarks', 'undergraduate throughput', 'academic clusters', 'exit velocities' and much more besides. Most of my colleagues despised this government-imposed vocabulary, but found themselves ill-equipped to resist it. It was all so different from Andalusia, where most of the people simply ignore the government in Madrid unless it offers them money or, better still, water.

All this was distressing enough, but the prospect of an external audit, courtesy of the triennial 'British Universities Survey of Teaching' [BUST], came as a most unpleasant shock in the grim month of November. Moreover, Connor and I were deputed to prepare the final documents for the BUST inspection, and to ensure that copies of all relevant documents were despatched to the six auditors. I was somewhat resentful at being asked to do the donkey's spadework in this manner, being new to the job and still rather green behind the ears. On the other hand, this was clearly an opportunity both to announce my arrival and to demonstrate my sociable and co-operative disposition to my disjointed workmates and my so-called line manager. It is often wise, as I am sure you know, to favour curry with a new boss. Most of the documents had, in any case, been drafted already, and our task was essentially to consolidate and edit. In private, Professor Boyle confided in us that he thought the material looked 'rather dull'. He therefore invited us to 'enliven it all a bit', and he lent us for comparison the 'cutting edge' documentation that had been submitted to BUST by the history department at the City University of Newcastle upon Tyne.

'You want us to sex it up?' asked Connor.

'If you must put it like that, yes, I suppose I do,' he replied.

It looked to us *una misión imposible*. Connor and I grew increasingly agitated as we read and read, amended and re-drafted, spell-checked and word-counted. Before long, we saw little dancing men in mortar-boards projected on to the insides of our eyelids whenever we attempted to rest. This, we knew, was not good, but we had to persevere. Then, with hours to go before our deadline, Connor's computer suddenly accused him of performing 'an illegal operation'. He was shocked and he slumped forwards onto the desk. Then, in his anxiety at what he naturally interpreted as an attempt to associate him with the popular practice of 'backstreet abor-tion', unsettling even to a lapsed Catholic, he extended a finger and pushed the wrong button on his computer. We lost the all-important 'Programme Specifications'. Heroically, Connor revived and began re-typing from an earlier draft, while I went to grill Dr. Phyllis Stein's brain regarding a couple of my more sticky passages. She was less than helpful.

Connor and I worked through the last night, anxiously burning one another's candles at both ends. The atmosphere was tense, and our combined judgement was fatally flawed. We had by now begun to think as one, and had each arrived at the department with a specially selected relaxant substance in our coat pockets. My contribution was a fine bottle of Bushmills whiskey, while Connor produced a matching pair of small, white tablets which, he said, would help us to 'put this department at the top of the BUST league'. Within ten minutes, we felt much more positive, and so set to work.

For the first hour, we read intensively, tinkered constructively and giggled uncontrollably. Then, Connor experienced a moment of self-doubt, and asked, 'Do you reckon we've "enlivened" it enough? It still seems like a heapashite to me, so it does.' I reinvigorated him by suggesting that we 'spell-check' the names of all our colleagues in a new and more adventurous mood. This instantly brought a fresh and exotic look to the jaded list. Grainne Toal became Groin Toad at the push of a few buttons. Sadly, we lost Hamish Vickery, but his replacement, Hermit Vicars, promised great mirth. Ardal McCardell took flight as Aerial Mackerel, while Norman Boyle, the professor who had burdened us, developed an Enormous Boil. Dudley Backle fell victim to Deadly Bacilli, but we chose to leave Ivar Orr exactly as he was.

Flushed with the success of this initiative, we turned our impish eyes to the long lists of courses that made up the bulk of the various 'programme specifications'. We decided not to interfere with the course titles at their first appearance in the repetitive documents, but to punish them for the monotony of their later re-appearances by intervening with all the severity of one of those tin-can dictators whose territories are forever being inundated by various forms of American marine life. On this occasion, the spell-check failed us by recognising most of the words, so we packed it off to bed and struck out alone. When we had finished, 'single honours' students could choose from the usual menu of courses, which included 'Age of the Normans', 'Argentina in the Age of Evita' and 'Monks, Warlords and Peasants'. At the end of the document, however, candidates for 'joint honours' could build their degrees from a far more inspiring list: 'Rage of the Mormons', 'Ballymena in the Age of Ryvita' and 'Monkeys, Warthogs and Pheasants', to name but a few.

At three o'clock in the morning, we printed our final versions and left them tidily on Miss Place's desk with instructions that they should be revealed to Professor Boyle in the morning, then sent by hasty post to the assessors. We also requested that our seminars for the next day be cancelled. Finally, we phoned a taxi from 'AAA Aardvark Cabs' and, pleased as poteen, we made our ways home.

Not surprisingly, we spent the next two weeks in a state of acute and dry-mouthed anxiety. Our head of department made sure that copies of all the documentation were available in the departmental office for consultation by colleagues, and he apologised for not yet having found time to read the material thoroughly for himself. He said, 'I flicked through it, and it all looked fine.' 'No hurry,' replied Connor. We attempted to postpone what seemed inevitable by discouraging the other lecturers from studying our work, and by hiding the relevant files whenever someone seemed to be snuffling around in the office. Miss Pelling said to me, 'You two are sweet - you just can't leave those documents alone, can you?' 'They are like our needy northern babies,' I said, 'and they need to be watched all the time.' We sustained this for a week, and I began to wonder whether we might actually succeed in avoiding dismissal. As Connor pointed out, however, we had so far succeeded only in resisting internal examination. We still had to endure a three-day visit from six outsiders, all of whom were being paid a bonus for reading the documents with a fine toothbrush and exposing any flaws or inconsistencies. He stared at the incriminating words on my computer screen, then concluded succinctly, 'Sure, we're toast'. I refused, as ever, to surrender, and I splayed out our options on the table before him: 'We're not finished yet, my friend. Either we come clean, or we wipe up the mess, or we simply let it all run.' Connor apparently did not like the sound of these alternatives, and for several minutes he once again buried his long face in my laptop.

Ultimately, it was all a bit of a damp squid. Six senior historians had each spent a full fortnight with a copy of our portfolio, and not one of them drew attention to the many anomalies and peculiarities exhibited therein. I realised with relief that the university system was in safe hands after all. In fact, the auditors commended us on 'the professional presentation of the material' and on 'the lucidity of the interpretative paragraphs'. They described our self-evaluation document as 'impressively animated and refreshingly honest'. One of them even said, in amusement, 'Do you really have a colleague called Ivar Orr? How splendid – his name rather flew out at me.' They observed some of our seminars, and spoke to groups of students picked by hand from Professor Boyle's fruitful tree. All in all, we received a unanimous vote of approval, and mutual congratulations were offered all the way around. There was only one genuinely uncomfortable moment. A man from Birmingham asked one of the staff committees what kind of material was covered in the module on 'Monkeys, Warthogs and Pheasants'. Professor Boyle looked at me with panic in his eyes. I looked at the floor and whispered a hurried invocation to St. Jude, the patron of lost causes. To my astonishment, he answered instantly, choosing to employ the privileged Connor McCann as his mouthpiece. Together, they launched into a speech that was as breathless as it was breathtaking.

'It is, I understand from Dr Toad, grounded in the 'new ecological history' of Ireland. At heart, it's about the implications of introducing alien species into a native habitat. It features not only the creatures of the title, but fallow deer, squirrels, rabbits, rhododendron, and so on. Of course, it also speaks to our own age, and it's very popular with the students.'

'It sounds absolutely fascinating,' said the man from Birmingham. Connor McCann had swallowed him in his nutritious entirety, and had also supplied me with the idea for one of the most successful undergraduate courses in the entire and wholesome history of history.[30]

Not surprisingly, Professor Boyle summoned us to his room bright and early next morning. Despite our astounding success, the frown on his brow was so heavy that we could barely detect his eyes. It was immediately obvious that our noble efforts had earned us none of your brown pointies after all.

'Do you two realise how close that was?' he asked, gesturing angrily towards the papers that were spread out like manure on his expansive and expensive professorial desk.

'We're really sorry,' said Connor. 'We lost all perspective and got drunk. It's my fault, not Jayzo's. I let it get to me,

---

[30] If you truly cannot wait, please hop, skip and jump your way to p.177.

and I brought the whiskey. I'm not offering any excuses, but we did both feel pretty stressed. And he's in his first term of teaching – so please don't punish him too harshly.'

'Don't instruct me on my disciplinary responsibilities, Connor. You are one person from whom I will not be taking advice.'

'I'm sorry,' Connor said limply.

The professor was exasperated, and allowed himself a rare expletive. 'You were supposed to 'sex it up', not fuck it up! You're a pair of hallions.'[31]

At this point, he looked straight at me, raising his brow momentarily in enquiry before it sunk once again onto his nose.

'Connor's lying about the whiskey,' I said. 'It was mine. He only brought the little white tablets.'

Professor Boyle's next question surprised me.

'What was it?'

'What?'

'The whiskey.'

'Black bush. Single malt. Twenty years old.'

'Good?'

'Certainly.'

'Good.'

His brow had ascended somewhat, and by golly wasn't that just the merest inkling of a twinkling in his previously indivisible eyes? He spoke again.

'I once inadvertently asked a barmaid if she had a black bush.'

---

[31] Irresponsible people, those who are good for nothing.

We chuckled nervously and glanced at one another.

'Christ,' he went on, 'aren't you two a couple of eejits?'

There ensued a peculiar five-minute silence, during which Connor and I shuffled uncomfortably from buttock to buttock and back again. We both wanted to stand up for ourselves, but I knew that subservience was politic. I glanced at Connor, put my finger to my lip and wisely held my tongue. At last, the Enormous Boil opened up once again.

'The way I see it, there's no point in recriminations, suspensions and dismissals. Not this time, anyway.[32] I'm going to be lenient, but only because you got lucky. If you do anything like this again, I will have no alternative but to drop the pair of you like . . . '

Here, there was a pregnant pause, at the end of which I obligingly gave birth thus:

' . . . like a tin of hot cats on a brick roof?'

The professor looked suitably surprised at my evident facility, and the conversation came to an end.

That evening, the staff of the department visited a pub for a rare experiment in communality. Connor and I were not exactly patted on the back for a job well done, but several of our colleagues did manage to force through their thin lips one or two of your cack-handed compliments. The month therefore ended well, and I felt more optimistic than I had done for some time. My buoyancy was returning, and my fellow academics were as accepting of me as they ever

---

[32] *Nota bene*, I thought, there is a warning in this.

were of anything in their peculiar half-lives. In these circumstances, I felt able to encourage and appreciate Begoña's commercial ventures with something approaching plausible enthusiasm. Her successes *were* impressive, but I was the one who brought in the more consistent wage and who would therefore be responsible for keeping the boat afloat if and when her coronation chicken went pear-shaped.

Chapter 14

In which Jesús commences his manful engagement with the spirit of modern Christmas and strives to raise the tone of his muscles.

The next few weeks were dominated by the long overture to our first Christmas as astute and avaricious urban consumers. Begoña and I knew that if we could survive and thrive in the intensity of the festive season, then we could truly regard ourselves as integrated twenty-first century city-dwellers. At home the mood was one of tumultuous agitation. The city centre was much the same, and it vibrated with commercial activity right from the start of December. The Christmas lights had already been twinkling for many weeks, while the shops were heavily and deliciously decorated *como putas de Sevilla.*[33] The power of Christmas was such that Bego and I even drew a little closer together again. Concord was in the air and our engines were beginning to roar once more. You will be delighted to hear that towards the end of the month we made love in an extraordinary way. But for this you must be patient. As a family, we spent several happy Saturdays down in the town, tossing our money

---

[33] Like tarts from Seville, a delicacy.

around willy-nilly and simply revelling in the atmosphere. Follow us, if you will, on one such trip . . .

The journey by car takes some considerable time because of all the empty buses that block the passage of more legitimate traffic. The citizens of Belfast look a little tense as a result, and at one point we stop to watch two angry men standing next to their cars. They scream incomprehensible obscenities at one another (I know it is rude because Concepción blushes) beneath a sign which bears the legend, 'Traffic Calming Measure'. I have an idea to buy for Begoña a recording of some music by a loyalist flute band, such as that which we heard in Bushmills. I keep my intentions private, of course, but I cleverly make a detour along Sandy Row to find a famously sectarian shop called 'Flutes 'n' Suits'. My womenfolk wait in the car, while I march with confidence through the door into a room crammed not only with the items mentioned on the sign, but with bowler hats, orange banners, sashes, music books, shoes and painted drums as big as the wheels of a tractor. The shopkeeper looks at me through a haze of tobacco smoke and I detect in his posture a certain scepticism when I explain the nature of my errand. He gestures towards a small cardboard container of compact discs, and he says something like, 'Have a hoke aroind in thur if yuu wan.' I do not know what this means, so I rummage gingerly in his box and hope that everything will turn out for the best. Soon, I identify two discs that seem to promise something like the potent, primitive music that Begoña and I found so energising when we visited the north coast. Curiously, they have identical covers and they feature the same groups and the same tunes (for example,

'The Sash', 'Orange Lilly' and 'My Granda Bit the Pope'), but one is ten pounds more expensive than the other. I ask the smoky man why this is the case. He points with a grumpy finger to the cheaper of the two recordings, and says, 'Thas juss floots 'n' drums, no wurrds. The other's gat wurrdds tooo, an thur's a rurr wee picture of Kang Bally inside the bax.' I still look unconvinced, so he leans towards me and growls like a bear, 'It's more *pravacative*.' I feel threatened by his obscure vowel movements, and I therefore purchase the superior of the two discs and haste a beaty retreat to the security of my car.

Once we reach the centre of town, we attach all three of the girls to a rope of medium length in order to guard against undesirable losses amidst the crowd. This works well, save for the moment when we accidentally entangle an elderly evangelist wearing a double-sided board that warns us, 'The wages of sin . . . is death.' He looks a little flabbergasted as he cuts himself loose with a penknife and scurries off into the throng. There are beggars outside every shop but, unlike the scrawny desperadoes we have heard about in Granada, these people are well-dressed and they have special containers for their money with tempting little slots. They even distribute colourful stickers with pictures of wheelchairs or boats or ambulances on them. What a strange place is this!

Concepción and Dilatación wander around in glee, their mouths open and their eyes bulging. They have, of course, visited the city centre once or twice before, but nothing has prepared them for the unadulterated splendour of this *fiesta comercial*. Temporarily, they are like poor, depraved children of the countryside once again, and they react to everything with an innocent freshness that almost strums accord on my heartstrings. They dance to the invisible Yuletide music that fills each shop like gas; they stare brightly at the homemade snow; and they plead indiscriminately for all manner of magnificent merchandise. Purificación, true as ever to her self, is somewhat less impressed. Instead, she wears a little frown and says she is troubled by the frequency with which we encounter Santa Claus. At one moment, she yanks on the rope, almost breaking my wrist in the process, and whispers in my ear, 'He's very fast isn't he Papá? That must be how he can do the whole world in one night.' This interpretation suffices until she sees two Santas at once, merrily seducing punters outside the Diggington's department store. She tinkles my bell again, and says, 'Hey, if that one's Santa, then who's that?' Somewhat crabbily, I explain that neither of these men is actually the real Father Christmas, a point that is neatly illustrated when one of them calls out to the other, 'Have ya a fockin' light thurr Jimmy?'

When we have bought all that we can cash and carry, we return to the car. Our shopping trip ends with a visit to the supermarket, during which we purchase strange festive foodstuffs and other necessaries. There are explosive crackers, luxury coffee without any caffeine, and mince pies with no mince. We also find a few Andalusian specialities: sugared almonds, dried figs, and dates which are sold in little boxes with 'Eat me' inscribed instructively upon their lids. I wonder to myself what other uses northern people have devised for these sticky fruits, but I keep the various possibilities to myself.

The sight of all this food makes the girls hungry, and they begin loudly smacking one another's lips. We therefore complete our excursion by taking them to one of the many 'Burgur U' stores. They feast on jumbo cheese and meat doorstops, served on a bed of yellow polystyrene. Begoña and I sniff these materials, but we cannot bring ourselves to eat any. The girls remain a step ahead of us, and each of them is also rewarded with a complimentary plastic stop-watch issued to all young *consumidores* as part of a fitness campaign being run by the American franchise. These are destined to become lost within our home and to go 'bo-peep' from their private locations at irregular intervals during the night for weeks to come...

The excitement of Christmas was, as you can see, ines-capable. It was not, however, my first priority at this time. Instead, I had to continue my efforts to advance and enhance the recovery of my reconstituted Achilles' tendon. I returned to the clinic, where the patronising doctor confiscated my special boot. He even refused to allow me to retain it as a toy that might help to keep the children off my back. 'Some of our patients,' he explained slowly, 'become over-reliant on their pneumatic walkers, so it is our policy to take them back, if you don't mind. And you shouldn't be carrying any children around for a while yet.' The physiotherapist, Abigail, was much more appealing: enticingly supple and arrestingly developed into the bargain. She pressed firmly on my foot and then, somewhat to my surprise, she suddenly began to flirtate before my very eyes. She said, 'I want you to resist me.' So I said, 'You want to make role play, chiquita?' To this, she replied with mock severity, 'Please take this seriously, Mr Sánchez Adventurer. I'll be the physio and you be the patient. Now, push against my hand, please.' When I did so, my leg felt enfeebled, though it was not quite as bootless as I had feared. The calf muscle was more floppy than any other part of my body had ever been before, but Abigail was reassuring. 'There's not too much wastage, sure there's not,' she said, in a low and seductive voice. Next, she demonstrated a number of exercises to me, the most surreal of which saw her standing on one foot with her eyes shut, while waving her other slim limbs around in a fashion full of passion. The purpose was to strengthen one's damaged foot, while simultaneously improving one's control over it.

'I'll never be able to do that,' I whimpered in despair. 'You can't teach an old dog to suck eggs, you know.'

'I bet I can,' she said, and I saluted her application.

Abigail also suggested that I join a 'gym' and begin some gentle work on something called a 'treadmill'. This sounded like a device for making flour from a donkey, and I wondered if she were either teasing me in some way, or more probably alluding to some fantasy that she was nursing.

A few days later, I took her advice and became a member of an institution called 'Bum and Bust'. I had never darkened the doorway of such a place before, and I was entranced right from the opening. I learned all the American jargon from their posters, and did hundreds of tummy crunches, gut wrenches, bum-bangers, butt-wangers, abdo-meanies, blubber-rubbers, flibberdigibbets, quaddies, kneebejeebies, flex-pecs, flab-jabs, ass-burners, toe-curlers and tongue-twisters. I also incinerated dozens of calories by cycling, rowing and running. I was particularly bewitched by the treadmill. Could there ever be a more exquisite symbol of the urban peasantry's liberation from the grim grind of productive manual labour? They perform repetitive and exhausting physical tasks in establishments such as this, building muscles that nobody needs, precisely in order to demonstrate this freedom from toil (though some, I admit, just stay at home and get fat instead). It is also a kind of conspicuous calorific consumption, and my participation in it made me feel strong, successful and rich. While straining my muscles, I was able to watch two channels of American television while listening to the latest songs from the girl-band, 'Nuclear Pussy', on a fabulously powerful music machine in the corner. 'Bum and Bust' is situated over the river, so that members can punish themselves while contemplating a view of the gentle Lagan and its spacious, underpopulated toepath. Altogether, it was good. My tendon was holding firm, and the construction of my state-of-the-art new urban identity was proceeding brick by brick.

Chapter 15

In the course of which Jesús spends time under water, under cover and under certain illusions, while making a new friend in 'Jumping Jack, the Spermicidal Maniac'.

Back at home, there was a mystical materialism in the air. We invited each of the girls to compose a list of the ten items they craved most achingly and, if possible, to place these in order of priority. Conchi headed her list with a computer game called the 'Game-girl C22' which, she explained, would enable her to experience life as a near-naked huge-breasted Amazon whose task was to evade the attentions of angry muscle-bound men with 'giant red guns that fire white goo'. Puri was not well-motivated, but her interest rates eventually rose somewhat following a little mean-spirited encouragement from her older sister. She expressed a vague desire for one of the new generation voice-activated 'Barbie' dolls. In particular, she hoped for an 'In Yer Face' Barbie, dressed all in black and capable of telling anyone who was brave enough to engage her in conversation to 'Go suck rocks' or 'Frick off.' Dila was silent and defiant when asked what she wanted for Christmas. If she opened her mouth at all, it was only to growl, 'You must never speak of this again.'

I was, as so often in my life, surrounded by women. From time to time, a man needs other outlets for his various hobby horses. I was therefore as happy as the proverbial sandbag when Connor appeared one Saturday afternoon, offering light relief and inexpensive refreshments.

'How 'bout a boys' night out, Jayzo?' he said with rather an obvious winkle in his eye. 'I was thinking we should have a couple of wee swallies, then take a look at the new sex shop in town, just for a laugh like?'[34]

I had already heard about this establishment. Some newspapers had covered up its grand opening, and it sounded like just the place for what the Irish call a 'good crack'. Needless to say, I had never seen anything like it, and I was charmed by Connor's courteous invitation. In the pub, I drank two glasses of wine and he consumed three pints of that well-named drink, 'stout'. With these beverages, we nailed our courage to the sticky post and prepared to insert ourselves directly into the centre of the sex industry. As a precaution, we both wore dark glasses and Santa Claus costumes, thoughtfully provided by Connor for the occasion (one never knows when one's students will pop up). On the pavement outside the shop, five or six middle-aged men and women shot fiery glances at any individual who dared approach. One of their home-made banners read 'Free Presbyterians Against Sin'. I asked them, 'Do you not mean "Free Presbyterians *From* Sin"?' but Connor pulled me away

---

[34] A 'wee swallie' is, I believe, a 'small swallow' or a 'quick drink'.

before I had my answer.[35] As we moved on, the angriest of the men shouted at us, 'Yuu arrre antering a dan of anaquity! Shame orrn Yuu!' He and his associate carried another banner which bore the concise legend, 'No Sex In Ulster'.

The exterior of the shop was unassuming – black glass and the words 'Belfast Sex Complex' in simple silver lettering. Inside, however, there truly was a world of wonders. Up until this point in my life, I had always considered myself sexually adventurous, something of an innovator when it came to topographical location and anatomical docking-point, but an hour inside this box of tricks taught me that I yet remained a dull, country conservative when it came to the penetrative pleasures. Connor was hardly less astonished than I, and we did not know which way to turn. We wandered erotically around the various attractions in a mood of deep *admiración*. One of the mini-shops, packed with pumps, harnesses, vibrators, butt-plugs, chains, electrical flexes, spikes, whips, saddles and milking gear, was called 'Weapons of Masturbation'. There was also a medical consultancy called 'Sore Point', a male escort agency named 'The School of Hard Cocks' and a separate store for adolescents known as 'The Early Yearning Centre'. We nipped very briefly into 'Offa's Dyke', the lesbian dating agency, but lingered rather longer in 'The Condominium'. Here, we studied the poster advertising a new super-safe ultra-stimulating American prophylactic called 'Jumping Jack: the

---

[35] He later explained to me that the 'Free Presbyterians' are members of a kind of church.

Spermicidal Maniac'.[36] After a minute or two in the tasteful fitting rooms, I decided to buy a box of these (our only purchase of the afternoon). If you think, by the way, that Spaniards do not use condoms, then you had better think again. We use them for all sorts of things.

The following afternoon, I had another adventure in the urban playground, but this one was aqueous. Begoña had to make a series of 'important business calls' so I locked up horns with my other good friend, Audrey. We took our combined offspring to 'Sink or Swim', the spectacularly renovated public pool on the Boucher Road. Conchi, Puri and Dila were immediately in their element, behaving as if they had swum in such places a hundred times before, but I found myself once again amazed by the inventiveness of our age. There were water-chutes called 'The Plughole' and 'The Hot Flush', artificial tidal waves, irresistible whirlpools, vicious typhoons, hologrammatic sharks, lifesize shipwrecks, real pirates, colourful underwater lights, virtual harpoons and blaring water-themed music, each piece carefully selected to mark one of the subtle shifts in the micro-climate. I was bowled over by it all, and began to wonder whether it was really a place for a man with an Achilles' heel. It struck me as quite wondrous that only one child – and not, I hasten

---

[36] As the leaflet explained, 'the unique and advanced chemical treatment on the inside of the condom means that no sperm is ever going to walk away from an encounter with the Maniac. It also contains a mild anaesthetic for the extension of male and hence female pleasure.' Furthermore, it promised that 'the dimples on the surface of the Jumping Jack will react with her natural fluids to produce a continuous series of rippling and pulsating sensations. Go beyond arousal, and don't plan anything strenuous for the following week!'

to add, my own – was seriously injured during the entire afternoon.

At times, I was overwhelmed and had to spend a moment or two recuperating in the more pacific 'paddling pool', set aside for the under-4s and the over-25s. Yet there was urban magic here too. Someone else's child chose to make an unsavoury deposit in the water, thus clouding the issue. In an instant, the attendants were there in their excitement to scoop the pool. Hurriedly, they moved us all away, then quickly tossed off into it with bucketloads of mysterious powders and fluids. Miraculously, the waters cleared within minutes, and half an hour later the toddlers were back in their pool, splashing deliriously around and undoubtedly swallowing many mouthfuls of its extraordinarily clean contents. It all left me feeling rather light-headed, and I struggled to assist Audrey with the challenging task of coaxing the larger children out of the waves at the conclusion of their merry-making. I noted with interest that she looked gloriously curvaceous in her costume. What is more, her skin was smooth as a whistle and substantially cleaner than a baby's bottom. In sum, Audrey was like the sexiest Mother Hen you ever clapped your hands on, and she was also marvellously unflappable. Eventually, I sat breathlessly in the changing rooms while my three girls skidded perilously around in the shower. I looked up, and caught sight of a faded old sign on the wall in front of me: 'DO NOT ENTER THE TOILET AREA DURING AN EVACUATION'. I have to say that I was confused by this. One of the other fathers nodded at it, and said, 'Tham darrk days are lorng behind us noiy.' I could only guess at his meaning, but I managed to say, in my best Belfast voice, 'Speak ferr yerrself, mayet!'

When we arrived home, there was a curious, slightly sweet, odour in the air, and I realised that Begoña had gone off somewhere.[37] Audrey came in for a glass of wine, while the children went on the rampage through my home. The two of us talked easily for some time, and Audrey explained to me what the 'Evacuation' sign truly meant. When I explained to her what I thought it had meant, she laughed contagiously. Just then, the full might of our two broods entered the kitchen in a frenzy of festive fanaticism. Audrey described them as 'wired to the moon' and she began preparing to depart. They all ran for cover, but we eventually hunted them down like wild boar and frog-marched her share of the party to the front door. At this moment, Purificación pointed up at the sprig of mistletoe that hung from the lampshade in our hall, and she said to me, 'Kiss her. Go on, kiss Audrey. You know you want to.' We both looked coy, but the others all joined in. 'Kiss her, kiss her!' Then, without words, Audrey and I moved momentarily together and our lips met. Hers were soft as the morning mist, and very briefly I tasted her. Her firm, full breasts pressed themselves for an instant against my chest, and I am ashamed to admit that I formed an internal picture of her maternal nipples, pink and periscopic. The children cheered.

---

[37] It turned out to be the smell of a new perfume she was testing. For the significance of this, read on in a hurry to p. 285.

Chapter 16

Which recounts how Jesús found the true meaning of Christmas but lost his native Andalusian ability to eat grapes.

My study of festive urban materialism continued with the School of History's Christmas Dinner, held that year in one of the enormous functional rooms at the Europa Hotel. Connor, flushed with his pedagogical success after our sexual outing, insisted that I attend as part of my continuing education. It was a most curious affair. We were, to my surprise, but one table amongst many, and the cream of Belfast's historians appeared to be under heavy *sedación* in comparison to the writhing mass of nurses and office-workers amongst whom we found ourselves. The wave of Mexicans passed us by, and we managed only the most apologetic cheer when our presence was announced by the hyperactive just-pubescent disco-jock. Professor Boyle fell asleep, everyone drank heavily to dull the pain of compulsory collegiality, and Dr. Down complained when he was served with turkey despite having requested the vegetarian option. Our cheerful waiter, obviously drunk, asked, 'What if I wurr to tell yuu that that thur turkey was a vagetarian herself? Wud that make it OK?'

At last, the dancing began and Connor and I watched as a

dozen uncomfortable academics filed out of the room, in search of a quieter bar. This left the two of us, and at last we began to have some good cracks. We invented a new dance, inspired by my recuperative exercises, and we beamed at one another as it spread around the room like hot potatoes. We sang songs that we did not know in screaming voices that we could not hear, and my bottom was pinched by an intoxicating lady from a waste management company. In short, there was such joy in the room, such profound happiness among workmates, and so much easy sharing of atmospheric bodily fumes that I even shed a tear or two. It was thoroughly enjoyable, and at the conclusion of the celebrations we wandered home in happy harmony with humanity.

The girls' school term ended with their nativity play, yet another bright new experience for us all. For once, Connor had not briefed me as thoroughly as I would have wished, and regrettably I was the only father without a video camera. I had little alternative but to watch from the outlines as the recording daddies jostled for position in the central aisles. At one point, two of them grew so irate that they turned their cameras aggressively on one another. Each filmed his opponent for two minutes during the coming of the magi, growling and pawing the ground all the while. I kicked myself for having arrived in a state of complete emasculation. I had let the family down, and was so dejected that I did not even hear Concepción deliver her only lines:

'Through many a danger I've had to pass,
I've followed the brightest of all the stars,
and now I'm here with my trusty ass
to do the new prince homage.'

I came back to my senses for the ensuing rock 'n' roll song 'n' dance routine called 'Everybody's doing the New Prince Homage'. Puri was an angel, and appeared embarrassingly vague throughout the proceedings. The school's smallest children were attired as stars, but their sparkling head-dresses irritated their scalps so severely under the bright lights that, by the end, they were all tearing their little fingernails through their hair in extreme annoyance. Tiaras were tumbling, and several of the troubled stars actually drew blood from their scalps. 'Heads are gonna roll,' Audrey whispered in my behind.

Christmas Eve dropped on a Sunday. In the morning, Begoña and I were keen to lie in our bed for a while, enjoying the calm before the storm. I therefore installed a DVD of double duration into the machine and encouraged the girls to partake. Bego remained asleep, but I was unfortunate in not being able to return easily to your Land of Noddy. Instead, I lay there counting goats as they searched for food on the barren slopes of my mind. My misfortune continued, however, for this supposedly soporific pastime set off a runaway train of thought that ended with my decision to wake Begoña up (and how!) by introducing her for the first time to 'Jumping Jack: the Spermicidal Maniac'. At first, she remained quiet, but then she gradually began to sigh and groan in that special way that ladies have. When she muttered, 'Why don't you turn on that English farm programme? You know, the one about Tom Archer's meat supply', I knew that my little dog was barking up the right tree (there was indeed a pussy in the branches). To be honest, I could not feel very much at all and I was a little disturbed at breaking my normal hard and fast rule of love-making. Nevertheless, I persisted with my efforts for the sake of the greater good. Begoña, in striking contrast, turned a deep crimson colour and began to pulsate like one of your neon signs. She was very, very hot, and having a wail of a time. In fact, I had to mute her delight by placing a pillow over her face and blowing up the radio to a higher volume. I reached my long-delayed but satisfying climax just as the vicar of Ambridge's cat died of poisoning. It really was a splendid coincidence.

During what was left of the day, a still refulgent Begoña took responsibility for the final Christmas preparations, while I applied myself grudgingly to the children. Without respite, they bombarded me with the most inane questions and comments, and a percentage of these, I regret to announce, remain lodged like bullets in my brain: 'Will Father Christmas not burn his arse off if he comes down that thurr chimney?' (Purificación); 'Papá, you know how everyone says the birds are Santa's spies, to see if you've been good? Well, what about that dead one we saw on the road – was it axecuted as a grass, or something?' (Conchi); 'We told our mammy that you snogged Audrey and she said, "For how long?"' (Dila). On and on and on.

By the late afternoon, I was becoming desperate, and so I bundled them all into the car and took them to the cinema. We watched the festive pre-teen blockbuster, *Jangle Balls,* and I was pleasantly surprised at its high artistic worth. Who would have thought that a film about an evil elf with metal testicles who tries – unsuccessfully of course – to destroy the spirit of Christmas could be both a comic masterpiece and a moving morality tale for the modern age? I was tired, and I had expected to snitch forty wanks on my soft cinema seat during the movie, but I found myself glued to it, just like the girls. I certainly could not say the same about midnight mass (we call it the Mass of the Cockerel), to which we dragged the girls with a Roman Catholic sense of duty that was ingrown, like one of your toe-nails. We sat on the hard-hitting benches for what felt like an eternity, and were only kept alive by the presence within the flock of an entertaining team of those loveable Irish 'stout louts' whose minds are always on lower things.[38]

Christmas Day itself lived up to all expectations. We filled one entire 'wheely bin' and sixteen 'jumbo garden waste bags' with wrapping paper and plastic packaging. Purificación asked, 'Does Santa come round again and collect all that stuff?' Bego replied, 'Yes, little one, on Tuesday morning – magic, isn't it?' The girls were demented with excitement and sometimes quite unreasonable. They would squeal with delight at each present, before rapidly becoming disilluminated. Luckily, we were able, at such moments, to spew forth additional gifts. Puri, for example, burst into tears when her 'In Yer Face' Barbie doll told her she was 'a disgrace to her sex.' And Conchi sulked when she could not exceed Stage 3 on her Game-Girl and kept being engulfed in the white fluids. She cursed it for having 'so much inaccessible capacity.' We relieved the tension by presenting

---

[38] In England, they have 'lager louts', but in Spain, there is no comparable sub-species.

them with spanking new electronic 'I-pods' so that they could separate themselves from the world at will. When the appeal of these faded, we issued the mobile phones so that they need never feel isolated again. Dila complained less vociferously than her sisters, which was a surprise, and she seemed for once to be happily consumed by her squeaking, squirting, breathing, breeding, growing, mood-responsive alien slime babies.

Begoña and I, not to be outdone, fell upon our own gifts from a considerable height of eagerness. She lapped up her flute music and her many fashion excessories. I was happy with my video camera, my 'Boysturiser' cosmetics and my male magazines ('Shark', 'Openings' and 'Slot'). My favourite present, however, was a pair of the new batch of Irish-designed Chinese-made solar-powered sensory sunglasses, which – as some fortunate readers may already know – 'utilise the very latest technology to assist individuals in understanding how they relate to their ever-more complex environments.' Each one looks like a stylish but otherwise unexceptional pair of your 'shades', but each also conceals a wealth of devices – thermometers, pulse rate monitors, microphones, sweat and hormone gauges, odour detectors and atmospheric readers – that enable concise and accurate messages to be communicated to the wearer *via* a translucent mini-screen, invisible to others, situated on the inward face of one of the lenses. Naturally, the glasses also adjust automatically to all levels of atmospheric lightning.

The pair that stared confidently back up at me when I ripped off the paper on Christmas morning were called 'WISCI glasses', the acronym standing for 'Wexford Indicator of Social and Cultural Integration'. I found them remarkably easy to use. To activate the main function, I simply placed them on my nose, touched a small pad on the left arm of the frame, and watched the screen as it displayed first a set of readings based on my various bodily signs, and then, more conclusively, an overall figure for my level of integration within my immediate environment (100 represented full and complete blending, while 0 suggested total *alienación*). I performed a series of simple experiments to assess the accuracy of my glasses. When I chastened everyone else out of the kitchen and watched football highlights on television while drinking champagne and eating sugared almonds, I achieved a score in the mid-90s. But when I lay on the floor for five minutes with my foot in the hot oven and thought about marking essays, my rating fell to 24. Even this was not my lowest score of the day, for when the televised football gave way to a 'Christmas Special' featuring Northern Ireland's best-loved TV personalities my score fell all the way to 6. Through these glasses, I could really see! Of course, the pleasure receded a little when Conchi pointed out that my new toy really told me no more than that I was feeling either happy or uncomfortable, but the few minutes of pleasure which they had brought into my life seemed to justify abundantly the £399 that Begoña had paid for them in one of her e-transactions.

It was a marvellous day, and we had survived our self-imposed test, passing mustard with flying colours. At night, we all fell asleep with our chins very much on the up. The rituals in which we had just taken part were so very different from those we had known before, but our cultural transmogrification was proceeding apace. When we lived in Andalusia, our gifts were always given at *Los Reyes* (Epiphany) and we kept them simple and practical in nature. Begoña would present me, for example, with a hosepipe and I might give her something like a funnel. The children received edible gifts, perhaps some *turrón*, a few *mazapanes* or, in particularly lean years, a sun-dried tomato. We did not send Christmas cards, but on Christmas Eve we would, if possible, eat a joint of lamb with the extendable family. And that was about it. Only one custom could we not bring ourselves to abandon when we moved to Belfast. In the past, we had all gathered around the radio at midnight on New Year's Eve in order to hear the chimes of *La Puerta del Sol* in Madrid. At each stroke of the bell, every one of us from the oldest to the youngest would eat a grape, quickly biting and swallowing it before the next chime rang through the air. In Belfast, on the last day of the year, we located the bells on our satellite, and we formed a pious circle around a big bowl of grapes. Back in Spain, we had never once found the operation problematic in any way, but now we were different and so was our world. Puri was the first to choke, followed by Conchi, Begoña and me. By the time the sixth chime sounded, the four of us were writhing on the floor, gasping for air. We somehow managed to begin striking one another firmly on the back, and at last the grapes began to re-appear, one by one, popping up into the air like half-chewed tree frogs fleeing danger. It was a moment of fright, and only Dilatación managed to contain all twelve of her grapes. She, perhaps, was a residual Spaniard yet.

Chapter 17

In which Jesús' children and Audrey's nipples loom ever larger.

On 1st January, I decided to attempt some of your 'New Year Resolutions'. I therefore sat for hours in front of my computer screen and wrecked my brains in my search for ideas. The harder I tried, however, the less successful were my attempts. I just could not imagine a way of making myself significantly better. Eventually, I flew in through an e-window labelled 'Help with NY Rezzies?' This dropped me into a frothing cauldron of self-improving possibilities where I stewed myself on a low heat for a considerable length of time. I even contacted an American guru called Girp Schneider, and he was kind enough to suggest that I 'take a long hard look at myself'. In the end, I managed a single, though important, declaration of intent:

1. Stop thinking about Audrey's nipples in every spare moment.

It was causing me considerable distress and I even considered going to *confesarme* (though I am ashamed to admit that I soon abandoned the notion). Sometimes, I believed that I could still feel their mesmerising imprint on my chest, and I went so far as to examine my mirror image for evidence (I took a 'long hard look at myself'). I would from henceforth tell myself that Audrey's nipples were probably less wonderful in reality than when they jabbed into my mind's eye, as they often did. They had, after all, been sucked to bits by a pair of hungry infants. She was still feeding the younger one, but I had politely averted my eyes whenever this rather primitive ritual had occurred in my line of fire.

When I contemplated my resolution, it occurred to me that each of Audrey's nipples in fact pointed the way to an additional issue in my life. One of them was clearly trained on the state of my marriage. I had to find a way of maintaining my recently renewed conjugal warmth, and I sensed that 'Jumping Jack: the Spermicidal Maniac' might have a substantial part to play in this. Yet I knew also that it would not be tactically astute to bring him into action too frequently. This was partly because of the risk to our mental and physical health, but also because one does not wish to establish something extraordinary as a new norm. With reluctance, I therefore decided to put this magnificent condom 'on the long finger' (as they say in Northern Ireland).[39] Audrey's other nipple pointed accusingly at my children. I had been spending too much time with them, and I was determined to encourage Begoña to return, slowly but surely, to her feminine responsibilities. This, I knew,

---

[39] Some of you might say 'on the back burner' (but please take care with your combinations, for if you put the long finger on the back burner, you are sure to receive an injury).

would be easier said than done. She was a moving target, constantly busy and rarely glimpsed. As we are wont to say in Spain, '*No es fácil saltar por encima de un perro pastor.*'[40] But I could not simply watch her leave us while I sat idly bye-bye. I was concerned that the girls might become somewhat manly under my potent influence, and more alarmingly I feared that I myself might be turning into one of your spineless northern nancy-boys. Of necessity, I shopped, cooked and washed for my annoying little daughters. I also had to spend a good deal of my time with women, and sometimes there was no alternative but to participate in conversations about soap powder, hair tinting, the fat fight, clothes shopping, maternity leave, menstruation and the menopause. This would not do.

Matters did not, however, go well with Begoña. One evening, early in the month, we were watching the so-called 'reality' TV show, 'Lord of the Celebrity Flies', as it approached its controversial and cannibalistic climax (I was rooting for the failed tennis player from Barcelona but I was, like him, to be consumed by disappointment). In a commercial break, Bego turned to me and said,

'Jesús, I am going to be away once or twice in the coming months, just for a few days each time.'

I looked askance.[41]

'The thing is that I have written a book, and the publishers want me to promote it in other countries.'

---

[40] 'It is not easy to leapfrog a sheepdog'.

[41] In Spain, we say, 'La mujer y la gallina, hasta la casa de la vecina' ('The wife and the chicken should go no further than the neighbour's house').

'Is it about dieting?'

'No, it is more intellectual, I think.'

I always hate it when ladies say things to me like this. She went on, 'It is all about the ways in which the internet is empowering women by allowing them to run businesses and make money from home, even while bringing up their families.'

'You may be raising money,' I said, 'but can you honestly say that you are helping to raise the children?'

'Oh, you are being unfair. I do my share.'

I snorted like a sceptical pig.

'What is your book called?'

'Well, the working title is *Male, Female, E-mail: Gender in Cyberspace*. What do you think?'

'I think it will make me the buttock of many jokes among my masculine friends.'

'Don't be silly, Jesús,' she said, 'most of your friends seem to be women anyway, and they will salute my efforts.'

Now, I affected the scowl of an owl.

After a moment, she put her hand in a very special place and said, 'The girls are all asleep. Would it make you feel nice if I went upstairs to fetch one of those little rubber things?'

'No, it would not,' I snapped. 'For that, you will have to wait.'

This was a new tactic for me, and it clearly unnerved us both.

'That is a pity,' she said. 'Well, what about if I were to make you some *Tocino de Cielo*?'

This was a weak spot of mine. *Tocino de Cielo* is the most

142

delicious dessert that we produce in Andalusia. It means, literally, 'Bacon of the Sky', though it contains no pork. It is actually rather like your crème caramel.

'I know you're thinking about it,' she said, in a teasingly musical voice. 'Ees very good, you know.'

I was temptingly sore. *Tocino de Cielo* had never failed to perk up my pecker. It was a battle of the mind, but I won through by managing to remain utterly resolute, on the outside at least.

'Pigs might fly,' I retorted, 'but I for one am staying firmly on the ground.'

I left the room with an appropriate flourish.

Conchi, Puri and Dila returned to their respective educational institutions early in the month, and they all settled again without strife. I was now managing the home-life of the Sánchez Venturas almost single-handedly (though sometimes, admittedly, I used both). When Begoña travelled to England for the first time, Conchi in particular felt the strain of her absence, and she wept every evening. This irritated me, of course, and I gently encouraged her to snap herself together, but because I am a good man at bottom I took her into the big bed with me. It seemed to me an inappropriate situation, but what else was I to do? A man must have his sleep. I have heard people say that there is something wonderful in the close proximity of a small, warm, needful child, but I am afraid I cannot concur. Puri and Dila, in contrast to their sister, seemed completely at ease with the 50% reduction in their parental allocation. Nevertheless, they too took to invading the master bed whenever they awoke in the night. On such occasions, my patience was stretched. Conchi would moan at the disruption to her sleep. Puri would return to the land of slumber instantaneously, but would then stab her foot spasmodically into my jewels with a debilitating combination of violence, frequency and unpredictability. She was just a wee slipper of a girl, but she had the hooves of a horse! Dila, for her part, would fill the night air with the mental torture of her nursery songs, and would scream furiously if ever I, in delirium, joined in: 'No, no, no!' she would cry, 'I'm the little one! I say "Roll over"! You don't sing!' I normally lay awake until they were all silent once more, at which point I would, if possible, extricate myself from their clammy clutches and haul my carcass off to the spare room. Here I would doze again, until one of them plummeted from the king-size bed with a floor-shaking thump and a shrill, lost cry. Nights like these were enough to overheat the sanest saint, but I was determined not to lose my temperature too frequently. Occasionally, when alone in the house, I would savagely beat up their cuddly toys, pummelling 'Paddington' without mercy and slamming 'Big Ted' against the bedroom walls until he begged to die. It was ugly but necessary, and at least it put me in touch with my masculinity.

I had to admit that, just possibly, Begoña had done a little more work around the house than I had previously conceded. All of a sudden, there seemed to be a fearful amount of shopping, cooking, tidying, ironing and laundry to do. I spent vast expanses of time trapped in what you so wisely call the futility room, and I began to think of the various appliances as collaborators in my *opresión*. I was also forced to become extremely disciplined, and every evening I made lists in a diary of all the tasks I needed to accomplish the following day:

buy tights for Puri, gift for her friend Hannah and tablets for worms

also honey-roasted academia nuts – Connor recommends

stop throwing soiled nappies onto front drive and fill in craters

prepare for interactive seminar on Inca child sacrifice

ask Audrey to sew Paddington's arm back on

And so on. I tried to complete some of my chores on the way to and from work, but they often dragged on into the long afternoons I spent with the girls. It was easier in the periods when Bego was at home, but even then there was a rather large thorn in my side of the rose-bed.

Chapter 18

In which Jesús struggles to hold on to his manhood while leaning on his friends for support.

On the subject of my gender function, I was sometimes prickly and defensive, *como un arbusto de tojo*.[42] One day, I took the girls into the 'MotherLove' shop in order to buy a new plastic cup for Dila, Puri having dissolved its predecessor in a chemical experiment. The girls were nagging for treats and dragging their feet, so I dispatched them to seek amusement in the powdered milk department. They grew a little rumbustious, and began to attract the attention of the formidable female security guard. At first, I tried to pretend that they were not in any way, shape or form my loin-fruits, but I was becoming increasingly annoyed. When a jumbo packet of 'Lucky Sucky' artificial baby-milk exploded in sensational fashion, I had no option but to intervene. I called the girls to heel, warning them that the paternal river was about to burst its banks as never before. Concepción said, 'It was a spontaneous blast – we weren't anywhere near it, so we weren't. This is a stitch-up.' Angrily, I marched them off, but as we emerged from the throat-

---

[42] 'Like a gorse bush'.

coating mist, I found myself face-to-face-to-face with the security guard and a small smartly-dressed woman whose badge identified her as the 'Manager'. She said,

'Excuse me, sir, but would you like one of my staff to help you look after your daughters while you complete your purchases?'

I do not believe that she meant any harm, but the normally charming way I have with the ladies deserted me for a minute or two.

'Would you have said that to me if I had myself been of the fairy sex, which I most conclusively am not?' I asked (here, I made an illustrative gesture).

'Well, possibly not, but you seem to be experiencing a little difficulty, sir.'

'No,' I said in a voice full of huff, 'You are the one with the difficulty – you do not like the fact that I am in your shop with my daughters on one hand and my unimpeachable manhood on the other.'

At this, both of my opponents coloured like rapidly ripening pomegranates. I spat out a question, exciting myself with the depth of my irritation.

'And while we are conversing, may I ask why your shop is called 'MotherLove'? This seems nothing short of discriminal, if I may be so bold.'

'Most of our customers are women,' squeaked the manager. 'It's as simple as that, sir.'

'Maybe that's because your blessed shop is called "MotherLove",' I snapped.

'I'll take note of your concerns,' she said.

'I would be grateful if you did.'

I had by now had enough, so I called the ghostly, milk-misted girls over to me and collected our belongings. Before we left the shop, however, I pushed them into the 'Mother and Baby Room' and incarcerated them there for a not insignificant period.

There was no doubt about it. I was living in a land of ladies. Virtually all of the parents whom I encountered at school were mothers. Regrettably, my children were all girls, and all their teachers at nursery and school were ladies too. Indeed, the only member of the school staff who was consistently male was the big Scottish headmaster, Mr. Fiscal Leeway. He was, like me, a figure of male authority, fierce and friendly by turns, but the children of the school did not spend much time with him unless they were either very bad or very rich. There was also, I supposed, the so-called 'lollipop man' but his informal job title and the colourful tool of his trade can hardly have generated a spirit of self-confident masculinity amongst the boys of Lagan Meadows.

I attempted to exude some self-confident masculinity of my own, reassuring myself constantly that it took a man who did not doubt his sexuality to surround himself with supportive ladies of all shapes and sizes. I tried to tell myself that there was no question of psychic *infiltración*. Anyway, my behaviour was in one sense thoroughly manly. Was I not building for myself a suburban harem, but choosing not to spread my seed with Pharaonic liberality? As the Spaniard is wont to say, 'If the pigeon coop has plenty of feed, it will have plenty of pigeons.' Each day, I conversed with various members of the harem, distributing my platonic favours around the playground and seeking to make each and every one of them feel special. Some of them, like the MotherLove mistress, doubted my ability to cope with the workload of a lady, and I told myself that this demonstrated – in the manner of a roundabout – that they considered me thoroughly manly. Others kept these understandable doubts to themselves, or even disguised them by saying things like 'You're doing a grand job', or 'My husband couldn't do what you do' or 'What have you done with your hair? It looks lovely.' No, there certainly did not seem to be any danger of my turning into a lady.

It came as a rude surprise, therefore, when I found myself confronted by the more orthodox masculinity of a burly bunch of builders. Begoña had spoken to them in December about the possibility of rebuilding sections of the brick wall that marked one of the boundaries to our back garden. In the festive flurry that had characterised that month, she had neglected to inform me of the builders' vague promise to undertake the work early in the new year. They materialised one morning, while I was baking some scones in my apron and comfortable slippers. I went to the door, thinking that it would be the post-woman, only to be confronted by 'Barny' and his stocky, dust-encrusted comrades.

'We spok to your missus,' he revealed, "bout a wall out the back. We've a loada bricks to leave off, if that's OK?'

'This is the first I have heard of it, but yes, the wall is calling plaintively for attention. If you wait for a minute, I will take you round.'

Hurriedly, I removed my apron and slippers and replaced them with a pair of rugged old leather boots, but the damage was already done. As I stood amongst them in the back garden, pointing out the decaying sections of the wall, I could feel the edifice of my own manhood crumbling and tumbling before their eyes. They were with us for a week, and they never mocked me overtly. Yet I detected the amusement and the scorn in their communal gaze. When I brought the girls home from school, the men's tools would droop conspicuously while they stared at me. If they caught a glimpse of me, chatting in the kitchen with one of my lady friends over an *espresso*, they would glance knowingly at one another. And one afternoon, they all trooped past the expansive windows of the futility room while I was sorting my way through a basketful of small pink pants in three sizes. I was devastated, and went upstairs to do 2000 of your socalled press-ups.

That afternoon, in the playground, I decided to ask three selected ladies – Audrey and her friends, Marion and Sinead – whether and what their menfolk thought about me. They all giggled, and declined to discuss the matter. I applied a little pressure, and they tried to look over my shoulder. Then Marion relented, and she said, 'I'm afraid my Dermot thinks you're 'a big gay love-boy', but I wouldn't listen to him, if I were you. I never do. I think he read in the paper that your wife is leaving you.' I looked stunned, and Sinead asked, 'It's not true, is it?' I said, 'No, it most certainly is not,' and walked away licking my wounded tail between my legs. As I did, I heard Marian say, 'Which part's not true? Did he say? Do you think he *is* gay?' After a moment, Audrey brought her nipples over to console me, and the attention, I must say, was most welcome. 'Don't worry,' she said. 'They're just not used to a man like you. Most of the fellas in Belfast are either tattooed psychopaths, lazy unreconstructed slobs, or wealth-obsessed careerists. Lovable rakers, the lot of them, but they're not exactly domesticated, if you know what I mean.'

'You can't teach an old leopard how to change nappies,' I said, to show her that I did indeed understand her perfectly well.

We continued the conversation over a cup of coffee. I said that I was now considering the possibility of renting a 'nanny' because I was uncomfortable with my present role. 'There are no two bones about it,' I added, 'the present arrangement is not working out for me.'

'Ackaway!' she said. 'You're only thinking like that because of what Marian said. You're great at it, and some of the other mums practically drool when they mention you.'

I looked doubtful, so Audrey expanded. Sinead had reportedly said that she could listen to me all day and that she loved the way I rolled my arse. 'You're very popular,' Audrey concluded.

'Come off it,' I yelped, 'I don't believe that any more than voodoo.'

She seemed surprised by my animation, but I proceeded regardless.

'Think about it. The average lady of Stranmillis does not really love a nappy-boy, or she would have married one. No, I have no wish to play with my so-called 'feminine side'. She is better kept behind bars in the deep fridge.'

'That's where you're wrong,' she said. 'And you shouldn't be afraid of that part of you. Just because Belfast women love their manly husbands, it doesn't mean they can't appreciate other attributes too. Maybe the 'nappy boy' – I prefer 'new man', by the way – is the one who better understands his woman, deep inside. And you should say 'woman', not 'lady' – it sounds old-fashioned, so it does.'

I was not yet convinced, so I summarised neatly in my own words what I took to be Audrey's intended meaning.

'You are saying, I think, that some 'women' like to think that the man who thinks like a woman knows what a woman wants in a way that a man who does not like to think like a woman does not. Have I got it right?'

'Roughly speaking, Jayzus.'

She had planted a little seed in the flowerpot of my mind. Could it indeed be true that inside every man there is a stifled woman trying to get out, just as it is undoubtedly true that outside every woman there is a stifled man trying to get in? I began to wonder, and I also decided to knock the nanny on the head.

As Audrey departed, Connor arrived. They had not met before, but they proceeded to delight me with one of those classical Northern Irish conversations in which complete strangers identify a whole string of mutual acquaintances. According to Connor, it does not necessarily work when the two individuals are from opposing religious traditions, though in many cases – as in Audrey's – there are 'mixed marriages' which extend the pool of interaction into the enemy camp. Audrey, it transpired, had met one of Connor's fifty-seven first cousins, and she vaguely knew his ex-girlfriend. Connor was familiar with several of Audrey's nephews, and also with the newly-qualified vet who had carelessly put her son's guinea pig to sleep while trying to rid it of lice. Such exchanges always warmed the muscles of my heart, as if the interconnections between my new friends formed some kind of safety net from which I would rebound if ever I should fall.

Chapter 19

In which Jesús gets to grips with local politics but strives without success to overcome a pint of stout.

My friendship with Connor continued to blossom, and it helped me to cope with my little *crisis de identidad*. Up at RUB, January was a month dominated by exams: stressful for the students, but merely tedious for us. There was a substantial quantity of marking to do, but we carried one another shoulder-high across the torrent of tedium. When I was not marking, I spent my time wading through hundreds of e-mails, mainly about penis extensions and mortgage rates (the twin preoccupations of the male academic). One correspondent kindly sent me a message entitled 'My girlfriend h0t'n'h0rny with a dolphin.' Naturally, I had to investigate this, but I tied myself in technological knots and ultimately had to turn the computer off in a desperate attempt to eradicate an undeniably memorable image. While thus incapacitated, I absent-mindedly failed to attend a meeting of the Faculty's 'Transparency Review Sub-Committee', to which Norman Boyle had appointed me in punishment for my role in the BUST affair. I promptly prepared my written apology, and was grateful to Connor for relieving me, just in time, of the notion that the committee's main area of responsibility had something to do with window-cleaning. He then insisted on fitting my computer with a friendly device called a 'spam-assassin', which saved me time and deprived me of pleasure in roughly equal measure.

Connor was profoundly committed to my education, and I trusted him like a brother. He even drew up a syllabus for me, and he headed the list for January with the words, 'Drinking a pint of stout'. I had little appetite for this, but he made it clear to me that it was an important rite of the male passage in Ireland. 'You're a great whiskey man,' he would say, 'but there's more to Irish alcoholism than that.' Somewhat reluctantly, I therefore accompanied him at lunchtime to 'The Blitz' (a World War Two theme pub). Connor bought us a couple of pints and a tin of powdered egg, while I found a table. The stout, I am afraid to say, tasted like a subtle blend of crude oil and sick, but it at least rendered the egg almost palatable. I tried to distract his attention while, little by little, I poured my pint into a nearby plant pot. I needed to engage Connor's mind, so I asked him about the attitude of Northern Irish people to foreigners living in their mist. What did the natives *really* think? At first he was cautious, and said that a man like me, with a positive attitude and a good job, had nothing whatsoever to fear. When I pressed on him, however, he opened up.

'Of course, it depends what colour you are, and what sort of job you have or don't have. If you were an unemployed Chinese man who didn't speak English, you'd not have such a happy time here. Racism is the new sectarianism. So much for the ceasefire.'

'But you think a sun-kissed Spaniard is acceptable?'

This was really all I cared about, and he laughed to see my selfish nakedness. He was becoming more thoughtful as our exchange deepened. Sometimes, he closed his eyes to think, and I was able to ply the plant with additional stout ('Guinness is good for you,' I whispered to it).

When Connor was ready to answer my question, this is what he said:

'Yeah, Jayzo, you're fine. You can settle here happily, so long as you don't make too much of a mess of the place. But whether an outsider can ever truly regard Belfast as home, or be accepted as one of us . . . Well, that's a more difficult question.'

'I have noticed,' I said, 'that when I say to Miss Place in the office that I am 'going home', she always thinks that I am talking about Spain. We have great confusion on this matter.'

'There you go – the problem in a nutshell. Perhaps we can't quite believe visitors from Spain would ever want to live here.'

Here, he glanced at my glass and added, 'Good, you're enjoying it. I'll get the next round in.'

At this point, I excused myself by saying that I had to collect Dila from her nursery. Unfortunately, I arrived twenty minutes too early, and the little termagant was outraged (her mood was already black because the nursery staff had foolishly tried to read her a story called 'Lulu's big hit', all about a little girl who learns to love her potty).

Under Connor's benevolent gaze, I was also becoming more confident and assertive in my understanding of local politics. The parochialism of Belfast became a pet bugbear of mine during this period, and I exercised it several times a day. I found plentiful evidence to fire my ire in the *Belfast Observer* (or BO), the best of Northern Ireland's daily newspapers. Its contents were dominated by articles and letters in which the mutual incomprehension of the two sides of society was made abundantly plain. Local politicians gazed obsessively at one another's infected navels while they spun in tight circles aboard the misery-go-round that was known euphemistically as the 'peace process'. Every few months, they all fell off and had to be coaxed back onto their plastic ponies by visitors from London, Dublin and Washington. And so it went on.

And yet, there were also hints of a new scent in the air. Around this time, the *BO* began to carry reports on what its pessimistic editors called 'a new and disturbing wave of sectarian violence'. 'Paramilitaries,' one report ran, 'are no longer content with mutilating and maiming one another's persons. On both sides of the divide, they have now begun to victimise the dependants of their enemies.' Here are some headlines, selected for your enlightenment: **'Loyalist dog assassinated'** (in this case, the Alsatian of a leading paramilitary was hit by a mortar shell while relieving itself on waste ground in the east of the city); **'Herd of Tyrone sheep dyed orange'** (this took place at night-time on a farm belonging to the father of a known PIRATE operative); and my own personal favourite, **'Mystery cricket balls rain down on republican households'**. In this instance, resourceful loyalists used a 'state-of-the-art bowling machine' to launch streams of so-called cricket balls over the 'peace wall' that separates the enemy communities in

West Belfast. The machine could hold up to three hundred balls at a time, and could propel them across distances of four hundred metres. It was also capable of directing them one by one with extraordinary precision through the living room windows and even down the chimneys of carefully targeted households and pubs.[43] Republican sources were forced to admit that, for once, the opposition had 'stolen a march' on them and revealed considerable creativity. 'We dadn't thank they had it in 'em,' said a vaguely familiar representative of the Ardoyne Residents Group, 'and I have to admit it's seriously humiliating to have yerr daughter's wedding wracked by a barrage of cracket balls. Fair play to 'em. It's time to gat our thanking caps orn, so it is.' These developments sounded like wonderful news to me, but most newspaper men were so intent upon pedalling their repetitive cycle of negativity round and round and round that they just could not appreciate it.

There were also some moderately pleasing developments at home. We had to deal with Begoña's third visit to England, but during her absence I realised with relish that Concepción was now having to work quite hard in order to summon up her night-time tears. One evening, she called for me from her bed approximately two hours after I had kissed her goodnight. I anticipated that, according to custom, she would be moaning about her state of deprivation. Instead, she had my *Concise English Dictionary* laid

---

[43] In Northern Ireland, cricket is a Protestant game, and when a ball lands upon the unwitting head of a local Catholic it is said to hurt in more ways than one.

out cold on her bed, and she said, 'Papá, I don't want you to take this the wrong way, but don't you think it's funny that so many rude words get specially written at the tops of the pages?' She explained that, having studied those words that were printed in bold above each column as a guide for the reader, she had come to the conclusion that some secret organisation must be highlighting the 'naughty ones' on purpose. I noted with a little squeak that she had written a list in the back of her school English book:

annals, bimbo, catholic, clitoris, cock, copulate, crampon, droppings, erotica, evaginate, fanny, gonad, harden, homoerotic, jockstrap, muntjac, nipple and nipplewort, ovary, penis, piss and pissoir, poofter, poxy, protestant, quim, scuttlebutt, shiitake, squelch, succubus, thruster, torpefy, uprush, vestal and virgin, wanderlust, wingding and yo–heave–ho.

I told her to go to sleep, but I did take the time to point out that not all of these words were actually rude. She said, 'Och, Papá, no offence, but you don't know everything – not all the meanings are in the dictionary, you know.' I refused to make concessions. Most of the words, I insisted, were perfectly acceptable in polite society. 'So I can leave them in my school book, then?' she asked, with an insolent smile. This presented me with a problem. In standing on my guns so bravely, I had shot myself in the foot. I decided to make a tactical retreat, after telling her in a stern voice that we would talk about it again in the morning. Conchi was a trial to me, but as I descended the stairs I noted with satisfaction that she had not mentioned her mother once (unless you are counting 'bimbo' and 'succubus').

PART III

Winter into Spring

Chapter 20

In which Begoña and Audrey both cause the hairs of Jesús to stand on end, though the two ladies otherwise exhibit their differences.

Begoña continued to spend half of her time away from home. Even when she was in Belfast, she was so preoccupied with the need to love and promote herself that she often allowed the little people to slip unnoticed from her mind *via* the tradesman's rear entrance. She thought she was the dog's knees, and this really got under my skin. In our so-called living room, Begoña was now more likely to appear on the television than in front of it. She was interviewed on the Friday-night chat-show hosted by a sycophantic local man named Michael O'Canavan. Begoña, I must say, looked mostly appealing in her elegant 'designer clothes' and her well-worn French boots of patient leather. At one point in the interview, Mr. O'Canavan was kind enough to present her with the opportunity to talk about me. At first, I was gratified, but the feeling did not endure.

'I think a lot of our viewers may be surprised to hear – given that you are so very busy with your various extraordinary projects – that you have a husband, and is it three wee girls?'

'Yays, sat 'ees right, Michael,' she said, 'and zay are – how you say? – the apples een my eyes.'

She was being deliberately sentimental, and exaggerating her comedy accent to illicit sympathy from the viewers.

'Och, isn't that lovely?' said the presenter.

Right on cue, the studio audience murmured in agreement, as if they actually believed what she had said. He went on,

'But, *Señora*, may I ask you that old clichéd question: how do you balance the needs of your family with those of your agent, your publisher and your many dieting disciples?'

'Oh yes, the work-life balance. Well, 'eet 'ees partly about rigorous self-discipline and 'ard work. But I also 'ave the most wonderful husband. He's called Jesús, and I love heem so much.'

The audience clapped, and Mr. O'Canavan said, 'Haysoos? What, like our Jesus? That's a funny name. Tell us a bit more about him.'

'Well,' she said, ''ee does so much to 'elp me. 'Ee does nearly all of the cooking and cleaning, and 'ee 'ees so good with our little girls. Zay adore him, and 'ee plays games wiz zem all ze time.'

I did not like the sound of this one little bit, and the hairs on my neck stood to attention as if preparing for combat.

'That's wonderful,' said Mr. O'Canavan. 'I'd have to say that there aren't many men who would do all that.'

'I know,' she said, 'but Jesús, 'ee is not like uzza men.'

I experienced a feeling of deep and desperate shame. This

changed a little, however, when the camera pointed itself at a very lovely young lady in the audience. She had a tear in her eye, and – if I was not mistaken – her tongue was lolling helplessly out of the side of her mouth.

I was still thinking about this when, a few days later, I conducted one of my private exercise sessions in our kitchen. Mobility and strength were, by this time, returning steadily to what the physiotherapist called my 'calf complex'. I found that dancing brought me on in leaps and bounds. The girls were all at school for the morning, so I raided the burgeoning music collection of Concepción and found the pre-teen 'hit' album by a group called the 'U-Band'. I shot up the volume and shook my thing as if there were no tomorrow. When I began to overheat, I reduced myself to a pair of pants and continued with the balancing-on-one-leg-with-eyes-shut-and-other-limbs-flailing routine. I was like a giant one-legged windmill, and when a familiar female voice said, 'Hello,' I fell over in surprise, prostituting myself all over the kitchen floor. Even before I opened my eyes, I recognised her tongue. Audrey was standing over me. To her credit, she was managing not to laugh at my expanse, and she added, 'Sorry, Dr. Sánchez Ventura. You didn't answer the door, but I could hear the music, so I let myself in through the back.' I went upstairs to augment my pants, leaving Audrey to make a pot of your tea.

Yes, indeed, she was becoming my primary female confidante, my safety valve, my escape chute, and we held regular tea-for-two *tête-à-têtes*. One memorable afternoon, she called in, and found me quarrelling with the girls over their respective bedtimes. Audrey could tell that my large bomb was primed, so she guided her children and mine into the living room, pulled a packet of chocolate biscuits from her coat pocket, and shoved Disney's 'Little Mermaid' into the machine where she rightly belonged. Having thus sedated the children, she returned to the kitchen, and said, 'Right, Jayzus, I'll pour the tea and you get it all off your chest.'

'*My* chest!' I said. 'What about *your* chest?'

She had to think about this, and so did I. Then she said,

'I wasn't the one who was tearing strips off the children. You need to relax. Sit down there, and close your eyes.'

This sounded interesting, and I therefore did as I was bid. She stood behind me and began to massage the sailor's knots in my neck and shoulders. The establishment of this tactile interface between the soft, supple form of her body and the rougher, tougher texture of my own generated in me a set of extraordinary physical sensations. At first, I tingled all over and felt the fine hairs on my neck rise up in excitement once again. Then, more embarrassingly, the hair on my scalp, which is normally quite peaceful, followed suit. Within a minute, the apparent circumference of my head had doubled. There followed a period of violent trembling that was also marked by extreme spasms, affecting first one limb and then another. As a result of the third such spasm, my knee rocketed upwards, hitting the underside of the table with immense force. The two cups of tea shook, but somehow they failed to overturn. Audrey removed her hands, and said, 'Are you OK?'

'I have really hurt my knee, but it will be fine,' I replied.

She sat down and sipped her still wobbling tea. She looked amused, and just a little flushed, but said nothing. For an age, we sat there in electrocuted silence, conversing without words. From the living room, the saccharine sounds of a Disney song drifted through to us, and we both recognised the rowing boat scene in which Prince Eric seeks within himself the courage to kiss Ariel:

> 'First you see her,
> Sitting there across the way,
> She don't got a lot to say
> But there's something about her.
> And you don't know why,
> But you dying to try,
> You wanna kiss the girl.'

I have to admit, I was struggling to resist the idea, and only the execrable grammar of the song enabled me to hold myself back. I am a man of letters, for God's sake, and I care about these things. In any case, Dilatación wandered in and announced in her comparably misguided English, 'I dud a poo-poo in my nappy.' The spell was broken, and Audrey exclaimed, 'Is she still in nappies? They must be enormous!' I was a little put out by this, and I took Dila upstairs while Audrey prepared to depart.

Chapter 21

Which opens with a squirrel and closes with a scallop.

At this time, the encounter with Audrey and the little mermaid often expanded to fill my mind and — I admit it with
shame — my trousers, but I had also to make some space
for the pettifogging concerns of my daughters. The early
part of the month was completely dominated by Concepción's
first ever school 'project'. It all began when Mrs. Murray
summoned the parents to school one evening, in order to
explain what P4 pupils should be aiming to produce.
Throughout her little speech, she referred to the audience
as the 'mummies', despite my aforementioned and still prominent masculinity. The general theme of all the projects was
to be 'the environment', and we were asked to assist our
children in the choice of specific topics, the location of
appropriate materials and the organisation of personal 'field
trips'. I tried to appear enthusiastic, but the more shop-soiled
parents who had already experienced the process with older
offspring either groaned or winced or slammed their heads
onto the desks after a fashion most theatrical. One of them
said, 'Mrs. Murray, do we have to? For the love of God!'
I suggested, in a tone that was both jocular and construc-
tive, that it might be appropriate, in view of the theme, for

some of the parents to 'recycle' the output of their older siblings. My comment was greeted with a communal 'Shhh' and assorted mumblings (I thought I heard 'Och, you're a queerr kinda tube' and 'Would yew everrr catch yerself orrn?' but I could have been mistaken).

Back at home, Conchi and I clashed acrimoniously over her choice of topic. She argued that the environment was a concept broad enough to encompass topics such as 'Nightlife in Belfast for the under-10s' and 'Why Northern Ireland needs its own Disneyworld'. I told her that this was not her teacher's meaning. Conchi was, by this stage in her development, a thoroughly urban creature, a lover of pop music, a connoisseur of juvenile fashion, and a devotee of numerous American TV shows featuring impossibly pretty infants who wrestled with 'issues' relating to drugs, sexuality and marital decay. It was regrettable that she had learned from such programmes a set of hand signals with which to signify that other people – namely me – were 'jerks' or 'dorks' or 'loserrrs'. This made me angry, and on one occasion I lost the cool of my normal cucumber. Gratifyingly, a brief display of masculine rage brought down a windfall from Conchi's tree, and I managed to persuade her that Mrs. Murray intended her to study the natural environment and not the constructed one. I asked Conchi whether her friends had selected their topics yet, and she replied, 'They're mostly doing pollution.' I wondered if she thought this would be interesting, but she made her 'boring' signal. This involved slouching and yawning, while arranging the fingers of her left hand into the shape of a small 'b'. I simply walked away, but as I did so I resolved in anger that Concepción's project would be on RED SQUIRRELS.[44]

Of course, I hoped that she would now leave me alone and apply herself, but she reminded me that I had to organise a research trip of some description. She had bricked me into the wine cellar, and I knew I would have to co-operate (after cracking open a bottle or two, of course). Our first attempt to observe the red squirrels in their natural habitat was ruined by a cataclysmic and utterly typical display of changeability from the local climate. Early one morning, we set off on foot towards the Belvoir Forest in beautiful pale winter sunshine with smiles on our faces, and silently I blessed the airline pilot who had carried us to this laudable land of milk and honey. Twenty minutes later, however, we sat huddled helplessly beneath a dark and forbidding conifer tree as a fierce gale lashed at our extremities and soggy northern sleet-balls crashed down around us like drowned sheep. The neighbourhood squirrels had more sense than to show their faces.

On Conchi's insistence, we tried again on another day, and this time we were more successful. On an impulse, we positioned ourselves in a different part of the woodland, closer to the river and more deciduous. We placed an old mat on the damp blanket of dead leaves, sat down and waited. For half an hour, we saw nothing and grew steadily more bedraggled. The patter-pitter of the rain was

_____

[44] I had heard on the radio that these creatures, though common in much of Europe, were increasingly regarded as something of a delicacy in Ireland.

interrupted only by my deep sighs and her shallow remarks. But then, all of a sudden, we heard a new and more auspicious sound. From somewhere above and around us came the noise of tiny scurrying feet, of little sharp claws on the coarse bark of oak trees. At first, we could not pinprick the source of the sound, even as it grew louder and more varied. The scurrying was now accompanied by squeaking and chattering, all suggestive of high sexual excitement. The animals filled our ears, but they still eluded our eyes. Then, at last, we saw them, racing frantically through the bare winter branches, high over our heads. The chase was on, but every time the male closed in on the bushy tail of his intended, she accelerated and changed direction (this is so often the way). They twisted and turned, stopped and started, and then, right above us, they flung themselves across a substantial gap between the final branch of one tree and the first of another. We saw their tiny, tufty forms silhouetted against the heavy February sky as they flew past, oblivious to our presence. We watched them for a further five minutes until they left our visionary field. As the final scuttling sounds faded, I glanced at Concepción. Suddenly, she was a little wide-eyed innocent eight-year-old again, and she whispered, 'Papá, that was amazing.' Had I been a lady, I might have been touched by this. But I am like a block of granite on iron stilts. I seized my moment of revenge, and signalled 'WEIRDO!' to her.

When she rewound herself from school one day and announced that the best project would receive a prize, I decided to intensify my involvement. The final stages went very well. There were certain creative differences, but most of these were resolved in my favour. I found Conchi's written expression somewhat pretentious, and so I told her that a more authentically 'P4' style would be preferable and more convincing. When necessary, I simply pulled generational rank and revised those sections for which I had allowed her to take responsibility. The resultant text, weighing in at fourteen kilos, was a sensation. On the day of the deadline, we delivered it to school by car, and every single one of the teachers came out to help carry it in.

Modesty prevents me from transcribing the project in full, so I will instead scatter a mere handful of the most informative nuts and bolts at your grateful feet:

'The red squirrel is one of Ireland's cutest creatures and may even have been present in prehistoric times. They live in our native trees, but red squirrels have been falling since grey ones came over from America in 1911. Soon the red squirrel may be extinct in Ireland, which would be very sad [Conchi had originally put "a cause of deep regret to all who value our natural heritage"].

'There are important differences between red and grey squirrels. They are different colours, for one thing. A red squirrel is orange, but a grey squirrel is sort of brown. Grey squirrels are big bullies and they eat all the food, so the red ones get even smaller and die.'

'They make babies in January and February when the males go crazy chasing the females all around the forest. I think the males like making babies more than the females. My papá says this is quite normal.'

On the Monday following, Mr. Fiscal Leeway himself

approached me in the playground. He reported that he had spent the entire weekend reading our squirrel project.

'What an astounding piece of work,' he said. 'I never knew squirrels were so fascinating. You must be very proud.'

'Well,' I said coyly, 'I must not take all of the credit – Concepción helped with bits and pieces.'

He laughed at my joke, little suspecting that it was not one. The prize – a colourful book entitled *Extinction and You* – was, of course, in the bag, and I realised, at last, that the rearing of children is not entirely without its compensations.

I was energised by this success, and I decided to revolutionise the 'school run'. It seemed to be taking longer and longer every day, and the traffic was so heavy that on some occasions we sat in the car for hours at a time. It was dreadlock on the Malone Road, so I attempted some of your blue skies thinking out of the left box. And here is what I did afterwards: I bought a lot of bicycles. Our social web had now been spun, and it seemed probable that I and the other little spiders could take to two wheels without fear of banishment. Connor McCann recommended a shop called 'Hugh the Canoe' on the Lisburn Road. I took the children with me, and Mr. Hugh was very helpful (he had no boats at all, but I was learning not to be surprised by this type of idiocy). It was easy to choose bikes for the big girls and for me, but Dilatación was, as ever, a problem. I had raised the bar for Mr. Hugh, but he sailed over it like a diminishing oriental gymnast off a vaulting horse. Leading us into the back of his shop, he unveiled a bright red bike trailer, big enough for the confinement of two smallish children. It could be attached to the back of an adult bicycle with a special clasp that was, he assured me, very safe (I said, 'There is no need to worry too much about that.') The mechanism was designed so that the big bike could fall right over without affecting the stability of the trailer.

'You can crash onto the ice and crack your head open,' he said happily, 'and the wains will hardly feel a bump.'

This scarcely seemed just, but I nevertheless bought it, along with the other bikes. Mr. Hugh told me that it was the first time he had sold such a trailer in Belfast, though in Copenhagen, he reported, it was impossible to cross the pavement on foot without being mown down by one.

That very afternoon, I loaded Puri and Dila into the scarlet chariot and dragged them along the river to the park near the Botanic Gardens. They were both entirely happy with the new transport system, and Puri was particularly thrilled by the attention that we received from great unwashed onlookers. Three men working on the road stopped to stare, and one said, 'Thassa fockin' clinker, boy!' Older children pointed at us and said, 'That's so cool!' or 'That's class!' At a pedestrian crossing, two old ladies peered into the chariot and cooed, 'Och, isn't that just lovely? Isn't that just super? Are you happy in there girls? I never saw the like!' Then, one of them surprised me by suddenly asking, 'Are you here on holiday? You're so exotic.' In the park, I took a short breather, but I also had time to notice a lovely piece of childish urban graffiti on one of the climbing frames. The little people of south Belfast clambered excitedly up a ladder, next to which was a bright blue metal panel upon which someone had scrawled in big black letters, 'I'd love to ride the arse off Shane Shanks'. Purificación looked at it too, her reading skills obviously improving at last, and she asked, 'Who's Shane Shanks?'

The chariot swiftly established itself as one of the stable fixtures in my daily life. We all cycled to school and nursery every day, and, as we approached our destination, Dila would laugh and jeer and point at all the people trapped in their cars. We were doing well, and I seemed to be rising to my domestic challenge with all the ascendancy of a griffon vulture on a warming morning. Indeed, I was now keeping my balls in the air so successfully that I sometimes wondered whether any of them would ever touch the ground again!

Gradually, I became more ambitious, until one day I bit off a little bit more than I could chew and nearly came unstuck on a bridge too far. Dila's nursery was closed for the day due to an infestation of educational inspectors, and I decided to pull her all the way to Portaferry at the far end of Strangford Lough. It was a long way – perchance seventy kilometres – and it took me several hours. During the last phase, we were cycling on a road that ran parallel to the shoreline. Connor had promised me that this was a very 'scenic' route, but my pleasure was dented by two things: firstly, it rained so much that I thought a mythical Irish giant had simply scooped up the contents of this mighty sea lough in his hands and dumped them, fish and all, on my head; secondly, I was completely and utterly exhausted, and my legs felt as mushy as some of your revolting peas.

Our specific destination was the 'Murky Depths' aquarium in Portaferry – which eschews tropical fish in order to concentrate on a feast of local creatures – and eventually we arrived. My vision was blurred, my speech was slurred and my jewels were benumbed. I could neither think straight nor walk straight. Sadly, we journeyed no further than the 'Touch and Feel' tank near the entrance before I realised that it was time to return home again. As we departed, I heard the guide telling the other boys and girls, 'The creature I am holding is another kind of shellfish. It is called a scallop. It has no brain, but it does have about fifty eyes. This means it can see us, but it doesn't know what we are.' I knew almost exactly how it felt. Of course, I was in no fit state to cycle back to Belfast. I collapsed on the road, but luckily we were eventually picked up and driven home by a kind lady with an empty box of horses.

Chapter 22

*This describes an unusual squirrel-fight in the history depart-
ment and also the brave attempt made by Jesús to swallow
an 'Ulster Fry' while swearing like a Belfast man.*

Despite the occasional moments of over-extension, I was
having a good time. At the university, I even conducted a
seminar so genuinely lively that it generated a violent confrontation. It was part of my brand new module on 'Green
History: Humans in Nature from 1500 to the present'. This
was not of course my normal *predilección*, but the students
flocked to it like lemmings. The initial sessions were hard
work, and the atmosphere was somewhat sullen. The participants eyed one another a little suspiciously across the
table, and nobody said more than a word or two. In my
glummier moments, I felt like the proverbial man who tries
to squeeze blood from a stone; but I also knew that such a
man must try, try and try again, for in the end blood will
out. Sure enough, the fourth seminar was very different.
As if by magic, the participants warmed up and then boiled
over, all within one hectic hour of intellectual exchange.
This was hands-on history in the top drawer! During this
phase of my professional existence, I was, of course, cutting
corners wherever I could, and the subject of the seminar

was therefore 'A Tale of Two Squirrels' (a case study in the introduction of alien animal species into Ireland). I had by now lost interest in this, but the work was already completed and I also had a prize-winner's certificate signed by Mr. Fiscal Leeway to prove it. This was my licence to operate, and I brandished it with confidence. I began the session by delivering a little lecture which provided the students with a witty wealth of background information. I then threw the subject up to general discussion, anticipating that my gesture would be met with the normal surly reluctance to articulate. I had, however, misinterpreted the situation somewhat (there is, as you say, a first time for everything). The students grew surprisingly loquacious, and they rapidly began to volley the various issues back and forth as if they really cared about them. This is what I heard:

'See tham thurr rad squarrels,' said Declan. 'Thurr s'posed to live hurr 'n' it's arr duty ter protact 'am, so it is.'

'What dyuu mean by that, zif I dadn't know?' asked William.

'Yuu wan me't spall it oit? The grey squarrels shud be shat, avry last wunnavem.'

Now a boy called Ian joined the discussion.

'But such greys as are hurr noiy have a right to remain, so they do. Thur naturalised, and snot thurr fault if thurr at a biological advantage, is it? Yer canna turn the clack back.'

It was going really well and I knew better than to intervene. I could not understand everything they said, nor why they were so spirited. They had not displayed the same level of engagement when, during the previous seminar, we had discussed the development of the Linnaean system of animal classification (I fell asleep during my own lecture, and when I awoke I found myself alone, the students having all passed quietly away). I knew, however, that I had finally succeeded in stimulating a real debate about history. I smiled from ear to ear, and felt a strange warming in my entrails.

The whole group joined in, sustaining the discussion for well over ten minutes. They talked about all sorts of things, eventually focussing on whether it might be possible to reduce or eradicate the population of grey squirrels by injecting an infertility drug directly into their nuts. A nice girl named Aisling was strongly in favour of this, but William said, 'I'll wager yewd like us all neutered, wud ye nat?'

This tempted Declan back into the debate, and he asked, 'Hude wanna mayet with yew, annywaze?'

William looked thoughtful, and said, 'Yuurr fockin' Ma.'

While I was contemplating the significance of this exchange, the fur suddenly began to hit the fan. Declan threw himself across the table and struck William squarely over the head with a large encyclopaedia of zoological history. William's chair tipped over backwards, and the two boys sprawled onto the floor. Soon, the other members of the seminar joined in, and various staples of the student life – books, drink cans, pens, mobile phones, baseball caps and rucksacks – flew around the room, this way and that. It was mayhem and I was taken aback. I crawled under the table in order to think, and created there a little oasis of tranquilitude for myself. Now, amidst the tumult, I remembered something that Connor had said to me: 'Listen to us carefully. We may seem to be talking about general issues, but half the time we're actually preoccupied with the particular politics of the north.' Was it possible, I wondered, that the students were not really talking about squirrels at all? This was one interesting question. Another one was 'What shall I do now?' For some time, I could think of nothing, and the thumping and thudding sounds that continued above me were like the irregular beatings of my troubled heart. I began to relinquish hope, but then I was abruptly and miraculously illuminated from within by an idea so remarkable that I actually began to shine.

I clambered out through the teeth of the battle, stood on a chair and shouted,

'This is all so PAROCHIAL! Why not think GLOBALLY? Grey squirrels are not PROTESTANT. They are, quite literally, AMERICAN. And who is taking over the planet? Why, yes, IT IS THE AMERICANS!'

Of course, I did not truly believe a word of this, or, to put my point more honestly, I did not really mind if it was true. My scarlet chariot, my breakfast cereal (novelty 'Choco Craps') and my recently-acquired 'frizbee' had all originated in America, and where would I have been without them? My rhetoric was tactical, but it had the desired effect. The seminar soon became quiet and reflective once more, and the discussion resumed.

'So the invasion of them thurr grey squarrels is a metafer fer the cultural imperialism of the US? I like it,' said Declan.

William received the baton and set off on his leg.

'MacDonalds, Kentucky Fried Chicken, iced lager, history

rewratten in Hollywood fillums etc etc . . . American culture is the real threat tuss orl – nat the local Prods or Taigs?'

'That is kinda neat,' agreed Aisling.

I warned them against pursuing this line of argument too aggressively, fearful that they might go out and start 'kneecapping' Bostonian tourists. But they were at least calm for the moment, and after they had left the room, Aisling put her head back through the door and said, 'We're all goin' fer a wee Budd in the Union, so we are. Dyawanna?' At last, I was making progress with my little charges.

The next day, Professor Boyle invited me into his office and asked me if I could tell him what had caused the commotion in Seminar Room 3. He had not only heard the sounds himself, but he had been telephoned by a concerned parent, whose daughter had returned home in a drunken state and with one of her eyes blacked out. I explained what had happened, and he expressed his surprise and concern that I had not recognised the problem rather earlier than I did. 'How long have you lived here now?' he asked. In my defence, I pointed out that behindsight is a deceptive filter: it makes the things that lurk at our backs – in other words, the past – seem comprehensible. 'The present is always a mess,' I said, 'and in the heat of that moment, there was little that I could have done to forestall the antagonism that arose in my nearly-perfect seminar.' I told him that, half the time, I did not really know what the students were saying anyway – especially the rough ones with the blood-shot eyes. I also said that I had been so delighted and excited to hear them talking freely that I had perhaps lowered my normally acute antennae for a time. Professor Boyle did not say anything to this, but merely shook his head as if he knew that he had been vanquished in argument by a more than worthy adversary. I pressed home my advantage, asserting, in a characteristically perspicacious moment of self-knowledge, that there was perhaps a distinction to be drawn between my intellectual understanding of the situation and my ability to integrate that understanding at the level of my interactive instincts. Now he commented kindly, 'Yes, Jesús, that is abundantly plain. But I wonder if it's perhaps more a gap than a distinction.' Encouraged, I said, 'It is one thing to know that you must avoid eye contact with a lion, but it is quite another to invert your eyes when he trots towards you in the clearing with his big teeth sticking out.' Again, he appeared to concede the ground to me. His only comment was to suggest that some of the students, on both sides of the divide, may possibly have chosen my course because they misunderstood what I meant by 'green' history. 'I think you've recruited a number of committed nationalists and their equally committed opponents. Our students don't normally behave like that – in fact, I've never seen the like.' I thought that a little display of emotional vulnerability might add a touch of humanity to my self-portrait, so I exclaimed, 'Oh, this country is a mad place with all the colour-coding and the thub-tumping! It passes over my head like ships in the night. Why don't you all just wear labels?' He said, 'We do, but not everybody reads them,' and I laughed obligingly at his lame joke.

When Connor heard of the squirrel debate, he decided for some reason to intensify my educational programme. He produced his syllabus for the month, and informed me that the next two items upon it were 'Eating an Ulster Fry' and 'Swearing like a Belfast Man'. The following Sunday, Begoña chanced to be at home, so Connor summoned me to his flat in the morning. When I arrived, he was already busy in the kitchen, where he had placed on the table a terrifying range of foodstuffs. For me, breakfast is a cup of coffee, a piece of bread and perhaps a slice of melon. Not surprisingly, I began to gag as soon as I saw what he was planning to cook. I said, 'Who else is coming for breakfast?' but he replied, 'It's just you and me, kid.' I sat down, and he began to fry things on his hot hob. I said, 'I have never seen you cook before. Are you turning into a "new man" or something?'

'No, no,' he said, 'that's your territory, isn't it? No, in Belfast, the typical man has no expertise in the culinary arts, except when it comes to the world-famous "Ulster Fry". Now, watch and learn.'

Into the frying pan went eight sausages and eight rashers of bacon, where they sizzled and spat like local politicians. When these items were charred, he put them under the grill to keep warm, and he filled the pan with something called 'black pudding'. This was followed by six eggs and a solitary mushroom that he claimed to have bought by mistake. Finally, he fried several slices of 'soda bread' and 'potato bread'. I looked on in disbelief. He then divided it all up and placed my share before me. 'There you go,' he said, 'Heart disease on a plate.' The situation was awkward, but I had to say something.

'I must apologise, Connor, but I truly do not know if I can eat such food at this time of the day. In the evening, I could swallow a whole pig, but in the morning? I am evolved to attend mass at this time.'

'Sure, you'll be grand,' he said. 'It's like this. Until you've eaten one of these babies, you'll always be making mistakes and watching your seminars descend into violence. Tasting is believing – the body and blood of Ulster. And don't worry. You can take all day, if you like. Anyway, your mind will be on Part 2 of the morning's lesson. Shall we begin?'

'Is it really necessary for me to swear like a Belfast man?'

'Nothing more so. You see, one of your problems is that you use words like 'damnably' and 'blessed' – they don't really do the job, so they don't.'

While we spoke, I was sampling a mouthful of each item on my plate. It all tasted good, but when I had been round the garden once, I was already replete.

'Don't give up, now,' said Connor. 'Remember what I told you.'

There was nothing for it, and I began my second circuit.

'So,' said Connor, 'what I propose to do is teach you three key sentences that incorporate some of our favourite expressions and swearwords – it's always good to learn them in context. I have chosen them in the hope that you will find occasion to use them as you worm your way further and further into our culture. Are you ready?'

I grunted in affirmation, and two pieces of bacon flew from my mouth and landed on his telephone. I was pleased to be relieved of them.

'How would you describe our colleague Mark Down,' he asked.

This seemed a curious way to begin the lesson, but I responded as honestly as I could.

'He's vain, and foolish into the bargain,' I suggested.

'No!' shouted Connor, "Eee's awa in the fockin' heed, a borrn fockin' eejit. Try it.'

I swallowed some gristle, and made a half-baked attempt.

'That's fockin' dasprat,' said Connor uncharitably. 'Put some fockin' dick into it, can ye nat, ye great binlid? Orr duu yuu wan me to give yuu a Belfast welcome?'[45]

I tried again, to much greater effect. Slowly but surely, I was beginning to warm to my task.

'That's better,' said Connor. 'But you need to work on that word, "fockin". It's the most important one we have. It kinda grows from the back of your throat, like you're about to cough something up. Now, what would you say if the wains were really getting on yer nerves? Not just annoying ye a wee bit, but really gettin' right up yuurr cont. What would you say?'

I was determined to avoid a second *humillación*, so I said, 'Will you give me that bloody remote control. I've just about had enough, so go up to your fucking rooms, right now, so you must.'

---

[45] Connor explained that a 'Belfast welcome' was a split lip. I had seen the expression once before, on a building in town called 'The Belfast Welcome Centre'. In my innocence, I had assumed that this was some sort of tourist facility. Now, I thanked my lucky stars that I had not ventured in.

I was rather pleased with this, but Connor was laughing so enthusiastically that a piece of black pudding had somehow found its way to the end of his nose, from whence it dangled alluringly. Eventually, he calmed himself and wiped it away with his sleeve.

'Now, try this: If yuusuns don't be gud yous 'r'all fer the fockin' glory hole, so y'are!'

I protested, 'I do not even know what that means. I can't say that.'

He explained that the 'glory hole' was, traditionally, the storage cupboard under the stairs, into which errant children could be placed for a period of punishment. I was intrigued. At home, we had just such a cavity, but we used it only for inanimate objects. I attempted Connor's second phrase, and made rapid progress. It was comparatively easy. I just pictured the children in my imagination, and out the words flew.

'Last but not least,' said Connor. 'Have you ever been served with substandard food in a Belfast restaurant?'

Of course I had.

'And what did you say?'

I was now on my metal, and I planned to rub it until it gleamed.

'I told 'em to fockaway off and play in the traffic.'

'Not bad,' said Connor, visibly surprised. 'But I want you to learn something more specific. In that situation, you could have said: "Thass fud is fockin' shite. Only tuu fockin' tatties, and wunnuvem a fockin' conker!"'

He explained that this was a complaint about the size and the number of the potatoes that had been served. When I had practised and memorised it, I asked, 'And what would

I say if there were simply too much fried food and I found it impossible to eat.'

He looked at my half-filled plate, and replied, 'Och, you couldn't really say anything. It'd be best to just keep eating so as not to offend your host.'

By the time I finished the meal, I was outrageously bloated and incapable of any movement that did not involve my bowels. It had been one of your abject lessons in gluttony. I remained stationary for several hours, then waddled home on heavy legs with animal grease gushing from my paws. Now, however, I was at least safe within the knowledge that Connor was beginning to rub off on me. I was becoming a true Ulsterman, capable of holding his own on every conceivable occasion.

Chapter 23

In which Jesús girds his loins in preparation for battle with the world-famous Lunchpack of Notre Dame.

Spring was in full swing long before the end of February, and even the dogs on the street agreed that it was the earliest one ever recorded. The most important difference between this season and its predecessor was that the rain became heavier, though perhaps more intermittent. Other changes followed from this. Hawthorn trees sent forth buds, primroses prepared to bloom, and a wildly misguided flamingo set up a shop on the shores of Belfast Lough. On the national television news, scientists queued up to warn modern man that he bore the brunt of the responsibility for such terrible occurrences with his continuous gaseous belching. Every night on the BBC, a little hairy Englishman coupled himself to a majestic blonde lady in his efforts to make this point stick. All over the world, viewers tried to imagine what the babies of this odd couple might look like. I was bemused by the climatic furore. It was clear to me that Northern Ireland desperately needed every little micro–degree of global warming that it could obtain. Most of the people who flew about in my orbit shared this opinion. They simply and sensibly ignored the controversy and celebrated any tiny improvement in their damp, cold lives. They knew that such progress was to be welcomed, and that we (I speak as an Ulsterman) were the direct beneficiaries of untrammelled American greed. From my vantage point in the north of Ireland, I naturally spared a thought for those living in the world beyond (such as it was), but I was justifiably preoccupied with the fortunes of my new found land.

In our own neighbourhood, the nocturnal forays of the badgers became more noticeable as the month progressed and twilight steadily receded. The temperature rose slightly, and, once in a while, the sun shone in between the showers. All over the place, builders were emerging from their partial hibernation in the darker corners of the city to begin adding extensions onto the already sizeable properties of the wealthier urban peasants. This 'nesting instinct' was strong on New Forge Lane, and proud home-owners performed colourful sexual 'displays' for one another, prancing and dancing in front of their houses with lawn-mowers, shears and strimmers. I half-expected to see the little hairy man popping up with his lady friend in toe! Yes, it was as if a new sparkle was tickling the fancies of everyone, even the most ancient, bitter and fetid of my academic colleagues. This was a magical time. At home, I once watched from the bedroom window for an hour, and kept a careful count as a pair of adult blue tits made seventy-six excursions to and from the nest in search of food for their precocious young. It struck me forcibly that, deep down, humans too – yea, even men – are merely dumb animals, biologically programmed to sustain their fledglings at the risk of their own independence. I felt a little bond with our delicate feathered neighbours, and contentedly I sighed. From down-stairs, I heard Dilatación yelling, 'Papá! I need you. I want more sugar puffs now! Are you not listening to me?'

'Shut the fock up! I'm busy!' I shouted, and slammed the door.

You will agree that each and every one of us experiences certain urges in the time of spring, and it was therefore my most fervent hope that I might, at some stage, be able to lure Begoña into shooting range. Unfortunately, it was not to be. Here is another of our infectiously concise Spanish proverbs: 'When I wanted it, you didn't want it; and when you want it, I don't.' [46] I was firing all of my bullets in the dark while banging my head against a brick wall, and I was less than comfortable. It was as if I were trying to fit my square peg into one of her round holes. Bego was frequently absent, but she kindly communicated with us *via* the pages of *The Orb*, that most detestable of London newspapers. It published numerous stories, every one of which she dismissed during her brief sojourns at home. 'If you can even consider the possibility that such things are true,' she said, 'then I will not talk to you about them.' And she was as good as her word. The worst of the stories appeared, as I recall, upon a Friday morning, a few days after she had left on one of her regular trips to Paris. Connor entered our room at RUB and said, 'Jayzus, you'd better see this before the students do.' He handed me a copy of the paper and directed me to the second page. There, to my profound surprise, I saw a photograph of Begoña with a glass of wine in her

---

[46] *'Cuando quise, no quisiste; y cuando quieres, no quiero.'*

hand, whispering into the enormous black ear of a very healthy-looking man. His hand was somewhere behind her, and the expression on Begoña's face led me towards some uncomfortable speculation regarding its precise location. Beside the picture there was a headline: 'NO SHRINKING VIOLET BEFORE THE LUNCHPACK OF NOTRE DAME.' I was very angry, and I asked,

'Who in the fockin' name of fock is he?'

Connor winced in sympathy, then answered.

'It's that big French athlete, Pierre Leconcombre. He's the fella who won the Olympics – 200 metres, wasn't it? Something like that. He's six foot four, born in Tunisia. You'd better read the article.'

I did so, and what a lurid piece of filthy fluff it was! I learned that Monsieur Leconcombre had acquired his nickname 'after that famous head-on footage of him winning a race in a tight sky-blue lycra body suit'. I still did not understand, but Connor was kind enough to satisfy me. 'It looked like an anaconda and two water-melons in a plastic bag,' he said. 'The man's hung like a horse.'

'He should be!' I snapped. 'That would teach him a lesson!'

The article also explained that my wayward wife, more beautiful than dutiful, had been seen in Paris with the freaky Frenchman on a number of occasions, 'and always with that same enigmatic smile on her face [see picture].' They had been wining, dining and, by implication, entwining for several days. They had shared aphrodisiac 'nooky-cookies' at a party. And she had even laughed pornographically when a journalist from *the Orb* asked her, 'Did Pierre pack your lunch for you today?' I imagined losing her to this prodigious athlete, and it made me feel physically sick. I thought about all the happy occasions upon which we had made all sorts of love in the bushes, and I resolved that, in the weeks to come, I would not go down without a fight.

My first instinct was primitively masculine. I would grow strong, sculpting my body into the most beautiful shapes that it had ever assumed. I would be harder and bigger than a cork tree. In this way, I would compete with the so-called Lunchpack, playing him at his own game. I also knew that, by releasing happy jumping endolphins into my bloodstream, I could hope to elevate my spirits. Even before the ill wind from Paris broke, I had for some days been feeling physically run-down, *como un erizo desafortunado*.[47] This was, I knew, my very first intimation of middle age: my Achilles' tendon was no longer perfect, and I was having some difficulty turning it around; my joints creaked in the mornings, and my knee in particular had not fully recovered from its contact with the kitchen table during the episode of Audrey and the involuntary hair extension; my teeth and skin had lost a little of their Latin lustre, and my eyebrows increasingly resembled a pair of hairy caterpillars crawling across a rotten branch; there was a slight twitch in my left eyelid, and I had three grey hairs that made me look extinguished. In pessimistic moments, I nervously imagined a future in which I might have to spend twelve hours every day stretching, flossing, bandaging, plucking, polishing, trimming and treating my many body parts, merely to feel

---

[47] Like an unlucky hedgehog.

comfortable with the idea of getting back into bed again. This would never do, and I allowed Begoña's conduct – which was either irresponsible or despicable – to drive my battle against mortality. I felt the poetic rhythms of repetitive endeavour: I ran and I ran; I cycled and swam; my marriage, if doomed, would go out with a bang; when self-doubt attacked me I whispered, 'You *can*'; and for the big Frenchman I gave not a fock. Within a week or two, all feelings of anxiety had been supplanted by an almost overwhelming sense of my own virility. I was well-heeled again, and I found rapture beyond the rupture. I reminded myself that, despite everything, I had the constitution of an ass. All I needed was the opportunity to fertilise my Begoña, but it was to be a long and heavy wait.

In the meantime, a shiny new neighbour moved into the big house opposite our own. He was an interesting 'fella', and I would like to introduce him to you (his small but pivotal part will later feature in my story). This man was so utterly urban and so thoroughly gifted in material terms that I am sure you will like him. Quite by accident, I developed one of your slight homoerotic crushes on him, though this was – I hasten to add – merely a thing of the spring. His lovely name was Ciaran Grady, and to my delight he began to mark his territory as soon as he arrived in the lane. He erected a three-metre high black metal fence and installed intimidating security gates, which he activated with an electronic device in his bulging pocket. Next, he installed his big dog, a magnificent growling, fouling Albino Doberman called 'Blade'. Mr. Grady was in his forties, but his girlfriends were all astonishingly attractive teenaged models. He also owned a speedboat, a jet-ski, a gleaming red sports car, two gigantic grey American pick-up trucks, and a Japanese machine called the 'Personal Elevator GVX7' that enabled him to hover thirty or forty feet over his own garden, for reasons about which I could only fantasise. In Spain we say, 'He who has a nice ring points everything out with his finger.' He drove like a loveable roguish maniac, and we christened him ZoBo (an abbreviation of Zoom Boy). At night, he managed skilfully to park all his vehicles on his driveway, and he stroked each one in turn before he went inside. It was a moving ritual, and I spied on him every night using my infra-red thermal-imaging telescope-cum-camera.

On several occasions, I tried to talk to him, but he seemed curiously elusive, almost as if he were afraid of me. Behind the mask, I realised, he had a shy face. In fact, we conversed on one occasion only, and both of us became rather inarticulate. It was as if our tongues were tied together! After he had told me about the chain of high-class escort agencies that he owned, and I had asserted the importance of my recent essay on the relationship between paint and reason, the conversation lapsed. I wanted to invite him in for a stiff one, but I had lost my bottle. Nervously, we both watched his dog, who was playing on the lawn with a dead cat. Dilatación was by my side, and I am sorry to report that she was scowling rudely at poor Mr. Grady. He broke the silence by asking me, 'Och, is she strange?' I said, 'She's a complete fockin' looper, she's awa in the heed', but if anything this made the atmosphere even more uncomfortable. Mr. Grady then emitted the following extraordinary remark:

'Sorry, but I was on my way to Mars.' I assumed that this was a reference to his personal elevator, but he climbed instead into one of his many cars, and drove away at speed.[48] It had not been the easiest of encounters, but at least the thin ice was now cracked.

---

[48] Connor explained to me, later that day, that 'strange', when applied to an infant, signifies 'shy or reticent', while 'Mars' means 'Mass'.

Chapter 24

Now, at long last, Jesús Sánchez Ventura applies his cavernous mind to the problems of twenty-first century parenting, and finds Mr. Blett Wankett wanting.

You will surmise, perhaps with mild annoyance, that I still had the children. They had not changed in any meaningful way, but during the spring my own behaviour towards them passed through something of a transformation. On one particularly rainy afternoon, I fell asleep on the lavatory when I should have been assisting Conchi and Puri with their homework. When I came to my senses with a splash, none of my daughters was in evidence. I summoned them, but there was no response. In a mood of irritation, I searched the house but again to no avail. I put on my coat and went out into the garden. Here, my attention was arrested by the sounds of children screaming in distress. 'Papá, Papá! Where arrre yew? We're in the garden hut, so we arre, and it's full of water! We're drowning, Papá!' Of course, I rushed over, pausing only to remove an unsightly daffodil petal from my shoe. The door of the wooden outbuilding was shut with jam, so I smashed it to pieces with an amenable wheelbarrow. Inside, my three daughters were in both a huddle and a puddle, and rain poured in through the roof at numerous junctures. The water was no more than half a metre deep, and I could not believe the disturbance that they were creating. Like a responsible father, I rebuked them for being such fools, telling them that I would surely put them in the 'fockin' glory hole' if they ever over-reacted again. As they filed past me into the rain, however, I realised that I had a warm feeling in my breast. It occurred to me that I actually regarded them with a certain affection, in spite of myself. I was genuinely pleased that they were not drowned or otherwise dead. Obviously, I was not going soft and squishy, but, as I looked around, it dawned on me that I had reached a watershed in my domestic life.

There were other, more important reasons, for a slight shift in my attitude to Conchi, Puri and little Dila. For one thing, it had been brought to my notice that some ladies in Belfast, and not only the older or larger ones, derived a kind of erotic depth-charge from observing a man who was nice to his daughters. For another, the girls perhaps needed a little bit more in the way of emotional succour than I had thus far been prepared to offer them. It was not their fault that their mother was becoming so sluttish. Once again, my sense of paternal responsibility began to gnaw away at my brain like a rat. I also had the misfortune to read a book called *The Mother inside the Father*, written by an American called Blett Wankett. It was full of drivel so disturbingly self-righteous and wrong-headed that I had to make a stand (and, if possible, hit him with it). I only purchased the book because I believed it to be a guide to your innovative northern sexual horseplay, and I was therefore perturbed to discover that it was instead a manual on modern parenting. For example, it said a father should not reveal his nakedness in the presence of his daughters when they were over one year of age. Now, I am no crazy brown-balled German nudist, but I nevertheless found this advice both offensive and impractical. Psychologically, it is neither possible nor desirable for a man like me to keep himself covered up at all times in his own house, even in such a cold climate. Blett Wankett also wrote, 'It is obviously important that both parents avoid the use of swearwords in front of the children, and preferably at all other times too. Too many of our little ones are punished at school when they innocently redeploy these words in the hearing of their teachers, and it is surely the parents who are to blame. So, my advice to all you moms and dads out there is simply to cut it out!' This put me in a rage, and I spoke out loud: 'How am I supposed to practise my Ulster swearing if I cannot speak freely in my own house? Tell me that, Mr. Wankett!' Finally, he warned that young children should not be exposed to 'cultural images or practices that were in any way violent, disturbing or sexually suggestive'. Where, I asked in exasperation, would I be if I banned my girls from watching their favourite DVDs? I will tell you the answer: in a big pile of shite. There was only one thing to be done: I must develop my own unique style and philosophy of fathering, using the girls as my experimental hamsters. And this is precisely what I did.

I acknowledge readily that my daughters' language had become more fruity since Connor had pointed the way to a more culturally integrated future. I do not, of course, wish to imply that I actively encouraged them, but inevitably they adopted some of my new expressions. Children learn from their parents: that is what parents are for. There were one or two sticky incidents in the wider educational world, but nothing for the teachers to write home about. Dilatación, for example, stooped to pick up somebody else's discarded hair elastic as we left nursery one day. She looked at it, and asked in a good, confident voice, 'What fockin' thing is this?' I made a joke of it, but the matronly minders did not appear amused. After this, I took the precaution of telling all three of my girls that the very rudest word in the English language was 'schnozzlehopper', and that they should under no circumstances use it. My hope was that, should one of them ever decide to swear in uncontrollable anger at her headmaster, she would call him this rather than 'big fockface' or some such.

In most circumstances, however, I was intrigued and relieved that the girls – like me – seemed to know almost by instinct that these were words that should not be uttered in the presence of teachers, other parents, vicars, priests, milkmen, neighbours, Mormons, gorgons, organists and the like. When a particularly prim so-called health visitor, Miss Algood, showed Dila a picture and asked whether she could think of any words that rhymed with 'duck', I practically filled my pants with fear. But my little one quickly said, 'Muck, luck, chuck' and made me marginally proud of her. Conchi was also in the room during this routine interview and, with a spark in her eye, she asked the intruder, 'Can you think of any words that rhyme with "rollocks"?' Luckily, Miss Algood could not come up with anything off the top of her cuff. It seemed to me that Conchi, Puri and Dila were all learning how to make choices about the appropriate verbal registers for use in a variety of situations, and that a small collection of unacceptable expressions would actually help them with this. How could they learn to exercise *discreción* if they knew no expressions that rendered it necessary, for fock's sake?

My starting point, as I experimented with a more committed style of fathering, was to assume that Blett Wankett was mistaken about everything. This helped me to focus my mind. I did not, for example, discourage the girls from taking a healthy passing interest in my manly jewels. Of course, I did not exactly waggle these in their faces, but nor did I keep them in close confinement. Instead, I answered their childish questions ('Can you drink through that?') as straightforwardly as I could ('Yes, I believe it could be done'). There was, it seemed to me, nothing to be gained from stifling a natural and inevitable curiosity. Once again, I occasionally found myself in mildly embarrassing situations as a result of my attitude, but if the busy-bodies whom you call Eve's droppers felt queasy and uneasy then I regarded this as their problem, not mine. One day, we all went into a public house so that I could practise my 'binge drinking', and Dila announced, 'I want to do a pee pee in the toilet.' I hurried her off without any great sense of optimism and, predictably enough, she changed her mind once we were in the toilet cube and emptied her bladder into her voluminous nappy. I realised that I too needed relief, and as I unzapped my trousers she said, 'Show me your wedding tackle.' I duly obliged, explaining casually that I was about to make use of it anyway. 'There it is,' I said, to which she replied in full voice, 'And the rest! Show me the rest!' We eventually emerged to find that a priest and a little boy were washing their hands vigorously at the basins. Dila and I walked tall, refusing to skulk and ask forgiveness. They, on the other hand, looked painfully embarrassed by what had just happened.

Mr. Wankett, I realised, had failed to understand that any experience can be interpreted on an infinite number of levels. My innocent little conversation with Dila, for example, would have had an entirely different ambience if it had been conducted between two elderly brothers (or, heaven forbid, between an attractive dietician and a well-endowed French athlete). For this reason, I permitted my girls to watch films from which Blett would have had me exclude them. They were familiar, for example, with the faintly erotic *Rearguard Action* and with the mildly frightening *Doomsday III: No Second Chances*. I noted with considerable interest that they simply filtered out most of the sections and themes with which they were not yet equipped emotionally or intellectually to deal. Logically, they interpreted most experiences at a level that was appropriate and meaningful to them, and if they were unable to find such a level, then they simply wandered off with their fingers up their noses. If any images disturbed them, then of course we turned the sound down. It was impossible, however, to predict what their tiny little minds would and would not enjoy: they all sat happily glued to the rather sinister musical, *Ashes to Ashes* (set entirely in a crematorium), yet they absolutely could not stomach *Dumbi* (Disney's 'instant classic' about a maladjusted cross-bred animal who travels back in time to establish his or her real identity). Surprisingly, they were thoroughly bored by *Lassie On Heat*, an old British film that I could and do watch over and over again. I could not tell what movies they would like, and I therefore permitted them to judge for themselves. The only so-called 'cultural image' that was banned outright in my house was 'synchronised swimming'. I was eager to conduct experiments on my happy hamsters, but I did not wish to warp their impressionable minds beyond repair.

I would not go so far as to say that I enjoyed my time with the children, but it had to be done. 'Why not make a virtue of a necessity,' I asked myself, 'and push over the boundaries of human knowledge in the process?' I decided that the best forms of father-daughter recreation were those that offered something in the way of stimulation to *both* parties. Fathers and daughters do not, by definition, enjoy the same things. Logically, therefore, we had to design activities that had multifarious appeal. Together, we invented a number of games that met this criterion, and we played them together for hours at a time. The most successful of these was 'Spin the Bin', which took place in our front garden. It was exquisitely simple. I would place a chosen child in the wheely bin and close the lid (it worked better when the bin was not completely full). Then, the other two girls – or 'monitors' – would shout, 'Spin the Bin!' and the fun would commence. Rapidly, I would rotate and tip the bin, first one way and then the other, while the monitors counted slowly to thirty. When this period had relapsed, I would stop, and the girl in the bin would have to guess which way she was facing (north, south, east or west). If she answered correctly, she would be allowed out of the bin and replaced by a sister. If she made an error, she would be spun again, and this would continue until she was either more successful or sick. They loved it – presumably because of the filth and the nausea – and I loved it too, because it allowed me, in a perfectly harmless way, to fantasise about the possibility of getting rid of my offspring once and for all.

Chapter 25

Here, Jesús' children bring upon themselves a myriad of misfortunes, and a crude attempt is made to lure him into the sinister 'PTA'.

My confident attitude to parental responsibility was, however, shaken during the second half of March by a series of minor physical accidents. None of these was exceptional in itself, but their cumulative impact was slightly unnerving (like being hit in the legs over and over again by pygmies on miniature bicycles). It reminded me with considerable force that, however committed one is to one's children, they will always find a way of disrupting one's life. First, Dilatación fell from a chair while trying to reach my whiskey and bumped her head. She seemed distinctly disorientated and I realised that she had suffered a chip off the old block, so we transported her up to the children's hospital. As the nurses examined her, Dila gradually became more lucid and, to our relief, started releasing a number of expressions from our favourite garden game: 'Spin the bin! It's north . . . no, west, yes, definitely west . . . can I come out now? I'm gonna boke.' As she continued, I saw the nurses glancing sharply off one another like some of your dodgem cars, but I assured them that Dila's words were in fact a sign of goodness. Within a few hours, we were home again, though the little 'eejit' had to wear a bandage for a week or so in order to cover up her purple patch.

Next, Conchi – while cooking our evening meal – put both her hands onto the hob, just seconds after the hot-plate had been switched off. She was very upset, even frazzled, and back we went to the hospital. Again, the damage was not serious and the nurse issued us with a tub of sorcerous white cream that eased the discomfort and allowed the hands to heal in a surprisingly short space of time. Once again, we required bandages. Finally, Puri joined the festival by stuffing a plump Californian raisin up each nostril. As she ran down the stairs to announce her achievement, she slipped and fell, twisting her left ankle quite stupidly. I was anxious to avoid another trip to the hospital, but my best efforts to extricate the raisins resulted only in a spectacular nosebleed. The nurses removed the little obstructions using a small nasal suction pump in a matter of minutes, and they strapped the ankle. As we departed, I heard them whispering to each other, but I assumed that it was just some of your nursy tattle-tittle. It was not all bad news, however, for I earned a great deal of sympathy from the 'yummy-mummies' of Stranmillis. Many of them were not backward in coming forward to offer help when they watched us trooping sadly across the playground like a line of maimed and barely mobile soldiers in a numbing black-and-white photograph from World War One.

In normal circumstances, I would probably have reached out a hand to Audrey for relief and support. I was, however, making an effort to hold her at arm's length. I had been quite seriously unhinged by my strange and disabling reaction to the touch of her healing hands. There was, I suspected, a message in the massage. My instincts were further reinforced by a very peculiar conversation that I had with another of the mothers. One afternoon, as I gathered my wounded troops together in the playground, the one called Sinead asked me – in the full hearing of everyone – if I would consider joining an organisation called the 'PTA'. I have to say that I was completely shocked by the brazen manner in which she dropped this acronym into our conversation. I had not heard of this particular group before, but I did not need anyone to tell me that the letters stood for something like 'Paramilitary Training Army'. I had lived in Belfast long enough to know how these things worked, but I was still shocked to see how inured the local people were to political violence. I did not want to place myself or my children in danger by expressing my outrage in overt fashion, so instead I tried to sidestep her bullets.

'Things are very busy at the moment, Sinead, I am afraid. You know, what with all these fockin' injuries 'n' all.'

She looked taken aback, as if she were not used to being rebuffed as she went about her malevolent business.

'Och, OK,' she said. 'A few of us just thought it might get you out and about a bit, help-you-through-your-troubles sort of thing.'

Now she was talking openly about the Troubles, as if they were not over. I could not believe my ears.

'A few of you?!' I spluttered.

'Yeah, just a few of the girls. I think it was Audrey who suggested it.'

'Audrey suggested that I join this organisation?'

'She did rightly. Audrey's very active in the PTA these days – she may even be taking it over next year, I believe.'

'I am sure you have got that wrong,' I said. 'It simply does not add up, and now I am non-plussed. Audrey would never involve herself in something like that! She does massage, you know.'

By this time, my little crippled trio had gathered around me, and in a slow-motion hurry we shuffled off to reclaim our bicycles.

Chapter 26

In which Nanny State comes to call and, armed with two long legs, lures our protagonist into a mood of ill-judged talkativity.

On the very first day of April, I received an unexpected visit from one of your 'social workers'. She showed me a plastic card, and of course I invited her into my home, but I was a confused trifle. I did not even know what a 'social worker' was. We do not encounter such people in the mountains of Andalusia. My visitor was very pleasant, immaculately presented, and she gave off an air of sensitive professionalism. Nevertheless, something about her made me feel suspicious. She claimed to have sent me a letter, but I had no recollection of it. She said her name was Christine Stewart, and I could not help but notice that she seemed to have lovely and exceptionally long legs. Of course, I behaved with my usual dignity, but my nerves were jangling like church bells during a typhoon. I made her a cup of coffee, and as I did so she sought to engage me in some 'small talk'. It emerged that she knew Audrey, though she assured me that anything I said to her would be treated in the strictest confidence. Now, I realised what was going on here.

'I might have known it! You're another one from the PTA, aren't you? Fock me, you people just don't give up!'

'The Parent-Teacher Association? No, I have no connection with them or the school.'

Parent-Teacher Association, my foot! Oh, this one was clever, and I would have to be on my guard. I attempted a sarcastic chuckle, but produced instead a lascivious guffaw that almost choked me. Christine Stewart moved one hand a little closer to her mobile phone. This gave me an idea, so I excused myself and went upstairs 'to the toilet'. In the bedroom, I made a hurried call.

'Listen, Audrey, I only have a moment.'

'What on earth's the matter? You sound spooked.'

'Just tell me this. What is the PTA, and are you involved with it? I have heard rumours.'

'Calm down, Jayzus. It's the Parent-Teacher Association — it raises money for the school, to help Mr. Leeway buy computers, sports kit and so on. I help out. What about it?'

'Thank you, Audrey,' I said, a little more calmly. 'I have one more question for you, if you don't mind.'

'Fire away.'[49]

'There's a woman here who claims to know you — Christine Stewart. She says she's a 'social worker' or something like that. Is she real?'

Audrey paused.

---

[49] This is an old Belfast expression, left over no doubt from the Troubles.

'Does she *seem* real?'

'Yes, yes, she's definitely real, but do you know her?'

'Yes, I've known Christine for years. Not well, but well enough. Her parents and mine are good friends. She's nice – a bit serious, from what I remember. She was involved in some terrible episode a few years back when they failed to intervene in a case of child-abuse, so I expect she's ultra-careful. Don't worry. It's probably because of all the wee accidents with your girls.'

'Are you serious? She's invading my house, drinking my coffee, and all because my imbecilic daughters fall over once in a while? What is this? It's practically some kind of joke!'

'Has she said what it's about?'

'No, nothing.'

'Och, don't panic. Just be yourself, talk freely, I'm sure you've nothing to worry about.'

I heard my visitor move her chair in the kitchen. '*Hasta la vista,*' I said, 'and thanks.' As I hung up the phone, Audrey said, 'Oh, and I think she's a lesbian' (or it could have been 'thespian').

I hurried back downstairs, and the intruder asked, 'Are any of your daughters home at the moment?'

'Only Purificación,' I said nervously. 'She's the middle one – I kept her home because she has a sore throat. She's not playing truant, or anything like that. She's watching a DVD in the front room. I expect she'll drift in and out of our consciousness, if you are agreeable. The other two are at school.'

She looked surprised. 'Oh, I thought I heard you talking to someone upstairs.'

'I had to make a quick phonecall to work.'

I searched my mind in desperation for some plausible detail with which to reinforce its cavity walls.

'I am addressing a workshop of part-time lesbians at noon, under the auspices of the university's Gender Group. They asked me, because I do a jobshare with my friend Connor and they thought I might have some insight.'

'Part-time lesbians?'

'Well, no. I suppose they must be full-time lesbians, but they only work in the university part-time.'

Anger flickered across her face, and if there had been a chain-saw close at hand she would probably have cut the silence with it.

'Do you need to go, then?' she asked.

'No, please don't worry. I have blown them off, if you get my draft. Anyway, Puri is sick – I cannot go today. Tell me, Señorita, have you ever been involved in the dramatic arts?'

It was not going well. Somehow, I could tell. At this moment, Puri slid into the kitchen on her stomach, clutching her throat and groaning, 'Must have water, must have water, before I burst of thirst.'

'Hello, Purification,' said Miss Stewart, 'are you not feeling very well today?'

Puri looked shocked to find a stranger among us, and she crawled over to me in what the people of Ulster call a security alert. She hugged my leg, and asked softly, 'How does she know my name?'

'Because I told her your name. It is OK. She just wants to talk to Papá for a while. Here, I will get you a drink.'

As I did so, Miss Stewart asked Puri, 'And what film are you watching today?'

My heart leapt into my mouth and I chewed unhappily upon it. I had no idea what was showing on Screen One, and I waited anxiously for my daughter's revelation.

'*The Bitch with the Itch*,' she said. 'It's all about a girl who likes to travel and do lots of other stuff too, but she comes home in the end. She's like my Mamá, but dirtier.'

It could have been much worse. I exhaled violently in grateful relief.

'I bet I can hold my breath longer than you,' said Puri.

At this, Miss Stewart almost smiled. Then she asked, 'And why do you like that film so much, Purification?' But Puri had now had enough, and she wandered off without responding. I said, 'I'm sorry about that. She can be a little vacant at times. She is, as you would say, the black hole of the family.' Now I was showing off, and Miss Stewart decided to restrain me by suddenly upping the auntie.

'Perhaps I should come to the point,' she said. 'I've been asked to conduct a preliminary investigation regarding certain reports we have received in relation to you and your daughters. Please don't be alarmed. At this stage, it's just a matter of routine.'

I looked shocked, and said, 'You want to illuminate me from your enquiries?'

'Something like that. We could either talk for a while here today, or we could make an appointment for you to visit me in my office.'

'Here and now will be fine,' I said, with the crisp air of a fresh lettuce.

'And would it be acceptable to you if I were to record our discussion, for my files?'

'I cannot believe this is happening. You must have some *real* work to do?'

I granted her request, then gathered myself together and recalled Audrey's advice about honesty. Now that she was no longer a terrorist, it seemed safe to trust her once again. During the next hour, Miss Stewart asked me one hundred intrusive personal questions about my life with the girls. It was like the Spanish Inquisition, and it made me feel just a little bit homesick. She listened attentively, but she also had a vindictive habit of remaining silent for a few seconds after I had completed each answer. This led me, again and again, to say rather more than I had intended. Sometimes, when I am nervous, I allow strange things to fly out of my mouth. Miss Stewart established that I considered myself a confident and able parent, but she also learnt that I tended towards innovation and experimentation, particularly in the matter of recreational pursuits. I am not sure that she approved entirely of 'Spin the Bin' and she frowned ever so slightly when I described the security-enhancing game called 'Would you still love me if I were called Barney Bumrush?' (another of our favourites, devised entirely by Concepción). In order to reassure her, I expounded some of my views on the significance of multiple levels of interpretation, but for some reason she still looked concerned. Rather than wallow in the silence, I told her all about yet another game, the utterly innocent 'WOP!' I loved it, and I think I managed to communicate my enthusiasm to Miss Stewart.

'I position myself at the bottom of the stairs, armed with five of those squishy-squashy indoor toy footballs.'

Here, I thoughtfully fetched one of them for her.

'The girls,' I continued, 'have to try and move across the space at the top of the stairs – which we call my window of opportunity, or WOP – without being annihilated. Don't look so worried! Those balls are remarkable: you can dispatch them with some force and they will cause little or no harm to a small child, even if you catch one right in the face. WOP! It is perfectly safe. They love it. Then, when all the balls have been collected by the girls, they hurl them down at me with all their mini-might. If Purificación were in better form, we would surely show you.'

'I see,' said Miss Stewart, 'and have any of them ever sustained an injury while playing these games?'

A small voice that was not mine said, 'Dila's eye went a bit black once, but she wasn't really blind or anything, and we didn't get her a guide dog, but Mamá says we can have a puppy one day. I want more water, so I do.' Puri presented me with her cup.

'And how do we ask nicely?' I said encouragingly.

'Just get me the water and I'll bog off again.'

Miss Stewart next asked about our recent spate of trivial accidents, but I insisted that the rumours had all been exaggerated.

'My information comes from the Children's Hospital, not from any rumours,' she said.

This made me furious, and I blew caution to the winds.

'*De puta madre*!' I exclaimed.[50] 'What busy bodies you all

---

[50] 'Of the prostitute mother'. This is something we say in Spain on special occassions.

have! They're my children. Northern nurses, my word! It is a wonder that anyone consults them. Do you know that if the girls had suffered such insignificant misfortune in Andalusia, we would simply have daubed them with traditional plant extracts, tied them up with old rags, and sent them out to play again? Why did I even attend the hospital?'

'You were being sensible,' said Miss Stewart.

'Listen,' I replied, 'these were incidents that could have occurred in any household, however responsible the parents.'

'Parents?' she said. 'But I understood that your wife was away?'

'Alright, parent in the singular,' I conceded. Her pedantry annoyed me, and I launched one of my favourite missiles. 'Would you be sitting at my table, asking me all of these invasive questions, if I were a woman rather than a man?'

She remained calm.

'It would make no difference – I am following a procedure that is applied whenever there has been a referral.'

'From the hospital?' I asked.

'We had one report from them, and another from a source which I am not at liberty to name.'

This woman really took the biscuit, and now I wanted it back. Slyly, I turned the table on her. She was bugging me, and I decided to put a flea in her ear.

'Oh, for all the saints! And do you have any children yourself, Miss Stewart?'

'Mizzz.'

'What?'

'Mizzz. I prefer to be called Mizzz Stewart, if you don't mind.'

I had absolutely no idea what she was talking about, so I simply restated my question.

'I am under no obligation to answer that,' she said, 'but since you ask, no, I do not have children.'

'I bet you don't even like men,' I added, perhaps a little imprudently.

'That,' she said sternly, 'is in no way germane to our discussion.'

I apologised with sincerity, and I tried to explain that it was not always easy to be a Spanish male with an Achilles' heel, whose enforced lifestyle led others to perceive him as some kind of sensitive, half-gay girl-boy, but who was actually a hot-blooded and lustful (though sexually conscientious, and hence frustrated) male, responsible for managing not only this contradiction but for raising three daughters almost unassisted in one of the strangest regions of Europe, while his wayward wife fluttered around the continent with a magnificent Moor whose gonads were on everybody's lips.

'I can see that,' said Mizzz Stewart with just a hint of sympathy. My next question did not emerge in quite the form I had envisaged.

'Have you any idea what it would be like to feel a man like me?'

'Not from personal experience,' she replied cautiously.

The atmosphere calmed down as a result of my disarming honesty, and the terminal exchanges were mercifully uncontroversial. As we left the kitchen, the calendar on our wall caught me in the eye: it was April 1st. This sent my head into a spin. I had heard about all the northern trickery that is perpetrated on this day. Had the whole thing truly been somebody's joke? On the doorstep, I asked my question. 'Are you truly a social worker?'

She really was good, and she managed to look genuinely surprised. 'Yes, of course. You saw my card. Why would you doubt it?'

'Come on,' I said, 'it's the first of April, and you're a friend of Audrey. I see what's going on. I know which side my cookie's buttered on around here. I may be foreign, but I'm no FOOL, you know.'

'Oh, I see,' said Mizzz Stewart. Now her head was spinning too. 'So, does this mean that you made up all that stuff about the violent and obscene games? That explains a lot, I must say.'

My head had stopped spinning, but now my mind was reeling.

'No, no, no,' I said, 'that was all true. I only just realised you were — what is the word? — spoofing.'

'But I'm not spoofing,' she replied. 'I'm really not.'

I paused in order to swallow this piece of bad news. She was not only a genuine agent of the state, but one who had found my explanations disturbing. It was a double-edged whammy.

'So, what are you going to do now?' I asked.

'I have to complete a report,' she explained, 'but I can say right away, off the record, that I will not be recommending any form of intervention at this point in time. You're idiosyncratic, perhaps a little odd, but your daughter is obviously fully at ease in your presence. That's the main thing. Just try to keep the accidents to an absolute minimum, will you? Then we can all relax.'

'So that's it?' I said.

'Not quite,' she replied awkwardly. 'I have to keep your case under review for a while, and I may need to see you and all your daughters together at some point. But I don't think you need worry.'

I watched while her extensive legs carried their cargo off down the driveway, and I went inside to find that Puri was in the process of taking a phonecall. 'It's the nursery,' she said. 'You forgot to collect Dila and she says it's the guillotine for you.'

Chapter 27

During which Jesús is insulted and Connor is consulted (with stimulating results).

Somebody else was cross with me too, though without any good reason that I could detect. On a Friday lunchtime, I stood at one of the junctions near the university and prepared to traverse the road. I had cast Mizzz Stewart far from my head, and I was in the most ebullient of moods, having just delivered a warm and witty lecture on Elizabethan mortality levels. I felt healthy, hearty and happy, and I wore a splendidly self-satisfied smile. My morning's work was complete, and there was still a whole hour in which to celebrate my existence before I had to begin rounding up my daughters. I waited for the envious little man to go green, and then I began to saunter across the street. As I passed the midway point, however, a shiny blue sports car came hurtling around the corner, and would have struck me down had not the driver, a young man in reflective sunglasses, depressed his brakes with a screech that pierced my ears. I was a little shaken, and gestured enquiringly towards the red light that he had just ignored. At this point, he drove his car towards me, and I backed instinctively out of the way. He sped past me in a haze of hormones, shouting aggressively through his open window, 'Fock off back to Dago-Land!'

This abuse from an imperfect stranger upset me even more than the experience of nearly being flattened, and my knees went weak. I suddenly felt introverted, isolated, shunned and shamed. I also felt painfully conspicuous, like some huge ungainly flightless bird at which everyone was staring. I wandered deliriously along the pavement, pecking randomly at passers-by. 'Catch yourself orrrn, big fella,' I thought to myself in the local idiom. I tried to work my way through the various questions and issues that this incident had raised. Firstly, what did his words mean? I sat down cross-legged on the pavement and activated the dictionary on my mobile phone in order to look up "Dago". I had heard this word uttered in my vicinity once or twice before, but had always presumed that it was a local contraction of the common expression, 'There you go.' I now realised, with something of a bumping, that it was a rude and colloquial term for 'a foreigner, esp. a Spaniard'. More pleasingly, however, it was derived from "Santiago", the famous saint whose name we Spaniards have always invoked while slicing other people's arms off. Perhaps if the stupid 'fockin' tube' in the sports car had known this, he would have been more respectful!

Was it possible, however, that I was executing him before he had received one of your fairshow trials? Had I heard him aright? Once in a while, I do make little mistakes with my ears, you know. Might he in fact have been a young intellectual, joyously reeling off a list of his favourite dramatists, literary theorists and artists: 'Chekhov! Bakhtin! Degas!

And . . . ' (I had perhaps missed the last one due to the noise of his hot engine)? The suggestion was more than plausible, but I could not be sure. I boiled it all over in my mind, and came to the conclusion that the man in the motor must instead have been a disaffected student who had heard me give a lecture or two, but had never met me in person. There was nothing to reassure me in this, and further questions arose within me *como burbujas de metano en el baño de un holandés.*[51] Was he unusual, a particularly bitter individual, and unrepresentative of the student community as a whole? Or was the passing friendliness and co-operative spirit of most of my students just a façade, a pragmatic deceit rendered necessary by the fact that I was in a position of power over them? Did they all, deep down in their hearts, despise me as a greasy Spanish dago who had no place in any one of the 6 + 26 counties?

These were clearly questions for Connor, and when I met him to learn 'How To Tell a Real Irish Joke' I took the opportunity to ask for an insider's interpretation. He laughed a little mockingly and promptly charged me with over-sensitivity. I was not prepared to take this lying down, so I stood up for myself.

'You would have been upset if it had happened to you,' I said. 'It made me feel like a fish out of water or a kangaroo that knows no bounds.'

He was still laughing, the rude bastard.

'Of course there are bigots here,' he said, 'people who'll resent you just because you speak with a funny accent and

---

[51] Like bubbles of methane in a Dutchman's bath.

you still can't swear properly. But you should give the rest of us a wee bit more credit than that. To most of your students, you're just a fella who's got a job over here. They enjoy your approach.'

This was more like it.

'Do you think so?' I asked with a charming and disarming air of vulnerability.

'Catch a grip, will you?' said Connor. 'Don't get all self-obsessed – it's an academic disease. Look around you – you're doing very well. Don't be letting him give you the nyrps. For fock's sake, pull your head out of your own arse and smell the daffodils.'

The image concerned me.

'And while we're on the subject,' he continued, 'here's a nice wee joke to start you off with: "An Englishman's home is his arsehole". Now, do you get it? Tell me the truth, now.'

Connor had a remarkable ability to cheer me up and to help me put my own trivial troubles into perspective. He was a walking tonic, and he often provided me with just the shot in the head I needed. I saw as much of him as was feasible, and the two of us enjoyed many open and honest conversations in a variety of local coffee-shops (he was still teaching me to eat greasy bacon slices in the morning). In Northern Ireland, he told me, the forging of a bond between individuals from divergent backgrounds is marked, in many circumstances, by an inevitable caution, an instinctive caginess in conversation. When Connor and I chewed the fat, how-ever, there was none of this, and we learned a great deal from one another. I told him my entire family history, right back to my ancestor, José del Antojo Repentino, who would have sailed with Columbus had he not nipped ashore for one last plate of fried quails' eggs just as the Santa Maria prepared to disembark.[52] Connor talked frequently of his own childhood in the controversial border town of Crossmaglen, and also of the history of the McCanns more generally. He seemed eager to discuss his family's past, and I was perfectly happy to lose myself in his incredible larder of anecdotes. Connor himself was profoundly disillusioned with local politics, and a sworn enemy of all who took up extreme positions in the warped world of Ulster's politics. 'Sure, someone should shoot the lot of them,' he would say with an air full of wist.

It intrigued me that Connor became quite animated, even enthusiastic, as he rabbited on about any number of horrific incidents from the Troubles. His eyes gleamed and glared, almost as if I had dazzled him with the bright light of intellect that burns continuously on my head. He told me of the assassination of his grandmother, and of the famous day upon which his uncle Gerard (this is pronounced 'Jurrrd') had broken all records by voting for Sinn Fein seventeen times in the space of three hours. At such moments, Connor was as well articulated as I ever knew him. His nose would twitch, his long ears would prick up and his big feet would thump about beneath the table, occasionally delivering me a sharp kick in the shin. If he had been talking about anything else, I would have described his mood as *nostálgico*. Eventually, I asked him, 'Do you miss the Troubles?' His

---

[52] You would doubtless call him Jo of the Sudden Craving.

first reply was a straightforward denial, but then he thought more carefully, and added, 'I suppose it was an exciting time, in a way. Life is cosier now, and I've moved from sectarian Crossmaglen to comparatively tolerant Stranmillis. It's a bit dull, so it is. Don't tell anyone I'm saying this, but I suppose some of us do miss it all in a way. It made us what we are, it made us special – life in the north is all about division. If we leave it all behind – as we must – then we might eventually be just like everyone else. There is something sad about that. When we lose our distinctive sense of identity, we might end up feeling less rather than more secure. We're famous for our bloody-mindedness. If we give it up, what will we be famous for then? Belfast will be just another shitty city.'

'You will still have the Titanic,' I said. 'Nobody can take that away from you.'

'Och, aye, I s'ppose so,' he agreed.

Chapter 28

Here, you will discover how Jesús functions in conditions of zero gravity.

Begoña's growth as a B-list celebrity continued apace, but she did do us the honour of returning for the girls' birthdays, all of which occurred in April.[53] She spent much of the time on her mobile phone, but at least she was there. Conchi and Puri had begun to notice that some of their friends – and particularly their friends' fathers – recognised Bego from her various apparitions in the media, and the little frisson of delight that this gave them made up for the fact that she was only occasionally available for comment. As residents of a modern city, it was of course necessary to stage for the girls a party of some sort. I opted for a joint celebration, and I discovered, to my relief, that there were many institutions eager to shoulder responsibility for the organisation of such events. There were swimming pools, bowling alleys, flight simulation centres, various places offering forms of laser combat, a big warehouse in which tiny tots

---

[53] This is nine months after the month of July and the annual *Concurso de los Roedores* in Picazón del Moro, about which time the young ladies of the pueblo become, by tradition, unusually receptive. See above, pp. 9-10.

could re-enact scenes from the Troubles, and, of course, the controversial "Rat World" with its six-page compulsory disclaimer form. Conchi insisted, however, that only two institutions, both of them newly-opened, truly deserved consideration: "Tingle Land", in which the metallic parts of the gigantic climbing frames and slides give off non-lethal but immensely exciting electric shocks to the pot-sized punters; and "Weightless Wains", the first zero-gravity children's party centre in the whole of Ireland. After intensive negotiations between the three girls, it was the latter option that won our custom.

There were thirty-two girls at the party, all aged between three and nine years. The good news was that none of them had any opportunity to enter our home, for all things were laid on by the friendly staff of "Weightless Wains". Begoña and I were on good terms for the afternoon, and we presented a united front to the world. On arrival at the huge converted prison in which the party was to take place, the girls were all sent to the toilet, and then fitted with special "space suits". Adult versions were provided for us, and a man in an alien costume delivered a speech about what we were and were not permitted to do once the festivities were underway. He was clearly having some kind of gas pumped into his slimy green mask and he spoke with a high and squeaky voice.

'Hello, boys and girls. Hoiy arre yuu orl today? Yuus are all welcome to "Weightless Wains". My name is Gark and I come frum the planet Crog45, so I do. Noiy, thur are one or two wee things I'd like yuus all to remamber. Number One: enjoy yourselves. Noiy, I can see the fewcha and I

226

know that yuus are all gonna have the best crack of yur short lives. But, and it's a big one [here, he turned around and revealed his giant pink alien bottom to the girls, at which they all giggled]: we don't want anny one er yuus to be ASTRONAUGHTY. And what do yuus all think that means?'

'No punching?' suggested Conchi.

'That's right,' said Gark, 'No punching. What else? Let's see if yuus can guess all the rules so as I don't have to tell yuus tham.'

The girls were all bright, and they were more than willing to accept the assignment.

'No gouging out of eyeballs?' suggested one of the Hannahs.

'No petrol bombs,' added Meabh.

'No kneecappings or crucifixions,' said little Janice, not to be out-done.

'That's right,' said Gark. 'Absolutely no violence whatsoever.'

When he had finished, the thirty-four of us were pumped, one by one, down a huge grey tube, passing through a number of peculiar valves and chambers, until we were quite literally fired out into our own special party room. Here, we were weightless, and for one hour and £1500 we drifted around, waving our arms and bouncing off the brightly-coloured ceiling, walls and floor. Within the chamber, there were many tunnels, hoops, ropes, trampolines and other playthings. There was a mini football pitch on the ceiling, and all around the place little plastic balls and toys floated delightfully. It was the most exquisite sensation, and Bego and I watched as the children wafted happily around with their eyeballs popping out. At half past the hour, a hatch in the floor suddenly opened, and a stream of synthetic, heavily processed party food came floating up to join the fun. The children could not eat this through their masks, but they were instructed to collect as much as they could in their "moon-bags", for later consumption. During the last part of our session, they therefore "swam" around the place, frantically trying to catch up with the chips, chicken nuggets, beef burgers, crisps, sweets, cartons of jelly and pieces of bright pink birthday cake. When there was nothing left, the operators pumped air into the chamber and we all plummeted to the floor for a feast. At its conclusion, a door opened and Gark reappeared, still well and truly inflated. 'Sorry folks,' he said, 'but yuus've all gat to return to earth noiy. Thur's another team of space travellers in the lobby, and I've to clean up yur mess before they can come in.'

Chapter 29

In which Jesús' love-making is less successful than his peace-making.

Back at home, there was a certain amount of vomiting, but essentially the girls were thrilled by their time in space. They were also extremely fatigued. One by one, they flopped onto their beds, and one by one they dropped off. It was unusually early, and I knew that a special moment had arrived. Here, at long last, was my chance to reveal to Begoña my renovated torso and to claim my stake in her. I had been presented with a window of opportunity and I meant to grasp it with both hands. I led her to the master bedroom. To my relief, she was more than responsive, especially when I opened my bedside cabinet of curiosities to call forth "Jumping Jack: the Spermicidal Maniac". Perhaps some of you northern nancies will be saying to yourselves, 'Why is he seducing her when his priority should be to rebuild his marriage through mutually conciliatory words?' Well, I will tell you: this is not a suitable strategy for *un hombre de Andalucía*. When push comes to shove, physical love is the best way forward. You must remember that Begoña and I had performed many erotic exploits in our memory banks, and I hoped that by stimulating her secret parts I could activate some recollections of our earlier days together. As soon as I began my efforts, the anaesthetic started to work, and I knew that I could probably, as you would say, go all night. I was certainly strong enough, and when Begoña felt me upon her she said, 'Oh, Jesús, you have been working out!'

She pulled the quilt over us, and in our makeshift tent of love there was deep pleasure to be had. When I was well and truly in the swing of things, I felt suddenly hot, so I manfully pushed the duvet off my sculpted shoulders with one of my chiselled arms. When I did so, I was surprised to see a row of three little female faces, looking at me from a distance of approximately one metre.

Undeniably, this represented a setback to my plan of rekindling our lost flame. Begoña's eyes were closed, and she was thus blissfully unaware of the audience. I therefore had some time to think. I did not want to arouse Bego's suspicion, so I proceeded with my activities while reviewing my options. Lesser men might have shrunk from their task, but I was made of sterner stuff. The girls were all smiling and did not seem unduly alarmed at what they were witnessing. All that was required was for them to stand quietly for half an hour or so while I completed my transaction. But could they manage this? No, they could not. After a minute, Puri reached impulsively forward and, in one single movement, pulled the quilt onto the floor. 'Let's get a proper look at what is happening under here,' she said. This intervention rather brought Begoña out of her ecstatic trance, and in a trice she exchanged one sort of gasp for another. The girls had moved even closer now.

'What are they doing?' asked Dilatación.

For Concepción, this was a matter of fact.

'They are shagging,' she said. 'He puts that thing up her butt and then he shakes it around.'

'No,' said Puri, 'it is not up her butt. It is up her fanny. You will see when he gets off.'

Now Begoña screamed, and the girls all fled the room to hide in their own beds. My wife was furious, and do you know what? She was furious with *me*. I told her I had not taught the girls any of this (which was the truth), but she did not believe me. I said that if she wished to control the things her daughters brought up, then she should come home more often.

'Oh, come off it,' she said. 'I am just doing what we came here for – living the life of a modern woman. You are jealous because you have not been so successful!'

I was very angry to hear this.

'Your behaviour is outrageous!' I informed her. 'It buggers belief!'

I stormed out of the room, banged my way down the stairs and switched on the 'Ulster News 24.7' television channel. The wretched children had bricked over my window of opportunity, and the following morning Begoña departed for the continent once again. She said she was involved in discussions regarding a reality TV show, and could not possibly miss the meeting. And that was that.

The news programme that I watched on that difficult night was, however, modestly encouraging. I had not been tracking the intricacies of the peace process with particular care, but here at last was something to make one sit up and prick one's eyebrow. I listened carefully as the newsreader made the following announcement:

'An innovative scheme could bring an end to the annual summer tension on Portadown's Garvaghy Road, said a spokesman for the Orange Order today. The plan will see a £3,000,000 sound-proofed tunnel constructed beneath the most controversial section of the road, so that members of the Order can march along their traditional route and play their customary flute music without disturbing the local Catholic residents. The chair of the Garvaghy Road Residents' Association has given the plan a cautious welcome. A similar scheme is to be implemented on the Lower Ormeau Road in Belfast, another of the key flashpoints. Our correspondent in Portadown is Lynette Ramsay . . . '

Miss Ramsay proceeded to canvas the views of various politicians from both sides of the divide, and there seemed to be something genuinely unusual in the convivial and almost consensual tone of their exchanges. 'We can do business,' said a large and surprisingly juicy Orangeman.

Within a week, the diggers were in and construction of the Garvaghy Road tunnel was underway. A building firm staffed predominantly by Protestants started at one end, while a Catholic company began work at the other. A similarly adventurous project was unfolding in Belfast itself, and people dared to hope. It had been a long haul, but now, at last, it seemed just possible that the metaphorical anglers of Ulster might be on the verge of landing the big fish called PEACE. The nervous residents of the Lower Ormeau district sat patiently beside the river and baited their own breath. There were one or two other optimistic stories during this period, and even the most cynical of old journalists was having to concede that the mood seemed to be shifting. A football match took place between the residents of Ardoyne and Glenbryn, and to the astonishment of the police it passed off in relative peace. There was one stabbing, one lynching and one none-too-serious tarring-and-feathering, but beyond this the rival forces relied on an arsenal of merely verbal abuse. The match itself ended in a thrilling 3-3 draw, but all commentators agreed that 'the score was far less significant than the fact that the game had taken place at all.' After the final whistle, the opposing strikers, each of whom had scored a hat-trick, split the match ball with a meat cleaver and, in a gesture of unprecedented good will, swapped wives for a trial month.

Elsewhere in the city, two battalions from enemy paramilitary groups staged a carnivalesque 'Fun Gun Run' which drew huge festive crowds onto the streets. Teams of one hundred individuals on each side spent a six-hour period jogging to and fro between a designated starting point in the city centre and the Lisburn Road police station, with the object of the competition being to establish which organisation could hand in to the authorities illegal weaponry of the higher value. In view of the fact that all paramilitary groups had previously decommissioned 'the totality of their weaponry' on several occasions, there was an impressive array of hardware on display. The honours were shared fairly evenly until the republicans produced two ancient "Skud" missiles that nobody had even suspected them of possessing. As the men of PIRATE struggled to transport these by hand along the Lisburn Road, a mixed crowd of Protestants and Catholics cheered and jeered almost as one. Concord was reaching dizzy new heights, spinning continuously upward. They also waved many banners, some of which, I noted with passing interest, were directed against the globalising trend and the hegemony of America: 'USA Burgur Off', 'UK Bulldog Now Yankie Poodle' and 'SOS: Save Our Squirrels'.

I wondered about the origins of all this creative and therapeutic endeavour. I vaguely recollected various conversations I had held with the burly men of Ardoyne, the unionist boys and my "Green History" seminar group, but my mind was, at that time, so addled as a result of sleep deprivation, marital mishap, sexual shortcomings and fear of anti-social workers, not to mention my academic duties, that I could hardly string two coherent thoughts together. Perhaps my natural modesty also deterred me from digging too deeply into the question. Certainly, I little suspected, then and there, that I had single-handedly brought the curtain down on top of Ireland's historic troubles.

PART IV

Spring into Summer

Chapter 30

Now, the valiant hero fights a ping-pong battle with some journalists until, eventually, he requires rescue on the wings of a phenomenal bird.

I felt happy in my new life. I was succeeding as a modern father, an academic and, above all, an Ulsterman who had been grafted onto Mediterranean roots. The Lesbian of the Long Legs was not troubling me, and the children seemed to be prospering. I was a big cheese in a small pond. Of course, I was still refining my persona in some respects, and applying the finishing touches to my reconstituted identity. Connor took me aside one day and warned me against swearing quite so exuberantly. He said I was now very proficient, but that in some respects I was becoming *too good* at it. He told me that I could afford to become a little more circumspect in my use of expletives, especially in front of my daughters and my colleagues. 'Look before you bleep,' he said with an ill-conceived smile.[54] Swear-words, he now insisted, were for special occasions, and their impact should

---

[54] Connor looked a little confused when, gently and moderately, I corrected him. I held him in the outermost respect, but I must add that his colourful bloomers did sometimes surprise and amuse me.

not be diluted by over-enthusiastic deployment. I was sensitive to his implied criticism, but I knew that he was merely fine-tuning his product rather than recalling it from the shops due to potentially lethal safety concerns. I would continue to better myself, and I felt unsinkable.

Within weeks, however, the wheel of fortune had spun again and this time my head was caught between its spokes. Begoña was, as so often, the cause of my troubles, the proverbial spanner in the ointment. Our abortive sexual encounter had left a sour taste in my mouth and there were little bits caught between my teeth. She continued to travel, and from time to time she splayed herself shamelessly across the centre pages of the London tabloid newspapers. The Lunchpack of Notre Dame still had her regularly on his antennae, and I had to accustom myself to the constant cycle of rumour and denial. I tried to put it all to the back of my mind, but every once in a while a spirit of annoyance animated my body. I am a man, after all. One morning, I was 'working' at home when the doorbell rang. I answered it, and came face to face with two very strange men, one carrying a big camera and the other a small pencil. When the latter opened his mouth and spoke like a character from 'Eastenders', I knew I was on one of your sticky wickets.

'We were just wondering if we might 'ave a word,' he said.

'Who are you?' I asked.

'We work for *The Orb*, mate, but don't hold it against us – just doing a job.'

I wanted to shut the door, but I had a little twinge of curiosity in my guts.

'I'd prefer it if you just departed,' I said.

'Don't be like that,' said Mr. Camera. 'It'll be wurf your while.'

'You see,' added Mr. Pencil, 'we've got some information for you, about your wife. We reckoned you might appreciate it if we kept you *abreast* of fings.'

The two of them sneered, smirked and snarled at one another like evil animated hyenas from a carton. They were clearly as thick as two short thieves.

'What information?' I asked.

'Depends on you, guv,' said Mr. Pencil. 'Here's the deal: we tell you, and you answer five of my questions in a for-ough and foughtful manner. Dave 'ere takes a few pics, and then we piss off out of your life. What do you reckon?'

'*What information?*' I repeated in a somewhat italicised tone.

'It's like this, see. We have it from a reliable source that your good lady wife has been indulging in a bit of the old rumpus-pumpus with Pierre Leconcombre, also known as The Lunchpack of Notre Dame (that's one of me own – d'yer like it?) It seems he's been playing her slot machine, and he's 'it the jackpot. We're running it at the end of the week, but we fought it was only fair if we chatted with you first.'

For once in my life, I stood in shocked silence. Mr. Camera pointed his lens at me and clicked into operation.

Mr. Pencil continued, ''Ere, we've got a foto 'n' all. A still, if you will, though I can assure you the two of them were far from stationary when it was taken.'

He reached into his pocket and pulled out a picture of

two people, one male and one female, one black and one white, apparently making love on a bed. It was taken through a window, and the heavily muscled man was flat on his back while being enthusiastically ridden by the slender woman. Her face was partially obscured by her own dark hair, but it did look very much like my Begoña. It showered shame upon my head, and I struggled to express scepticism.

'Hold your horses,' I said, 'this is a piece of tricky photography. I have read about you and your elk. You are both nutcases and this is a thin cashew of lies! Did you take it yourself?'

''Fraid not,' said Camera, 'it was sent us by a contact of mine – 'e works in Paris. Good bloke – straight up.'

'Rather like the Lunchpack himself with your missus,' added Pencil.

If I had ever truly possessed the plot, I now lost it.

'*Vete a la mierda*!' I shouted.[55] 'I will split your heads like a pair of pomegranates, you impudent, low-born and slanderous villains! I will slice you into slitherines! I will make you eat some of your own humble crumble before the sun settles down for the night!'

I simply had to attack somebody, for my honour was being impugned and lampooned at one and the same time. It was an urge more overpowering than anything I had experienced before, and it sent a pulse of uncontrollable masculinity through me. In that moment, I was an ancient

---

[55] This means 'Go to the shit!'

warrior, a fearless hero, El Cid facing the Moors at Alcocer.[56] My allegedly feminine side was taken by force, violently raped and utterly vanquished. I was overcome by my own manliness. Words soon failed me, but actions spoke louder. I reached for the only weapon that was to hand – Conchi's pink tennis racquet – and I prepared to do battle. My one problem was that the photographer, who had delivered the most offensive line, was in truth rather large and powerfully built withal. The so-called journalist, on the other hand, was a scrawny little runt of a man, thin and puny of limb. Sensibly, I concentrated my primal urges upon him. The fury of my assault was so extraordinary that, rather surprisingly, Mr. Camera ran for cover. At the time, it seemed to me that he had simply fled. On opening a copy of *The Orb* next morning, however, I realised that the cover for which he had run was provided by the overgrown shrubs at the side of our house. Curse all plant life! From here, he evidently trained his lens to take pictures of us and compiled a pictorial catalogue of the proceedings. The newspaper printed these in the manner of one of your comic strips – six individual images, with explanatory captions beneath:

1> Dr. Sánchez Ventura's face is a picture as he first hears the news of his wife's alleged infidelity.

2> He cries 'Santiago!' and strikes our plucky little reporter with a tennis racquet, opening a three-inch gash in his head.

---

[56] 'The man born in a favoured hour cried out at the top of his voice, "Strike them, my knights, for the love of mercy! I am Ruy Díaz the Cid, the Battler of Vivar!"'

3> Advantage Dr. SV: he continues his assault, leaving our man all but insensible.

4> Match point: the scholar struggles to divest the journalist of his trousers . . .

5> . . . and straps him to a magnolia tree with his own belt.

6> Game, set and match! Dr. SV lays down his racquet and urinates triumphantly upon his vulnerable victim.

The editors exploited the situation for all it was worth, and almost unbelievably they managed to situate themselves on the moral high ground by reporting that they had no plans to initiate litigation. 'It is well understood,' they wrote, 'that Dr. Sánchez Ventura was extremely upset, and our reporter has agreed to forgive and forget, despite his various injuries and crippling laundry costs.' I was, of course, intensely proud of my actions, but this self-righteousness made me sick. I also wondered what Begoña would say when she heard of the hostilities. I hoped that she would be impressed by the ferocity with which I had done battle, but you never can tell with ladies. Anyway, it was her own stupid fault for being such an errant, arrant whore, and she did not have a leg to stand on. That night, I turned and tossed myself in bed for hours before I fell at last into a restless sleep.

I dreamt that twenty-four historic tennis champions from your Wimbledon tournament were beating me barbarously with their racquets before a cheering audience of journalists. The centre court vibrated to the dull sound of graphite on bone. Björn Borg was icy and expressionless as he struck me. Boris Becker was there too, clubbing me with the full force that his massive Germanic frame could generate. Roger Federer was on a Swiss roll, and his attack combined fury and grace. Over in one corner, a pale English boy called Jim or Tim, whom I did not recognise, kept asking the others, 'Please can I have a go now? Oh, go on, gi'us a chance,' but as I drifted in and out of consciousness, I heard Andre Agassi say to him, 'Go home, "chicken boy",' at which everybody laughed.[57] The pain was acute, and eagerly I anticipated death. Then, all of a sudden, a giant but elegant bird flew over the court, casting a shadow over us all. It settled beside me, and said in a powerful, piercing voice, 'Leave him alone, for I will sustain him. Your blows shall be as nothing.' The players dispersed in awe, and I peered up at my rescuer's plumage, the most striking feature of which was a warm russet patch on its neck. As my eyes closed once more, I felt myself lifted gently from the grass in a long, slender beak and placed within the softness of feathers. And then we were airborne . . .

---

[57] It sounded like a joke, but unusually it passed right through me.

Chapter 31

Which recounts what happened when Jesús came upon a woman in the woods.

The giant gentle bird flew in and out of my mind's eye on many occasions during the daze that followed, but I was at a loss to comprehend its significance. I sought to do what Connor called 'getting his head sharred' by making long runs in the countryside. Mrs. Naughtie, our increasingly kindly neighbour, was always willing to preoccupy the children, thus freeing me to take my body out and about in the big wet yonder. One drizzle–dampened afternoon, however, I should perhaps have stayed at home. I set off alongside the river towards Stranmillis in a mood that was bleak and black. Little by little I began to feel my mind unwind. The endolphin-effect was enhanced by the timeless meandering of the river, and by the music of many songbirds, concealed from view in the rich, throbbing greenery on the Lagan's banks.[58] In the woods, I paused amongst the bluebells in order to remember the episode of the lustful squirrel. I negotiated my way through the undergrowth in search of

---

[58] In Andalusia we sometimes eat such creatures, and just for a moment I forgot myself and felt a little peckish.

my favourite tree, an ancient oak that stands in its magnificence some way from the path. I put one hand on the gnarled trunk, and performed some of the exercises that had been recommended to me when I was down at heel. Then, to my surprise, I heard a familiar voice.

'Nice legs, shame about the sad, doggy eyes.'

My eyes alighted on the fine form of a woman whom I knew. 'Hello, Audrey,' I said. 'What are you doing here?'

She too was out running, and had evidently glimpsed me from the path. I had not cast my eyes upon her for some time, and to my alarm I realised that she looked firm, fresh and fruitful. She was dressed simply and without affectation in a pair of light blue trousers and a white cotton shirt upon which was emblazoned the stimulating motto, 'Handmaid in Ireland'. It was worn rather thin by frequent use, and just tight enough to reveal her more than comely figure. As she approached my lonely location through the trees and flowers, I could do nothing but notice that she wore a pink brassière beneath. She stood a little closer to me than was strictly necessary, and I leaned with a certain awkwardness against the tree. Naturally, my manliness was responding to her lady-like presence, causing me significant discomfort. I faced the classical male dilemma. If one rearranges one's jewels in such moments, one immediately draws attention to one's stimulated state and one had better be ready to accept the consequences, for good or ill. If one does not attempt such a manoeuvre, however, the pain will eventually become acute, and one risks losing pride and consciousness simultaneously. I chose to take this risk, and I felt my *amigo especial* straining to escape from his solitary confinement.

'I haven't seen you much lately,' Audrey said softly. 'Are you having a bad time?'

'I am unusually perplexed at the moment,' I conceded. 'Have you seen the newspapers this week?'

'One or two,' she said. 'It'll settle down.'

Audrey moved a step closer, and her aura began to envelop me. It was as if she were touching me. She was not, and I knew that she was waiting, quite rightly, for my green light to flash. An age seemed to pass. I do not relish telling you what next occurred, but some things, as you say, are better out than in. Giddily, I allowed one of my hands to traverse the small but crucial distance that separated it from Audrey's waist. My fingers rested against her stomach for several trembling seconds, and in my dizziness I wondered if she had even registered their presence. Softly, I moved my hand across her, stroking the cotton of her blouse and, by implication, the warm, supple, feminine flesh that presumably lay beneath. Slowly, I manipulated the material through my fingers until, for the first time, my skin touched hers.

At this moment, a shapeless jogger thudded past on the path. We stood quite still, our various large brown eyes all converging in mutual exploration. And then the impostor was gone.

Audrey's stomach, simultaneously firm and soft, deepened my trance as I caressed it with the lightest of touches, terrified of popping the magical bubble. When my fingers reached the tantalising lower swell of her breasts, she closed her eyes and whispered almost inaudibly, 'If you go any further than that, you will have to make love to me.'

'Do you want me to stop?' I asked.

'Do I look like a woman who wants you to stop?'

'Is it safe?' I wondered.

'No, it's dangerous.'

'But I have no protection, no raincoat for my toy soldier. My pocket rocket lacks insulating foam, and Jumping Jack is recuperating at home.'

'Why don't you stop talking? You needn't worry. Anyway, I don't believe in the infallibility of the condom.'

I lost myself in this obscurely ecumenical moment, and only one course of action presented itself to me. The time had come to go the whole hog. It was as if nothing mattered nor even existed beyond our two bodies in the damp, dark woodland. I did not think of my girls, nor even of the prospect of taking my revenge against their mother. It did not even cross my mind that here, at last, was a wonderful opportunity to embed myself, not only culturally but *biologically*, in Northern Irish society. Instead, I thought only of the unearthly pleasure that awaited me within Audrey's garments. I stroked the smooth perfect curves of her breasts, I kissed her neck, and with a deft flick of my tongue I unfastened the strap of her brassière. Gently, I freed her breasts and played softly with her nipples between my fingers. They felt warm and alive, and I thought for a moment of new-born mice, squirming in their pink helplessness. Audrey gasped (had she had the same thought?) and then she sighed most exquisitely. She turned around, and leant backwards into me. I held her breasts in my hands more firmly now, enclosing them and squeezing their fullness. She moaned, and pressed her buttocks against my almost hysterical male parts. Rhythmically she applied pressure, occasionally turning her head back towards me so that our lips and tongues could indulge in moist, warm exchanges. I was beside myself with desire and, for the one and only time in my life to date, I went off in my shorts.[59]

'Was that what I think it was?' Audrey whispered.

'I am not sure. What do you think it was?'

I was playing for time. The whole encounter now hung in the balance. It was touch and go.

'It felt like you jumping the gun,' she complained. 'I hope that's not you finished now?'

'Of course not. There are plenty more fish in the sea.'

I was mildly disconcerted, but by no means panic-stricken. If there is one commodity of which I have never been short, it is able-bodied semen.

'Good,' she said. 'Come over here.'

She led me by the hand to a patch of wild garlic, fragrant and dripping, secluded and seductive. The fine rain pattered down around us, though the trees afforded some shelter. In the distance, we could hear the incessant drone of the city, but it could not touch us here.

Audrey turned to face me, and kissed me robustly and resoundingly on the lips. Our tongues wriggled and our teeth clonked. At intervals, we came up for air and began to undress one another. Training shoes, socks, shirts, shorts and sweaty pants formed a druidic ring around us. Naked at last, Audrey lay down on her back and gazed up at me with all the calm confidence of an experienced international goalkeeper. I can

---

[59] I mean, of course, that I shot my seeds, rather than that I departed the scene.

still see in my mind the pale beauty of her body against the lush green-and-brown of the forest floor. We made love within a mile or two of the city centre, unseen and unsuspected. I managed to delay my inevitable explosion much longer than I had anticipated, even without the restraining influence of little JJ, the man of rubber, and I had never before made a woman groan, grunt and snort quite as Audrey did on that afternoon. Beneath me she squirmed and gasped, and with her hands she grasped at the dark fallen leaves that carpeted the ground around. She took handfuls, and rubbed them into my back.[60] After a while, Audrey inverted me and pretended to be the dominant partner. She pressed into me, and I teased her nipples relentlessly with my tongue. This released by reflex from within her warm droplets of milk, which fell within and without my mouth. They tasted sweet and, in that moment, it seemed to me the most natural and beautiful thing that could possibly have occurred. Audrey reached her *orgasmo* in a wave of ecstatic peaks, while I ascended one mighty summit. When we had finished, we lay together on the ground, her head resting on my chest and mine on hers. We gazed up through the trees to the grey sky above. We said nothing, not even when an intrepid mountain biker passed by on the path, but each of us knew that this was a meeting we would not be repeating. Eventually, we dressed lazily in the drizzle, kissed once more, and went our separate ways.

---

[60] In the cut and thrust of the encounter, I realised that your so-called precocious ejaculation is grossly under-rated and hardly deserves its bad press.

Chapter 32

Regarding the lingering aroma of wild garlic and the identity of Jesús' fantastical feathered friend.

The following Friday, Connor once more entered our room at RUB with a copy of *The Orb* under his arm. My heart skipped a beat, then dropped abruptly into my boots.

'Cheer up, Jayzo,' he said. 'You've a face like a Lurgan spade, so you have. I've got something you'll like.'

He opened the newspaper and pointed towards one of the articles. It was only a short piece, and there was no picture. The headline read, 'Nothing In It, Says Lunchpack'. I read on. Monsieur Leconcombre had withdrawn from the talks concerning the television show, and had accused its producers of manipulating him to the detriment of his happy family life. He said, 'They have forced us to pretend that we are having *une liaison dangereuse*, and they even gave us lines that we were to say at the parties. I have had enough, and now I am going home.'

'Oh my word!' I said.

Connor looked perplexed. 'What's wrong? Aren't you relieved?'

'At present,' I said, 'I actually feel cheated.'

'But why?' he asked.

I could not tell him what was in my mind. For the first time, I gave my friend one of your porkers.

'I really don't know.'

'And while I'm asking the questions,' proceeded Connor, 'why do you smell so strongly of garlic? It's boggin', so it is.'

The smell sat heavily upon me for days, despite my obsessive attempts to eradicate it.[61] After each shower, I would summon my daughters and ask, 'Has it been washed away now?' Time after time, they would reply, 'No, you're still a complete minger.' I told them a version of the truth, which is all that one can expect in Ulster. They therefore knew that I had fallen over in the woods while out for a run, tumbling downwards through a bank of aromatic flowers. Then one grey afternoon, I stood in the school playground with a group of the other mothers, awaiting the emergence of our various children. Dila was at my side, saying something about how she had seen a policeman with no bones who had been all floppy. Audrey and I were endeavouring to behave as if all was as it had been before, though there was a coyness there that had no precedent. We were determined to keep the cat in the bag, but we nevertheless exchanged fertile glances, each of us surreptitiously checking the other for signs of embarrassment or regret. This left the art of conversation to the rest of the group.

'What's that smell?' said Deirdre. 'Who's been on the garlic?'

---

[61] Lady Macbeth was not a patch on me!

Audrey blushed. I looked away. Everybody else began sniffing the air. Dilatación prepared to pronounce.

'It's my Papá,' she said. 'He fell over in smelly flowers in the wood and now he's always stinky.'

Everybody laughed, but Marion was still flaring her nostrils in another direction, *como un perro de caza*.[62] 'That's funny,' she said. 'I could swear it's coming off Audrey.' Now the glances were whizzing around all over the shop like bullets in one that sold china. Dila ignored my attempts to silence her, for she had decided to settle the matter. 'I think Audrey fell over in the woods too,' she said. There was more giggling, to which Audrey responded by saying, 'No, love, but I did eat a very smelly meal last night. I expect it was that.' At this moment, the school doors opened and hordes of children came rampaging out. Puri performed her usual trick, which involved creeping round behind me, then running head first into my coccyx. I had never before been grateful for this distinctive mode of greeting.

I did not feel truly guilty for what had passed so fluently between me and Audrey in the woods. How could I bring myself to regret an encounter of such profound erotic beauty? More troublingly, I knew that Audrey and I would probably never have made love without my perception that Begoña had abandoned me for the Moorish giant. This, I now knew, had been a false perception, though it remained undeniable that Bego had tortured, humiliated and misled me. She was by no means an innocent party, but I had now exceeded her in disloyalty. I was troubled by the emotionally

---

[62] Like a hunting dog.

complicated situation in which I found myself, and I had another dream about that big and peculiarly reassuring bird. Its markings were very distinctive, and I determined to establish whether or not any such creature truly patrolled the planet's airways. I sought out my copy of *The Birds of Ireland*, and began leafing through its pages. Along the way, I encountered an unlikely gaggle of pink-footed geese, together with white-billed divers, storm petrels, whooper swans, shovelers, wigeons, velvet scoters, corncrakes, killdeers, turnstones, treecreepers, spotted flycatchers, buff-breasted sandpipers and lesser yellowlegs. There was great diversity, but I could find nothing that resembled my dream-bird. And then, on page 117, I saw it: the 'red-necked phalarope (rare)'. There could be no doubt. It had the same dark and slender beak, the same pale underparts, and the same dark back with the buff stripe. Most distinctively of all, the bird of my imagination clearly possessed the same 'red foreneck extending up sides of neck to rear of ear coverts'. In fact, the only significant difference was that the real bird was not three metres tall at the shoulder and capable of human speech.

I read on with interest, and discovered certain remarkable parallels between my own life and that of the red-necked phalarope. Like me, it could be 'surprisingly approachable'. Like me, it sometimes gave 'short, low-pitched prek or whit calls', and it was occasionally prone to 'spinning in circles or up-ending'. More uncannily still, I noticed the phrase, 'chick-rearing performed by males only'. This distinguished the species from most other birds, and the male phalarope evidently paid the price for his domesticity by being "drabber" than his partner. My soul felt warm. I had evidently found a kindled spirit, and I eagerly sought information on the bird's place of habitation. I learned that my chances of meeting one in the flesh were slim, yet I refused to be deflected. The red-necked phalarope had not nested in Ireland for several years and, even in better times, had been 'an extremely rare breeding species, present only in the summer and only at a single site in the far west'. It had, therefore, been a "blow-in", just like me, and my instinctive belief that this bird had lessons to teach me grew still stronger. A little more research revealed that its former breeding ground, "Annagh Marsh", was on the Belmullet peninsula in County Mayo. At this remote location, peculiar environmentalists, unable to find mates of their own, were busily attempting to lure the birds back by preserving the patchwork of open water, swamp vegetation and marsh that together constituted the phalarope's idea of a desirable residence. Thus far, they had laboured without success. I consulted a map of western Ireland, and learned that the Belmullet peninsula was virtually an Atlantic island, connected to north Mayo only by a narrow strip of land. I peered at its placenames – Gubastuckaun, Doonamo Point, Knocknalina, Illanleamnahelty, Ooghwee, Spinkadoon – and felt the landscape calling to me with an excitable tone ('Ooghwee!) There was also a village that delighted in the exquisitely topical name of Blacksod. This settled it, and in optimistic mood I determined to go off on one of your adventurous and wild goose chases.

I consulted Connor at RUB the next day, and he advised me that the entire Belmullet peninsula was now within the recently established "Spirit of Connaught" theme park. This encompassed a substantial portion of the ancient province, and was the initiative of a huge Dublin-Frankfurt conglomerate of holiday companies called "CeltoVax". This organisation had pumped euros intravenously into the region, arguing successfully that huge and easy profits could be made by luring and hooking foreign visitors. Enthusiastically, the inhabitants of Connaught agreed to tow the line. Connor found me a copy of the standard "community contract" on the internet, and I studied it with carefulness. Residents of the park agreed that, at weekends, on bank holidays and during the entire month of August, they would:

1. 'Whistle or sing ancient Irish melodies when perambulating about their communities. NB Particular attention is drawn to "I Buried my Wife and Danced on Top of Her", the designated theme tune for the park as a whole.
2. Attend Mass in a state of either (a) obsessive reverence or (b) extreme but good-natured drunkenness.
3. Speak in Irish (or something that might pass for it) when in conversation with other natives; but address visitors in English, telling them tall tales about strange speaking fish, ancient giants, little people, freedom-fighting ancestors, banshees etc.'

There were 162 additional guidelines, but the room at my disposal is too small for their comprehensive *regurgitación*.

Connor encouraged me to go, advising that one could

not fully understand Ulster unless one also acquainted oneself with the twenty-six counties of the Republic. It was, he said, a conspicuous lacuna in my knowledge, and he apologised for not having drawn attention to it sooner. Concepción, on the other hand, was less than positive about my plans for a trip to Belmullet. Of course, I did not really want to take any of the girls with me, but what choice did I have? She said that my projected tour would cause her to miss Grace's birthday party which was going to be "class" because they were having a disco and everyone said that Rufus (the stud horse in her year group) was a really good dancer. I refused to relent, and after a while Conchi was partially carried along by her little sisters' excitement at the idea of going on a hunt for a bird with a red neck that Papá had dreamt about. And so, one Friday afternoon, I packed them all into the car and set off westwards.

Chapter 33

Concerning what befell when Jesús finally met the bird of his dreams, a story as implausible as it is true.

We journeyed through dark, heavy showers and pockets of bewildering sunshine. I attempted to amuse the girls with my conversation, but they were frequently disrespectful. On the road, we passed under a walkway, and I said with a voice of cheer, 'Look, girls, it is one of those bridges that is just for Presbyterians.' They all began to laugh, and Conchi said, 'Och, Papá, you mean "pedestrians".' Crossly, I switched on the radio and concentrated my mind on the news that a republican group in north Belfast had stolen two giraffes from the zoo, and then released them onto a Protestant street in the east of the city. Here, they had terrorised the residents for two hours, principally by consuming their shrubs. A tearful woman from the afflicted neighbourhood said, 'It's a disgrace, so it is. From wurr I'm standing, the Troubles ur getting wuss, not better. You shud see my forsythia!'

After three long hours on the road, we entered the 'Spirit of Connaught' theme park by passing through a large plastic rainbow that arched elegantly from one side of the road to the other. A waifish maiden, white of skin, black of hair, and clad in traditional Irish dress, stopped our car and said, 'Good sir, will ye spare ten euros for a starving mudder of eleven?' I told her that I would not for I had nothing to give. At this, she leant her head closer to the window and I winced, anticipating the proclamation of some ancient and malevolent Celtic curse. Instead, she said, with just a trace of irritation, 'I'm not really a beggar. It's the entrance fee – ten euros, please sir.'

As we travelled onwards, the girls bombarded the back of my head with inanities until I could stomach no more. When I spotted an elderly priest leaning against a wall beside a hand-written sign that read 'WANTED – HARD FILL', I stopped the car and ran to him in a desperate quest for adult conversation. I asked him if he knew of a pleasant place for lunch, and he kindly recommended an establishment called 'World of Famine', just a few more kilometres along our road. I invited him to join us, but he said, 'No thanks, I'm paid a retainer for standing here – no offence, but it's a contractual matter.' We located the recommended establishment without difficulty, and admired the artificial human figure who balanced precariously on its roof. His single leg had been made from an old rake, his limbs from coathangers, and his head from an orange football with a visible puncture. He looked too weak to move, but his faded black shirt bore the motto, 'Slick FM – We Rock All Night'. Most of the visitors were attending a guided tour of the various peasant hovels before lunch, but the girls said they were 'absolutely starving' and so we made one of your B-lines for the so-called T-room. This offered a range of potato meals based on recipes from all over the planet, and some of them were surprisingly edible. The walls were imaginatively decorated with evocative objects from the local past: a plastic tricycle, a shiny red violin, and the head of a bison. In one corner, a couple of musicians performed a rather lascivious Irish song about a woman from Dublin with a taste for cocks and muscles.

Later that afternoon, we finally reached the Mullet. For some time, I drove around in circles, cursing the map and all who had a hand in it, while the girls, hungry for visual stimulation, gouged their eyes on a feast of Connaught curiosities: a young man on a bicycle, being pulled along with breakneck celery by a small bus; a neat white cottage, the front room of which was packed, from floor to ceiling, with hay; and a sheep that had been dyed half green and half red. Eventually, I located another of those thoughtfully-positioned leaning locals, this time a ruddy-faced farmer, and stopped to ask for directions. He was in the process of feeding a bacon and avocado sandwich to a dog on a lead, but he willingly suspended it for a moment in order to assist me. This little man was extremely courteous, and told me where to go in no uncertain terms, but he also said that Annagh Marsh was 'a queer wet place, only fit for banshees, birds and beards'. I was unsure of his meaning, partially because he sported the most hilarious comedy accent you could possibly imagine.

The farmer's directions proved viable, and before long we had made our way to the last known nesting site of the red-necked phalarope in Ireland. Of course, I knew in my guts that we would not find one, but I withheld this infor-mation from my notoriously jumpy offspring. We leant on a locked metal gate and peered through it to an expanse of soggy grassland, reedbeds and open water. Silence sat upon the world, and it felt for a moment as if all life had been ground like nutmeg to a halt. Then Concepción spoke.

'There aren't any birds at all in this God-forsaken place, so there aren't.'

'Be patient, child,' I said, 'Perhaps Dame Luck will smile upon us.'

This was a good line, and I sensed that I had the beating of her at last.

'Dame Luck is a Lame Duck,' she replied.

'Ock, of course there are birds,' countered Puri, 'you just have to go and find them. Come on, Papá, we need our welly-boots on.'

As if to commend her optimism, a big bird with a bent beak flew over us, and its plaintive, liquid warbling filled the air. It settled some way off, amongst the reeds. I consulted my book and successfully identified it as a curlew.

We donned our boots, and the girls all managed to surmount the gate after a thoughtful leg-over from me. On the other side, I reluctantly held Dila's hand, and for a time we made reasonable progress through the dismal marsh. We headed towards the curlew's cry, squelching and slurping with every footstep. It was heavy going, and soon the brown water of the bog began to invade our boots. I now began to get cold feet about the whole project. Then, in the twinkling of an eye, interesting events began to occur. First, there was a new bird call – a sort of "whit" or perhaps a "prek" – from a position just a little to our right. Then, predictably enough, the manifold shortcomings of my children came home to roost. Before I could react to the new bird, there was another call, loud, insistent and very close. It sounded like this: 'Papá, help, my boot's been sucked off by some fockin' animal! Come quickly, I'm drowning, so I am!' Purificación was in trouble. She stood on one leg in the marsh, the other leg flapping around in the air as she desperately tried to maintain a balanced outlook on life. I released Dila's hand and waded towards her, but before I arrived she collapsed backwards into the swamp with a satisfying (to me) 'SPLAT'. I expected her to scream, but instead she lay quite still, as if comatose, and gazed blankly at the grey clouds overhead. She had obviously failed to make good her shortfall, and – worse still – I suspected that her mind had been boggled. As I lifted her up, we both heard Dilatación fall over behind us, at which the smallest of my burdens let fly with a shriek that fairly rented out the skies.

This was when matters began to go awry. The primordial scream of Dilatación terrified our mystery bird, which now shot up like a deranged firework from the reeds with a shriek of its own and flew in panic, straight at Concepción. Both parties attempted to swerve at the same time, and the terrified bird hurtled right into Conchi's thick mop of uncombed black hair. She yelled and shook her head in a violent display of ill manners. The bird struggled to escape, but with each desperate manoeuvre it merely worsened its predicament. I watched aghast, and tried to squelch my way closer, somewhat hampered by the presence of Purificación on my right shoulder. By the time we reached Conchi, she had her eyes closed and was emitting a curious 'arp–arp–arp' call. The bird now looked resigned, like a disgraced politician who knows his term in office to be over. I glanced at Dila to confirm that she had not been sucked into the ground completely. She remained both visible and docile (for one reason or another). Next, I set Puri down on a spongy tussock, and peered at Conchi's latest hair accessory. It looked half dead, but it had a wonderfully warm and rich russet patch on its neck.

I knelt down beside Conchi and hissed, 'Stay calm and don't move a millimetre. Do you know what it is? It's our phalarope. Can you believe it?'

'Get it off me,' Concepción growled.

Attracted by the spectacle, Dila had somehow hauled herself out of the mire and now she leant heavily against me. Puri drew closer too, and we all contemplated the bird, which stared impassively back at us. Gently, I cradled it in my loving hands and tried to make reassuring phalarope sounds. Puri and Dila soon joined in, and we 'whitted' and 'preked' as convincingly as we could (though Conchi was clearly saying 'whet' and 'prik' instead, while staring insubordinately at me). Our efforts seemed to keep the bird calm, though it also seemed possible that it was preparing to shuffle off this mortal coil. Either way, the world had slowed once more.

Not for long, however. Moments later, the superficial tranquillity was broken by yet another new sound. An angry male voice was echoing through the heavens. 'What in de name of God do you tink you're doing?' it asked, adding, 'Dis is a nature reserve, and access is restricted.' We looked wildly around us, alarmed by the belligerent tone. A large figure, shrouded in dense hair, was advancing upon our position.

'Heaven help us,' I urged. 'What is that?'

The girls were trembling.

'Is it human?' asked Conchi.

'It's half man, half beard,' whispered Puri, 'and I think our number is up.'

Fortunately, we were over-reacting: it was only an Irish ecologist, but he certainly cut a frightening figure as he swelled up out of the primeval swamp. His boots came up to his nipples, where they were greeted by his descending beard. He had clearly evolved himself with precisely this landscape in mind, and now he was making warlike gestures with at least two of his arms.

'Did you not read de sign?' he asked. 'Dis is an important breeding ground, and we're trying . . . '

He stopped abruptly as he caught sight of Conchi and the pretty bird on her shoulder.

'Holy Mary!' he exclaimed. 'It's a phalarope – a male. Dat's de first one we've had here in nigh twenty year!'

Momentarily, his joy trumped his fury, but when I tried to clamber aboard the bandwagon of his positivity, he ran me over like a dog.

'It is beautiful, isn't it?' I asked. 'Are you the Keeper of the Swamp?'

He had questions of his own.

'What have you done to it? What kind of irresponsible eejit are you? Are you aware dat you've placed my life's work in jeopardy?'

I tried to deal with each of his enquiries in turn, but

263

soon sensed that he was not truly interested in my responses. This made me angry.

'It may be your life's work,' I said, 'but it's my sole mate. I dream about this creature day and night, and it rescues me whenever the sporting superstars punish me with their racquets. You only love it because your weird beard prevents you from mating with a member of your own species. I love it here in my heart.'

This shut him the fock up, I am proud to say. He did not speak for a full minute. Eventually, he said, 'We must release de bird immediately. See if it's hurt, den hope for de best. And I'm going to want to take your details.'

'I have already tried to ease it free,' I said, 'but it is well and truly enmeshed. I do not know what we can do.'

'You've done plenty,' he snapped. 'Now listen, I want all of you to stay here quietly while I go back to my van for some scissors. We'll have to cut it free, and soon. No loud noises. No sudden movements.'

With this, he slomped off towards the road, and I turned my attention to Conchi.

'Now, do not panic. I believe that the nice swamp-gentleman intends to trim your locks.'

She was not happy.

'No, he can't, he mustn't. You'll have to stop him. Fight him if necessary. Like you did that newspaper man. He's not properly qualified. Look at him, for God's sake. He patently knows nothing about hair-care.'

I was so anxious to induce co-operation that I broke out in a rash promise.

'We can rectify the situation at home. I will make it up

to you. The best hairdresser in Belfast will come to our house.'

I felt a slight twinge in my wallet, for I knew that this would not go cheep (my coiffeurs were not exactly overflowing at this time). I added, as an afterthought,

'But it's your own fault. In future, if a bird flies at you, just stand still.'

Man of Bog now returned, armed not with scissors but with a large axe. By this stage, Conchi looked terribly annoyed, but her new image consultant scared her so effectively that she accepted her fate in grim silence. I had to admire his style. When he had finished, she looked a pitiful mess, with most of the hair missing on one side of her head. Man of Bog now attempted a rare gesture of tenderness.

'Would you be wanting me to do de udder side?' he asked.

'No, I wouldn't. Leave me alone.'

To my shame, I now began to giggle like a girl.

'It is not that bad,' I said. 'Those lop-sided hairstyles are quite fashionable at the moment!'

'What do *you* know?' she hissed.

The delicate phalarope was still in my hands, and it remained there while Man of Bog carefully pulled the last strands of Conchi's severed hair from its legs, wings and neck.

'Why is its neck red?' asked Dila.

'It's embarrassed. Wouldn't *you* be?' replied Puri.

Man of Bog now examined the phalarope and pronounced it mercifully free from life-threatening physical injuries.

'Now, let it go, very gently, onto de ground,' he

instructed.

I did as I was told, but the bird was strangely reluctant to depart. It merely sat there, occasionally twitching its head. Then, to the wonderment of all, it walked calmly over to me, and pecked three times quite deliberately at my boot.

'It's trying to tell you something, Papá,' said Puri. 'Just like in that film about the girl dog who's always being chased by that gang of boy dogs.'[63]

'No,' said Man of Bog, 'it's disorientated. Something's not right.'

As if to prove him wrong, the phalarope suddenly flapped its wings, took off, and flew three perfect fluttery circles around us. Having completed this precise manoeuvre, it turned tail and flew away from us, heading north-east with a fresh air of purpose.

'It wants you to go too,' said Puri. 'It's telling you to leave this land while you still can.'

Sadly, I began to wonder if both she and the bird had a point. I looked around me at this watery world in which human footsteps turned instantaneously into deeply depressed puddles. What was a man of Andalusia, born in the sun and raised on the vine, doing in such a place as this? For the time being, I had no answer, and so I buried the question in the shifting desert sands of my mind, hoping that it would quietly disintegrate there, but knowing in my loins that, for lack of moisture, it would not.

Our business in Mayo was nearly at an end. Man of Bog subjected me to one further diatribe, during which he

---

[63] See above, p. 202.

promised to inform the newspapers and then hunt me down like a common criminal if the phalarope should fail to return. I did feel an uncertain sympathy for him, and obligingly I presented him with my real name (though in anagrammatic form).[64] With confused thoughts rampaging like Visigoths through my head, I shepherded the children back towards the car, and we began our long homeward journey. They were all weary, troubled and filthy, and for hours they would not leave me in peace. I told them that they would feel better when I got them home and sponged off them, but it made little difference. Conchi, in particular, had been plunged into a state of vanity-insanity, and she snapped incessantly at my Achilles' tendon all the way home.

---

[64] The best that I could do under such pressure was Steven Charan Zeus-Jus, but he wrote it down without complaint.

Chapter 34

*Concerning what happened when Jesús stretched out his legs
to show the fathers of Ulster a thing or two.*

I received a phone-call from our social worker shortly after
the saga of the disappearing phalarope.

'Yes, yes, the Fool of April,' I said as she re-entered my
atmosphere. 'Of course I remember. However could I
forget?'

'Sorry to bother you,' she said, 'but I need to arrange a
meeting in the next few weeks, with you and all three of
your daughters. And your wife, if she's available. Do you
recall, I mentioned it as a possibility?'

'*Madre mía!*' I cried. 'Can you not leave us alone for five
little minutes? Just because one of them caught a rare breed
in her hair — it could have happened to absolutely anyone.'[65]

'You're probably right, but I should have followed up on
our initial conversation anyway.' She paused. 'When would
suit?'

---

[65] I assumed, correctly, that she had heard about the incident. *The Belfast
Observer* had run a story with the headline, 'RUB Spaniard Traumatises
Endangered Bird'.

I feigned sudden anxiety. 'Sorry, I must attend to a pressing matter – Dilatación is trapped under the fridge again. And Puri is trying to rescue her with a pitchfork. I shall say *hasta luego*. You know how attentive I am. I will call you back.'

Somehow, I neglected so to do. Mizzz Stewart made a number of clumsy advances, hammering away at me but unable to pin me down. For once, I had the enthusiastic co-operation of the girls. I explained to them that she was, in reality, an alien named 'Vog' from the planet SocServ, and that she fed voraciously on the enthusiasms of little children. It was imperative that we avoid all contact with her, for the security of the Earth. They were much taken with the idea, and willingly scurried off to secrete silently beneath their beds whenever I shouted 'Vog descending! Hide like a rhinoceros!' Meanwhile, I would explain to Mizzz Stewart that they had all gone out to participate in wholesome recreations such as pond-dipping, flower-pressing, bird-watching, rabbit-culling and ecumenical dancing. Vog may only have appeared a couple of times, but I knew full well that in northern Europe this amounted to an open-shut case of full-on sexual harassment. I was also aware that she would eventually succeed in dragging me down the long dark tunnel of justice, but I had no intention of smoothing her passage.

Fortunately, I had other and more uplifting fish to fry. The Lagan Meadows Primary School held its annual "sports day" early in the month, a glittering new experience for us all. After disposing of Dila, I rambled up to the school playing fields in order to join a humming throng of parents.

For once, the daddies were publicly underpinning the mummies, presumably tempted by the competitive nature of the event and the prospect of a vicarious fixture of adrenaline. I circulated amongst my female friends, distributing oral favours, and I was introduced for the first time to some of their husbands. Audrey's man, Sean, had something in his eye that may have been suspicion, but he was tolerably cordial, all things considered. I did not speak to him for long, and we both welcomed the distraction of the morning's first races: sprints for the children from the school's nursery class. The girls all trotted obediently down the track, looking sideways at one another with friendly but quizzical expressions ('Is this *really* what they want us to do?') They could not have cared less about the race, and they seemed oblivious to the encouraging cries of their parents. I studied the adult etiquette with care. I sensed that some of the other fathers might be seeking opportunities to pour scorn upon me, and I had no wish to make a receptacle of myself. The expectation seemed to be that intensely competitive urges would be packaged and presented to the world as emotions of universal benevolence. There was a lot of parental repression underway.

The nursery boys, on the other hand, repressed nothing and, in comparison to their feminine class-mates, were like another species altogether, a crowd of flesh-ripping carnivores in amongst the meadow-munchers. The closing stages of their race saw two miniature sprinters vying for supremacy in adjacent lanes. Then, when one seemed to gain a crucial advantage with ten metres to go, the other reached across and grabbed his collar, tugging him to the ground before crossing the line unchallenged. The judges then outraged a section of the crowd by awarding them joint first place. This was not the only race in which blatant cheating was rewarded with high honours, and thus the children learnt one of life's most important lessons.

Indeed, the scope for cheating became progressively more extensive as the morning proceeded. Straight sprinters chose between false starting, obstruction and drug abuse (there was a boy in P5 whose urine was crying out for analysis). But in the races requiring the balancing of strange domes on one's head, or various manoeuvres with hula-hoops, or hopping with a beanbag between one's thighs, the opportunities for deceit were myriad. The P3 beanbag race was won, for example, by a boy called Adam who had devised a method of cramming the small pyramidal cushion right up between his buttocks, so that he could run and not hop. It was several minutes before the object re-emerged in the wake of his villainous performance. None of the children who emerged victorious in the hoop-skipping races actually skipped through their hoops, except in a very tokenistic fashion at the beginning and the end. The winner of the P4 dome-balancing contest had to have the red plastic hemisphere removed from his head by force, and we all saw the string-like white substance that lingered suspiciously in his hair.

I also noticed that some of the older girls, unlike their little sisters at nursery, appeared to be almost as desperate for success as the boys. The empirical evidence suggested that boys are born competitive, while girls learn to be so. Lastly, it was abundantly plain that for the unlucky few

– the dumpy, gangly or excruciatingly nervous kids who brought up their rears in every race – sports day was an *humillación*. There were fallers and stallers, wailers and failures, weepers and creepers, all visibly traumatised and in need of consolation from their mothers. I have heard it said by soggy northern liberal types that all sporting contests should be abolished at school, in order to protect the sensibilities of such souls, but I say, 'That is life, kid – you learn or you burn.' Conchi and Puri exerted themselves keenly enough, but both came second in their races. I was furious with myself for not having coached them with greater creativity and expertise. Luckily, however, the family honour was comprehensively restored by my own efforts in the final race of the morning. 'Would competitors please come forward for the Fathers' Race?' said the Master of Ceremonies, to my unmitigated jubilation.

This, a straight sprint across sixty metres, provided a most fitting climax to the proceedings, for it brought together the most competitive members of the entire herd. I had no inkling that such an event was in the offing, and my preparation was therefore next-door to non-existent. Interested daddies, sixty-five in total, gathered on the specially extended starting line, and all but one of them maintained the pretence of harmless fun as they chatted to one another. Needless to say, I was the silent one, and I stood alone and resolute in my lane, systematically stretching the various muscle groups in my understandably agitated legs. I was a little anxious about my Achilles' heel, but I knew in my heart that I could not afford to look this gifted racehorse in the mouth. No, this time I would have to milk it for all it was worth. On completion of my exercises, I glared down the track at the finishing tape and I focused my mind upon it, excluding all other considerations. I developed a little of your funnel vision and I was determined not to be sucked into the deceitful exchanges of the other fathers. Mr. Fiscal Leeway called us to the line. A few of the participants coughed nervously as an expectorant hush dribbled over the crowd. I should have known that the other competitors would falsify their starts, and more importantly that they would not be called back for jumping on the gun. My appealing naïveté meant that I began running with a two-metre disadvantage, but I managed not to panic. I raised my head gradually and concentrated on establishing a good rhythm. I lifted my knees high, pumped with my arms, and relaxed all non-essential muscles. My face was a picture of relaxation, but my limbs were like sculpted bronze (if a little more flexible). At twenty metres, I was already hauling over the others, and by forty metres I was out in front, away and clear. I was flying, and the ladies in the crowd were going literally insane (three of them were later institutionalised). I broke the tape with my pectorals throbbing to a chorus of your so-called 'ooze' and 'arse.' I drew gradually to a halt, and turned to offer my condolences to the other daddies. They looked understandably disgruntled, and I can honestly say that my heart went out to them. I was anxious not to appear patronising, but I made a point of patting each of them on the back in turn while saying, 'Hard luck, mayet' in my best Ulster voice. Audrey's husband was, I must say, rather more generous in defeat than were some of the others, and he offered me an encouraging 'Up Yours!' as I went walkabout amongst the ladies.

After a victory of such moment, I found it rather difficult to deflate my bulging air-sack, and I soon realised that I simply could not wait an entire year for my next athletic adventure. Then I asked myself an intriguing question: what was to prevent me from competing in the fathers' races at the sports days held by other schools? This was a relatively quiet time at RUB, for the exams were already finished, as was most of my marking. In the mornings, the girls were all fully occupied in school and nursery, and I could not really motivate myself to indulge in any scholarship of my own. This, surely, was an opportunity too enthralling to miss. Furthermore, exposure to a wider cross-section of local society would surely advance me along the obstacle-strewn road towards complete cultural absorption. So I telephoned the Belfast Education and Libraries Board, and told a secretary there that I was an international academic engaged in a study of primary school provision in Northern Ireland. She obligingly e-mailed me a full list of schools, and it was then a simple matter of phoning a selection of these, posing as a parent who had mislaid the information regarding sports day. Before long, I had compiled a punishing fortnight-long itinerary of races at seventeen different schools.

My first outing, to the Botanic Primary School, was mildly stressful. I won the race by half of its total distance, but I nearly exposed myself when the teacher at the finishing line approached me with a clipboard and said, 'Can I just take your name for our results sheet?' I had not expected this, and stupidly I told the truth. She then asked me for the names of my children. I said, 'Concepción and Purificación Sánchez Ventura,' and she looked first surprised and then suspicious. She said, 'Those aren't names I recognise, so they're not, but your face definitely looks familiar. Would you wait here for a minute?' She turned away, took five steps and then stopped abruptly. Before she could rotate, however, I had vaulted the fence with my bicycle and was out of sight. 'You must refine your strategy,' I muttered to myself as I sped off towards home.

My performances at the other schools were far more polished, and I affected a range of local accents in order to escape discovery. All in all, I am proud to report that I emerged victorious on fifteen of the sixteen remaining occasions. The fathers of Ulster did not know what had hit them. I wore a variety of clever but unobtrusive work-related disguises in order to guard against public *reconocimiento*. At Dundonald, I triumphed as a postman who had just completed his roundabout. At Donaghadee, I romped home as a radiologist. At St. Kieran's, the heavy overalls of a council workman restricted my freedom of movement somewhat, but I still pulverised the field with all the concentrated and pounding aggression of a pneumatic drill. My only defeat came at St. Aloysius Primary School in Lisburn, and the memory of it still rankles my ankles. Here, I was soundly beaten by a 6ft 4in American called Clunt Biskitt who, it transpired, was not a school daddy at all but instead a "college football star" from Los Angeles, visiting Belfast on an international exchange of Christians. As readers will no doubt recall, he also went on to win the 400m hurdles in the Madrid Olympics (the first white man to do so in years). Biskitt had agreed to offer some voluntary sports coaching in the school, and had been asked by the Principal and PTA to do them the honour of participating in the Fathers' Race. Naturally, I complained, but was told that the children had wanted to see 'the big fella' run, and that it was all 'just a bit of fun'. Like fock it was!

Chapter 35

In which Jesús loosens his marbles as Mizzz Stewart turns up yet again like a bad-smelling penny.

The day after my last race, I attended the history department's final Examiners' Board Meeting. It was a lamentably poor substitute for my athletic exertions, and I felt restless in my bones. With the gift of behindsight, I can say that my bloodstream was still coursing with adrenaline, something that can only have exacerbated my feelings of unease. It is less clear that either of these factors fully explains or justifies my behaviour on that very peculiar morning. For some time, I had been doubting my vacation as an academic, and asking myself again and again the self-same question: 'What is the purpose of my professional life?' True, my book on paint had been well-reviewed in its English version by the academic community, but it was without doubt a commercial disappointment, selling fewer than two copies in the open marketplace during its first month. Fellow historians were falling over one another to compliment me in learned journals, and they almost seemed to delight in the fact that nobody else was reading it. They said it was 'challenging', 'not by any means an easy read' and 'rather inaccessible, but no less brilliant for that.' The book sold for £125, and the most extensively quoted section, I noted with suspicion, was the so-called "blurb" that the publisher had gushed onto my jacket. I had proved my credentials as an intellectual heavyweight, but had I done anything to alter the ways in which Everyman and his lady-friend experienced the world?

With such thoughts drifting like Portuguese Men-of-War in the water on my brain, I glanced around the table and contemplated my colleagues. At the far end, Mark Down, our pudgy pink Examinations Officer, was in his element, chairing the meeting and using his heavy hands to heap scorn upon those students whose marks were wayward or hopeless. The tedium might have been broken by the morning's occasional group discussions of particular issues, but since these were invariably about "preponderance", "conceptual equivalents", "aggregation" and "differential weighting", it was not. On and on it went . . . 'Differential weighting for Godot,' Connor whispered to a glazed model of myself.

The first three hours were just about bearable, but I began to lose my mind as we pushed on beyond this. I could have swept the sand from an Atlantic beach in the time we had been sitting there. 'So that's a 2.1 at 70, just missing the first class because the candidate only has 6 marks in the upper bracket, one of those curious anomalies that our system throws up.' Dr. Down was still speaking. He loved anomalies, having no children of his own. The pressure was building steadily inside my normally self-contained head. 'And if she appeals against us, then so be it,' he said happily. The atmosphere in Seminar Room 2 was oppressive. There is nothing quite like the smell of unwashed, unwanted academics huddled together in a stale room. The windows were tightly shut, for fear of student spies dropping from the eaves with burnt ears. I gazed out, and watched a carefree couple kissing, tongue-in-cheek, beside a lamppost.

'This candidate would have just scraped a 2.1, but our external examiner saw fit to bring the mark for HIS247 down from 66 to 55, which drags the overall average back to 57.8, and so we have yet another 2.2 at 58.'

'That is a pity,' said Professor Boyle with genuine sincerity, and Dr. Down conjured up a cruel little smile.

For me, the distinction between thought and speech now began to dissolve. Until this point, my groaning at their droning had taken place strictly within the four walls of my head, but I fear that it had now begun to encroach on the exterior world. I was attracting one or two glances, and I recall a fleeting, fast retreating realisation that they thought *I* was the peculiar one! I next imagined that there were visitors from another planet hovering over the School of History in an invisible, invincible space craft, preparing to take me and me alone away from all this. Telepathically, they encouraged me to prepare myself, and I knew that the finger of destiny was stimulating me. I closed my eyes, put my hands above my head with fingers extended, and hummed a high note. Then, three octaves below, I softly began chanting 'The time is ripe. The time is ripe.' I had expected the beam from their tractor to feel warm and enveloping, but when it began its work the sensation was much more like that created by a sharp jab in the ribs from Connor McCann.

I opened my eyes, and found that the glances of my colleagues had matured into stares.

'What on earth are you doing?' asked Dr. Down, with unveiled contempt.

'Awaiting transportation to another planet,' I responded truthfully. 'And what are *you* doing?'

'I am trying to chair an important meeting, and your behaviour is exceedingly disruptive.' He glanced sideways at Professor Boyle, and muttered, 'He's been nothing but trouble since he came.'

'What are you trying to inseminate?' I asked, quite reasonably.

There was no answer.

Connor was leaning towards me with his eyes agog and his lips ajar. His spirit counselled caution, but it was too late. I was angry, all bottled up, and it showed in my fluid outburst. I could not contain myself, and I sprayed the room in the following manner:

'Ock,' I began, 'you're awa in the fockin' heed, a borrn fockin' eejit. If ye will nat shut yer gapin' gawb, yer fer the fockin' glory hole, so y'are. And another thing: thass fud is fockin' shite. Only twa fockin' tatties, and wunnuvem a fockin' conker.'

They all looked suitably stunned, like baby Canadian seals. Connor's face was now in his hands, but I heard him mumble a question that began with the words, 'What kind of monster . . . ?' The rest of them met my tirade with the violence of silence. Nobody spoke for at least a minute. Then, at last, Professor Boyle attempted one of his famously emollient ejaculations:

'I'm afraid to say, Jesús, that such language is not acceptable. It is very warm in here, and I know you've a lot on your mind. But even so. Why not go for a walk and come back in when you feel a little calmer? You and I should perhaps have a proper conversation later on today?'

His tone was so soothing that I began to regret my diatribe almost immediately. I nodded sheepishly, bleated apologetically, and allowed myself to be herded from the room by a still-yappy Dr. Down. I did not return for three days, by which time – to my surprise – the meeting was finished.

The next day, I took the girls out to the Giant's Ring in the afternoon and we ran up and down the steep grassy slopes of the ancient circular earthwork. When they were tired, we sat on top of the bank in the drizzle, and, like Neolithic hunter-gatherers at the conclusion of a fruitful foray, consumed our Belgian chocolate biscuits and mango juice. They knew that I was unhappy, and before long they began to irritate me by offering unwelcome consolation and advice.

'You need a mamá,' said Dila, 'to look after you.'

'Perhaps you should get your hair cut shorter, and maybe put in some highlights,' suggested Concepción. 'You'd be surprised what a difference it can make to your self-esteem.'

'A boy at my school says you're a single parrot, and that's why you're so scruffy,' added Puri.

'When will Mamá be coming home?' enquired Conchi.

'Just a few more days,' I said. 'She can't wait to see you all.'

'Papá, do dogs *know* they're dogs?' wondered Dila.

I searched for an appropriate answer, but before I found

one Puri changed the subject with another, slightly less taxing, question.

'Papá,' she said, 'if we sit up here in the open, isn't it easier for Vog to find us?'

'Don't worry about her,' I said. 'This is a magic protective ring and nobody from the planet SocServ can walk upon it. Her feet would fry up like bacon in a matter of seconds. And even if she found us, we know what to do. You just have to remember not to be enthusiastic about anything and not to say anything funny. Then she cannot feed, and she will probably die.'

'A most painful death!' chortled Purificación.

Speak of the devil and pop! goes the weasel. A few days later, we arrived home from the shops during the afternoon to find Vog squatting hopefully on our doorstep. She had cornered us, and reluctantly I allowed her over my threshold. The girls played their parts far too well, and the next hour was excruciating in consequence. We assembled in the living room, and I endeavoured without any success to relax. Conchi and Puri were calm by comparison, and highly focused on their goal of surviving the encounter. When our visitor asked if she might speak to the girls alone for a few minutes, they stifled shrieks of alarm and begged me to remain. They also kept a close eye on Dila, evidently fearing that she might let the side and thus the planet down. I was permitted to hold my ground. Vog began smoothly enough, but she became visibly more agitated and intense as her many questions were answered, one after another, by the deadpan trio. I tried to jolly them along a little, but they stuck doggishly to the script.

'And did you have fun when you went birdwatching in Mayo?' asked Vog.

'No, not really,' said Conchi.

'Boring, actually,' agreed Puri.

'Now, you had a wee accident didn't you, Conchi? Can you tell me what happened?'

'Whoosh,' said Dila with a sudden burst of energy, 'she took a bird right in the head!'

'Shh!' warned her sisters.

'Nothing really happened that I can remember,' said Conchi. 'There was a bird, but it wasn't very interesting at all.'

'It got stuck in her hair,' I explained. 'A freakish accident, and we resolved the matter with the Keeper of the Swamp, as you probably know.'

'And do you like your new short hairstyle?' asked Vog, desperately trying to stimulate some conversational flow.

'It's OK I suppose,' said Conchi, 'but I wouldn't exactly say I'm *enthusiastic* about it.'

She peered curiously at her interviewer for any signs of malnourishment.

'Purification,' Vog went on, 'are you looking forward to when your mummy next comes home?'

'Not very much. I suppose it'll be OK.'

'Have you not missed her?'

'Not really.'

'I suppose she's alright if you like that sort of thing,' added Concepción.

Vog looked at me, so I explained, 'They may be just a little resentful, but they are always happy to see her.'

The creature from SocServ glanced at her notepad, and coughed nervously.

'Is she dying?' whispered Dila.

'Not yet,' replied Puri, 'but soon.'

And so it went on. I could tell that Mizzz Stewart was nervous as she and I stood in the driveway at the conclusion of the encounter. 'I have certain concerns, Dr Sánchez Ventura,' she said. 'Last time, Purification seemed such a lively child, but this time they're all so flat and unresponsive. I've never seen bright children behave in such a manner.'

'I expect you think they've got a touch of your so-called asparagus syndrome, but I can assure you that they have not. I told them to be polite, and that was the result, I'm afraid. Please do not forget, they were born into a different culture.'

Obviously, I could not tell her that she was Vog from the planet SocServ, no matter how ingenious the notion may have been.

'To set my mind at rest,' she went on, 'I think I should see each of them individually, perhaps without your being in the room, and I want to call somebody else in to observe. I'd be most grateful for your co-operation. I'll be in touch during the next day or two.'

And with that, she left the scene, allowing me no time to respond. Shell-shocked, I crawled back inside to a hysterical greeting from the triumphant triplets. 'A most painful death!' they chanted.

Chapter 36

In which Jesús fulfils his wife again, to the justifiable relief of the eager reader.

Begoña had been in Rome for some days, locked in negotiation with the marketing people at one of Europe's most fashionable manufacturers of cosmetics. I learned from the newspapers that the company had been selling smells for ten remarkable years, and was planning to produce something fragrant and steamy with which to mark its territory. This was as much as I knew. I was, therefore, rather taken from behind when a sudden eruption of publicity poured boiling lava upon me. It was announced in the so-called media that Begoña had been chosen to promote "Decade", an alluring and innovative new perfume for slightly older ladies. This was evidently quite an achievement for Begoña, and the tabloid papers were brimming over with it. Journalists phoned me with offensive regularity. I deflected them by pretending to be a very pretty waitress from my past life with whom I had once grappled memorably at a *tapas* bar in Granada. I would pick up the phone, and coo like a turtle dove, '*Hola*. My name is María Inmaculada. How may I serve you, Señor?' On one occasion, the phonecall came not from a newspaper, but from my fast-growing Begoña.

'I *knew* you were lusting after that little cat, but you denied it, didn't you? Well now we know the truth,' she said sharply.

'In Ireland,' I countered, 'we will never know the truth. Calm yourself, Begoña. *Qué pasa?*'

'I am well. Have you heard the news?'

'*Sí, sí.* Congratulations on being selected as the Decade front-lady. How does it feel, and what does it mean?'

'It is very exciting, but I will have to spend some time in Rome.'

'You surprise me.'

'I *will* surprise you,' she said. 'I have negotiated a very favourable contract, so that I can be at home most of the time. I work one week each month for a large package of euros, and the rest of the time I belong to you and the girls.'

'That is wonderful,' I said, though my heart was less sure than my tongue. 'You have decided to be a wife and mother again.'

'Well,' she said, 'it is partly for that reason, of course, but also because my contract prohibits me from undertaking any other promotional work. I can keep the Earl of Sandwich because he is so local, but I will have to sell Shrinking Violet.'

The girls evidently believed that the return of their mother would iron out any little ruffles and creases that existed in their lives. They prepared for the Day of Jubilation by obsessively cleaning those parts of the house which they imagined to be Begoña's favoured locations. The metal frame of the seat beside her computer was soon gleaming with the ostentatious smugness of American teeth, though the room around it still looked freshly burgled. They rearranged the cushions on Bego's armchair, chased all the dust mites from her side of the bed into mine, and polished the bathroom mirror until you could almost see your face in it. They also tidied Bego's underwear drawer on an hourly basis, pausing only occasionally to dress up in its contents and prance around the house shrieking 'Do you like my booby baskets?'

We collected her from the International Airport on the evening of Friday, June 26th. We had to shovel our way through a pile of reporters and photographers just to get near to the arriving door. Begoña had taken the clever precaution of sending out a look-alike actress to act as one of your decoy ducks. The plan was that Begoña herself would then slip out unnoticed to resume her family life. Unfortunately, the actress was extremely convincing and mostly appealing. We were halfway back to Belfast, singing happily in the car, before our mistake became apparent. 'That's not my mamá,' said Dilatación, and we hurriedly bent double-back on ourselves. Begoña was not happy when eventually we found her, surrounded by slobbering press hounds not far from the check-in desk of RockBottomAir.

Strangely, however, I knew immediately that our relationship was secure. There was now a lot of water under our bridge, and only a little dash of somebody else's spilt milk. It was, as ever, a matter of biology, chemistry and physics. I knew that if we still clicked in our bed, then all would be well. The fiery gleam in her eyes told me that she wanted me to scale her fortress and bash my way once more to the banqueting hall. Even in this mad modern age, there is nothing a lady likes more than this. So we drove home in euphoric mood pursued by howling hacks, and barricaded ourselves into the house for a stimulating weekend of personal *reconquista*.

At first, of course, Begoña's attention was completely consumed by the selfish girls. Then, towards midnight, they fell asleep in the living room, one by one, and we carried them up to their beds. Concepción survived the longest. She sat on the sofa with wide eyes, but eventually she lost her thread in mid-sentence: 'There's an alien called Vog who's trying to eat our enthusiasm, but we think she's . . . '

'Listen to that,' said Bego, 'She's completely delirious. Here, you take her up – she's too heavy for me.'

When I returned, we opened a bottle of champagne and charged headlong at our glasses. For the next eleven hours, we talked in an open and uninhibited manner that reminded me of a time in Andalusia, long before. We agreed to ask alternating questions, and we undertook to be completely honest.

'I will begin,' she said. 'Question One: have you missed me?'

'I realise now that I have,' I said carefully, 'but at the time it felt more like anger. Some of it has been *insufrible*. Have you any idea what it has been like for me?'

'Have you any idea what it has been like for *me*,' she countered, 'to be living under such perpetual public scrutiny?'

'That is your choice,' I replied. 'You have ploughed your own furrow, and now you must lie in it.'

She looked pensive, and went to turn the heating up.

This was a good sign, implying an intention to disrobe. When she returned to the room, she picked up the bottle of champagne.

'You surely have not finished that glass already,' I said inaccurately.

Begoña took a hearty slug out of the bottle, and strolled over towards me. She looked ravenous in an expensive pair of jeans and a flimsy vest of cream. She placed her hands purposefully on the arms of my chair, and slowly she leaned towards me. I stared hotly at her uncontainable breasts, which plunged enthusiastically in my direction as she drew nigh. She also had a substantial pedant dangling from her neck, and I received a sharp blow on the nose for my trouble. Begoña put her lips to mine, and injected me with at least 50 millilitres of champagne. I was not prepared for this, and I choked violently. She was amused, and her body rocked and reverberated under the influence of the fulsome, open-mouthed, head-back, swashbuckling belly-laugh that I remembered so well. What is more, she then took horrible advantage of me and my friend Jumping Jack as we gathered ourselves together.

'And now, it is my turn,' I said a little later. 'Question Two: was that the first time you have made love since we last had the pleasure together?'

She looked me straight in the eye, and said, 'Yes, *totalmente*. I am and will remain your faithful wife. *Eres el único corcho en mi botella y el único conejo en mi madriguera.*'[66]

---

[66] You are the only cork in my bottle and the only rabbit in my burrow.

This was like sweet music in my ears, but I was also slightly troubled. My dread of Question Three motivated me to concentrate on Question Two until one or other of us lost concentration and/or consciousness. I felt guilty and my crest had fallen somewhat, but I masked my true emotions with a display of incredulity.

'But what about all those parties with The Lunchpack of Notre Dame? Are you seriously expecting me to believe that nothing happened?'

'Nothing whatsoever. The whole thing was a giant *fabricación*. They told us what they wanted, and we obliged. Didn't you read about it?'

'Yes, of course. He took his legendary penis away and the whole thing folded.'

'That's right,' she said. 'I was relieved. Do you know he puts a courgette in his pants when he runs? He told me. It is in his contract with the sports shoe company. I never even kissed him.'

'Are you serious?' I asked. 'He never felt the rough edge of your tongue?'

'Never. Not once.'

'Is anything real?' I wondered, but Begoña was already leaving the room in search of a second bottle of champagne. I watched her go, in all her curvaceous nakedness. I knew that my own cork was ready to pop again, and so I followed her. '*¿Tienes un puesto vacante para un artesano con experiencia que lleva sus propias herramientas?*' I asked.[67] And she did.

---

[67] Do you have an opening for an experienced craftsman with his own tools?

'Question Three,' said Begoña, when we regained the sofa. 'What have you been up to in my absence?'

I knew exactly what she meant, but noted that her carelessly vague wording provided me with a lifeline and a loophole all in the same package. I visited my mental store, hoping to find some intriguing and suitably deflective information. My mind has been known to betray me at such moments, but to my relief I found that the cupboard was far from bare. There was plenty that I could tell Bego before I needed to consider admitting that I had sipped the breastmilk of another man's wife (put like this, it does not really sound so terrible). Indeed, the anecdotes came tumbling from the shelves as I pushed open the door. I told her almost everything, and watched her interest in my sexy life dissipate with every passing *revelación*. Now it was her turn to appear incredulous, and even I found it a little difficult to believe that I had accomplished so much while she had been away. I had alienated all but one of my colleagues, purchased a chariot, stimulated genuine political progress, possibly rendered the red-necked phalarope extinct in Ireland, won a whole string of Fathers' Races, and nearly lost the children to a social worker. What is more, I had beaten up a reporter and eaten up an Ulster fry. All this within the space of six months! It was scarcely plausible, but I assured Begoña that every word was a close approximation of the truth. She was particularly troubled by the detail about Mizzz Stewart's intrusions, and this despite the fact that I withheld the entertaining Vog sub-plot.

'Is that all finished now?' she asked.

'No, I do not think so. She is still on the warpath. Perhaps you can talk some sense into her. She will probably listen to a woman. It will be OK.'

I had made the mistake of reassuring her too convincingly, and now her mind turned to the vexed question of my sexual fidelity.

'There is one aspect of my question that you have not answered,' she said accusingly. '¿*Soy la única gamba sobre tu tenedor*?'[68]

'It is not your turn,' I objected.

'This is not a new question,' she insisted, 'and you must respond.'

My mind whirred and whistled into action. What was I to say to this? Was honesty the best policy, or was it in truth the very worst? Should I explain that I had indeed made love to another woman, but that my judgement had been clouded by an intense and indignant jealousy that was not of my own manufacture? By chance, I had recently read a newspaper article in which a psychologist revealed that a normal person tells 273 lies a day, without even realising it in most cases. We lie to our children in our desperation to induce *cooperación*. We lie to our colleagues in our anxiety to conceal our inadequacy. And we most certainly lie to our wives when we have been playing in our so-called away strip. I made a rapid calculation, and reckoned that I had only told 272 lies so far that day. This clinched the matter, and I replied with confidence, 'Yes, of course, my fork is only for you.' Bego was not even suspicious, and she said, 'I never really doubted you, you know.'[69]

---

[68] Am I the only prawn on your fork?

[69] I carry the burden of this calculated deceit with me to this day, but somehow I soldier on.

'Question Four,' I said. 'Do you think we will always live here, Bego?'

'What, now that you have offended every significant social grouping in Northern Ireland?'

'That is not fair,' I said. 'What about the paramilitaries? I have not offended the paramilitaries. They like me. It could be much worse. The political situation is actually improving. This is not a bad place to be, you know, and most of the locals are very friendly.'

'What about the weather? It rains nearly every day. I don't think I'll ever get used to it.'

'Of course you will. I am acclimatising steadily, and the girls have stopped complaining about the conditions. They're little ladies of Belfast now.'

There was an aggressive knock at the front door, which we decided not to answer.

'Then there are the journalists,' said Begoña.

'We would get that anywhere, especially now that you are the Decade woman. It has a nice ring to it. I am proud of you, you know? Your achievements are not to be sniffed at.'

I was on the verge of suggesting that we postpone discussion until after we had rested, but then Begoña volunteered a more promising solution.

'OK,' she said, 'what do you say to this? We'll stay for another year or two, settle down a bit, and then make a decision.'

'That is most agreeable,' I said.

I led her to bed, pausing only to show her my appreciation on the stairs.

Chapter 37

In which Jesús is staked out by his enemies and forced to acknowledge that his best friend is a walrus.

It became a veritable siege, just like the famous one that almost strangled the city known to sensitive souls as '(London)D/derry' in or around 1688. I had read about this – rather hurriedly, I must admit – in preparation for one of my historical RUB seminars. The rats, I recalled, had grown so hungry that, in the end, they had resorted to eating apprentice boys. Memories, in that part of the world, are long. An Ulsterman never forgets, and he stores ancient grudges in his trunk.

We were prisoners in our own home. The phone rang every few seconds, and the computer collapsed under the weight of a million unwanted e-mails. Press-hounds, mongrels to a man, were on duty out in our road, sticking their snouts through our locked gate and drooling onto our driveway. Cameras clicked whenever Begoña glided past one of the visible windows, and the only privacy we enjoyed was at the rear-end of the house. The children throve on it with an innocence born of idiocy, and I was for once able to turn their energy to my advantage. Their battle-cry was 'No Surrender!' and, under my guidance, they constructed on our back lawn a catapult which hurled apples, nectarines and frozen bread-rolls over the house and into the road with passable accuracy. I had never before seen top-of-the-range French lingerie put to such arousing use.

For several days, the lane was impassable and shopping impossible. Fortunately, we were able to maintain the children at a minimal level of nourishment with our frosty beef burgers and our processed novelty potato balls ('shaped like real potatoes'), but our remaining supplies of bread and fruit were earmarked for military use. Begoña and I knew that none of this would last forever. I was able to trap pigeons and hedgehogs on the back lawn, using a laundry basket, a length of string and a broom. The resultant kebabs were just edible, but before long the local wildlife all ran out. It was imperative that I found my way to the shops, and Begoña suggested that I consider passing through the rear gardens of our neighbours. I duly phoned Mrs. Naughtie, ostensibly to apologise for the disruptive presence of the press, but actually to ask whether she would object if I tunnelled my way into her backside wearing an Irish dancer's curly black wig before borrowing her car for a trip to the supermarket. Mrs N. was as co-operative as ever, and even offered to do our shopping for us, but I had a dose of your cabin fever and I needed to weave myself a spell on the outside. Conchi and I set to work with our spades. When the hole was big enough, I squeezed my form through it. The girls created a "lemons from the heavens" diversion, and I drove off towards the shop, my artificial hair squeezing my head in a manner that rendered my eyes unusually protrusive.

I crossed the Lagan on the Governor's Bridge, and

travelled along the Annadale Embankment. To the side of the road, preparations were underway for the biggest bonfire I had ever seen. In my domestic confinement, I had quite forgotten that the anniversary of the Battle of the Boyne was looming and that loyalists across "the province" were looking for inflammatory artefacts to incinerate. Connor had advised me that it was customary for blow-ins, sensible Catholics and middle-class Protestants to leave Belfast during this portion of July. 'You must get away for the Twelfth Fortnight,' he had urged.[70] It seemed unlikely that we would manage such an escape, but I calculated optimistically that a state of virtual house-arrest was probably the next best thing. I slowed the car in order to peer at the monumental bonfire, and was bewitched by remarkable range of its contents: sofas, armchairs, cushions, tables, carpets, desks, lamp-shades and curtains, planks, garden waste, books, rocking horses, a dead dog and at least one cello. As far as I could tell, most of these objects were in good working condition (with the possible exception of the dog).

The supermarket was unpopulated, save for a couple of comprehensively tattooed men in the pasta section. One wore a so-called "Rangers" shirt, and the other sported the full "Celtic" strip. They were conversing loudly, and, at first, I thought they were preparing to fight. As I drew closer, however, I realised that they were united in laughter. One of the men had a two-legged Alsatian on a lead, and they were both looking sympathetically at it. The dog's

---

[70] By this, he meant the period around the world-famous twelfth of the month.

owner said to the other man, 'Ock, aye, it was a guddun, right enough! I'll get yew back, but. Yurra wee fockin' chancer!' The two of them stared at me somewhat rudely as I heaved my bulging trolley past them.

On the way home, I listened to a local radio station and heard one of the reporters explaining that the Annadale bonfire was, for the first time in many decades, a "good news" story.

'This year,' she said, 'the atmosphere attending the bonfire is described by locals as relaxed and positive. This part of south Belfast has not seen the upsurge in sectarian tension that has marred early July in recent years. I'm here with Mr. Dougie Glass, one of the organisers of the bonfire. Mr. Glass, what do you think has contributed to the change of mood?'

'I can't be sure. There's just a wee bit of a feeling that violent sectarianism has run its course. Everything's just far less tense this year, so it is. We've even had Catholics from the Lower Ormeau calling by to leave us furniture, deceased pets and the like, for the bonny, you know. There's been nothing like that since before the Troubles.'

'Yet as we know from all the previous false dawns, these shifts can be fragile. How would you feel if something happened to jeopardise the new mood?'

Mr. Dougie Glass paused, trawling his mind for the right words.

'Ock, I'd be shattered,' he said eventually.

When I thought about it, I realised that I too had noticed this momentous alteration in the temper of the town during the previous weeks. The atmosphere had become a little calmer, and some of the new graffiti was less antagonistic than the old. You could see it on people's faces.[71] Belfast's Troubles seemed finally to be fading, but as I drew into the Naughties' driveway with flyaway eyeballs and an extremely itchy head I remembered that I still had a multiplicity of my own.

I had not spoken to Connor for several days, but a visit from Norman Boyle brought my lanky friend right back into the picture. The professor fought his way through the press-pack and dodged up the drive under a hail of bunfire. He stepped inside.

'How on earth do you put up with this?' he asked.

'It will pass,' I replied breezily. 'They cannot stay this interested forever.'

'Listen, Jesús, I'm afraid I have some disturbing news.'

'You're going to put me in that sack, after all?'

'Dismiss you? No, no. Actually, I'm fairly keen to keep you. God knows why.'

'Because I have a certain nuisance value?' I suggested.

'Maybe so. No, it's about Connor.'

'Connor? What is it? Has something happened to him?'

'May I come in?'

We went into my study and Professor Boyle closed the door. I offered him a chair, and awaited his pronouncement.

'There is no easy way to say this. Connor is not who he says he is, and he has disappeared.'

---

[71] I recalled one piece of artwork that had formerly conveyed the precise instruction, 'Kill all Taigs'. More recently, however, some gentle soul had thoughtfully replaced the word 'Kill' with the word 'Fock'.

'What on earth are you talking about? He always runs away during the Battle of the Boyne. He's a yellow-livered coward. He told me so himself.'

'No, this is different,' he said. 'I had a phonecall this morning from a very senior policeman. He told me that our Dr. McCann is in fact an internationally renowned confidence trickster, wanted for questioning by detectives on five continents, including Antarctica.'

I sat in befuddled silence, then heard myself mutter, 'If it is true, then I am a Turk!'

'I know this is hard for you to believe,' Professor Boyle continued, 'but it seems to be true. He's known variously as the Cheetah, the Leech, the Stonefish, the Cobra and the Walrus.'

'But he is my best friend,' I insisted.

'I'm sorry to say that he is nobody's best friend. The police think he may originally have come from Northern Ireland, but they're not even sure of his real name. I have just checked the references he supplied when he applied for the job – none of it adds up. He's a con-man, one of the best. He's said to have millions stashed away in untraceable bank accounts, and he's been missing for two years.'

'Since he joined RUB?'

'That's right. The police didn't think to look for him here, but then an anonymous caller – they didn't say who – suggested that they run a security check on a certain member of the history department. When they did so, they discovered that "Connor McCann" didn't exist until he took up employment with us. The rest followed from this.'

'OK, let us assume for the moment that they are right. What kind of crimes has he committed?'

'Apparently, he has yet to be convicted of anything, but only because they can never find him. The evidence is ready and waiting. He locates individuals who combine wealth with personal insecurity or instability or simplicity, and then lures them into an elaborate web of plausible lies. He's a spider, a money spider. By the time his victims realise they must squash him, he's long gone, and so is their silver.'

'Long gone silver,' I echoed helplessly.

He looked at me with genuine concern before proceeding.

'Here in Ireland, he's implicated in the mysterious disappearance of seven million euros from the accounts of a bank in Dublin. They've got DNA, and it matches some found in a separate investigation in Hong Kong. I have to ask you this: did Connor ever ask you for money?'

'No, quite the reverse.'

'You asked *him* for money?'

'No, no, no. I mean only that he was always very generous to us. Where do they think he is now?'

'Ock, they don't expect to see him again in Belfast. They're still looking, but he's probably left the country under yet another false name.'

Professor Boyle left me to wallow in my mud-pool of misery, from whence I phoned our bank in order to check the family funds. I found to my relief that everything was in order. I was vigorously vibrated by Professor Boyle's intrusion into my personal spaces, and I spent the rest of the day in a condition of trembling preoccupation. His bombshell shook my already shaky grasp on the concepts of *truth* and *reality*. Were these anything more than myths? Was everything merely artifice and appearance? Perhaps my life as related in this book was merely the product of some fantastical delusion (could this *really* be true?) In a rush of creative energy, I sat down and wrote my inflammable diatribe, *The Shaming of the True*, which draws generously on the comedies of Shakespeare in order to build its distinctly post-modern argument. Perhaps you are clever enough to have read it?

Conversely, I found it difficult to identify a single so-called untruth in anything that Connor had said to me. His attention to detail had been *extraordinario*, and I marvelled at the mind of a man who could construct for himself such a coherent and plausible identity. But why, I asked myself, had he befriended me, of all people? I was at a loss. I was not particularly rich, and by no effort of the outstretched imagination could I have been described as insecure or unstable, let alone simple. When Audrey telephoned us in order to offer what she called a "food-drop", I told her the latest news. She was audibly bamboozled, and assured me that she had detected nothing untoward when she met Connor. We were just beginning to chew on the meat of the conversation when a much deeper voice suddenly sounded in my ear.

'Who's this?'

'Hello. It's Jesús Sánchez Ventura. Is this Sean?'

'Just keep away from us will you. I know your gayem, mayet.'

With that, he hung up the phone, thus adding an additional heavy weight to my already unwieldy sack.

Begoña comforted me to the best of her abilities, but I remained unusually muddled. Moreover, our living conditions now seemed to me life-threateningly claustrophobic. I was a big fish in one of your small pies, and I began to wonder whether some dramatic escape might after all be possible. The urge intensified after we received the first of several calls from Vog, urging us all to attend an appointment with her. During one conversation, I stood by the kitchen window and watched the girls loading a rare but stoical hedgehog onto their catapult in the back garden, demented with the excitement of battle.

'You cannot see us now,' I told her, 'we are under siege and nobody is in the mood for therapy. Why must you be always trying to catch the odd man out? Call us again when the smoke has settled.'

I heard her say, 'Dr. Sánchez Ventura, this is becoming a very serious matter. I don't want to . . . '

Then I put the phone down, unplugging it for good measure.

Chapter 38

In which Jesús is to be observed cycling under Orangemen and leading his dependants through an exercise in harmless escapism.

My plans remained shrouded in a web of secretion. Begoña was feeling fragile, having upset her stomach, and I knew that she would probably pooh-pooh the whole idea (I merely promised her a 'surprise holiday' in the sun). Conchi and her sisters might well have relished my scheme, but they were loose cannons at the best of times and it therefore seemed unwise to load them. A dramatic acceleration in the schedule suddenly became necessary when, one morning, I peeped through the drawn curtains of our bedroom to monitor the size of the press-gang. There were still eight or nine journalists and photographers, but I also noted with anxiety the presence of Vog and a be-suited male colleague, two policemen, Audrey's husband, and a police van displaying the description 'Wildlife Crime Division'. We had to make our move.

Around midday, I gathered up my womenfolk and finally drew them into my loop. When this operation was complete, I sent Bego, Conchi and Puri under the fence with two tents, five sleeping bags and a limited quantity of luggage.

We called once more on the services of Mrs. Naughtie. They climbed into the car, buried themselves beneath blankets, and prepared to depart for our rendezvous point, down by the Waterfront Hall. I had never before seen Mrs. Naughtie drive, but she bravely took the wheel and successfully smuggled her passengers out. Dilatación and I remained at home in order to distract the attention of our visitors from the departing vehicle. We continued to ignore their attempts to contact us, and the front gate remained firmly locked, but we collected the milk and switched household appliances on and off so that they would have no cause to doubt our presence.

For my next trick, I phoned my other neighbour, the delightful Ciaran Grady, (*alias* ZoBo) and asked of him a substantial favour. He was unsympathetic at first but, to his external credit, he eventually agreed to assist us, and he created a very memorable diversion indeed. He began by releasing his white Doberman dog, Blade, into the road. It lumbered around hungrily, sending Vog and the others into a paroxysm of panic. Then Zobo dispatched his current girlfriend, the reigning Miss South Armagh, to lure the hound of death back into the garden by throwing a stick for it. Miss SA wore what I presumed were her night garments, and she looked rather fetching. Our moment of multiple post-modern truths was drawing nigh, and, as I watched the local beauty queen being slobbered over by a large beast, I felt my resolve stiffen. Instinctively the photographers began to snip their pictures, and I prepared to cut them down to size with my own execution. Our persecutors re-grouped, now with their backs to us. I remained at the window to witness one further development. Blade grew still more amorous, and began jumping up at Miss South Armagh, pawing playfully at her negligée and snarling in mock aggression. Within seconds, it was an all-out wrestling match on Zobo's front lawn. The audience clearly believed that an actual mauling was taking place, and I have to admit that if I had not set the whole thing up myself I too would have assumed that the blood was real. Vog, loose-brained liberal that she is, decided that she simply had to intervene, and I knew that our chance had come.

We left the house by the back door, and I loaded Dila securely into her scarlet chariot. I mounted my bike and rode it round the side of the house in *silencio absoluto*. The sounds of combat from across the road provided our cover, and surreptitiously I unlocked the gate. Once in the lane, I pressed the pedals for all I was worth, propelling us with some considerable speed towards the Lagan toe-path. We were almost round the corner, and thus out of reach, when Dila, like a fool, shrieked 'Wheeeeeeeeeeeeee!' at the top of her voice. This had not been in my script, and just as we disappeared from view I heard a man shout, 'Come back here yer fockin' barrstard, I wanna word with yuu.' The first cars caught up with us within minutes, but the road is narrow and they were unable to pass. The drivers hooted and the passengers yelled, but they could do no more than watch in helpless frustration as I crossed the bridge into the car-free, bollard-protected zone of comfort on the other side of the Lagan. I was making good my getaway, for the time being at least.

I knew that there were other points of access to the

network of riverside footpaths, and that our escapade was still closer to its beginning than its end. I was swimming in adrenaline, and my legs pumped up and down like huge industrial pistons. I did not see another soul between New Forge Lane and Stranmillis, and I generated an exhilaratingly steamy head. 'Go faster, go faster!' screamed Dila, and I obliged. The sweat was flying from me as we sped along Lockview Road, where Vog and the gang had their first opportunity to intercept us. We saw three cars turn menacingly towards us from the roundabout, but as they manoeuvred to form a barrier across the road, we jinked onto the path for short-cut pedestrians that connects Lockview to the Ormeau Embankment. In the time it took the drivers to turn their vehicles, we made it all the way to the internationally renowned Ormeau Bridge. That is how fast an articulated Spaniard can travel! Here, I knew we had only to cross the road in order to reach another corridor of security.

As we approached the bridge, however, a terrible and apocalyptic scene presented itself to us: thousands of middle-aged men in bowler hats were marching over the river in time to the music of flutes, blocking the way to the next section of the path. The combination of high and low sounds had once charmed me, but now it made me feel as if I was being thumped repeatedly in the stomach while a disease-carrying mosquito whined and dined inside each of my ears. Nor were these the only sounds. The route of the Orangemen was lined by a noisy but essentially good-natured crowd of protesters, waving flags of green, white and gold. Many of them were jeering and pointing at the tarmac beneath their feet. Another group was singing a song called "Going Underground" in raucous four-part harmony. To make matters worse, two substantial policemen stood on the grass, monitoring proceedings and evidently guarding the entrance to some kind of tent. It was a traumatic moment, and I cycled up and down along the line of protesters, desperately seeking some way through. I glanced back along the embankment, and saw that several cars were approaching the bridge. Vog was leaning out of one of the windows, shouting 'We only want to talk.' It occurred to me months later that I should perhaps have granted her an audience, but my dander was up and I shouted back, 'You'll never take us alive-alive-oh!'

The motley band of busy-bodies piled out of their cars and began walking towards us. 'Fock, it's Vog,' said Dilatación, who was at last beginning to understand the nature of the game. 'Don't worry Papá, I'll be really boring,' she added. At this moment, a burly hand grasped my shoulder from behind, and I thought it had my number on it. To my relief, however, I turned to see that it was Seamus, my guardian angel from Ardoyne.

'¡*Buenos días, amigo*!' he said in a silly accent.

He caught sight of the approaching group, and reverted to his workaday voice.

'Yuu wudden have gat yourself in bather again, wud yuu noiy?'

'Just a little,' I panted. 'They are all hunting me for one reason or another. But I am a good man, here in my heart [at this point, I struck my chest]. I have to reach the Waterfront Hall. It is very urgent, but I can see no way through.'

It was just as it is in the old American films. The villains were walking towards us, but every time I looked in their direction they had somehow failed to progress. This added suspense to my situation, and it gave Seamus a moment to think.

'The tonnel! The tonnel!' he exclaimed. 'Yuus can go doiyn the fockin' Orangemen's tonnel. It's nat fanished yet, so it's nat, but thur's a builders' access point just over thur, and another on the other side a bat further doiyn. Yuu can cross under the road and gat into the Markets. Come with me.'

'But what about the policemen?'

'You leave tham to me. I've been annoying Peelers for decades, so I have.'

I had assumed that the metal and canvas structure standing on the grass belonged to the police. It was securely fastened at all points, and a large red and white notice warned, 'Authorised Personnel Only'. I now realised that this in fact marked a temporary entry point into the new Tunnel of Unionists. Seamus orchestrated the operation in a matter of seconds. Two men at the back of the nationalist throng began throwing their fists at one another, and shouting 'Yer a fockin' traitor' and 'I'll fockin' kill yuu, ye wee shite.' An attractive middle-aged woman then screamed for assistance, and the two policemen moved hurriedly away from their post. Seamus next recruited three additional men from the crowd, and they all set to work removing the signs and opening the strange tent. To my astonishment and delight, they produced from nowhere a pair of metal-cutters, a crowbar and a small incendiary device. The police, with their minds on other things, failed to react to the new disturbance until it was far too late.

'Turn left,' called Seamus, 'and may the road rise up to meet yous! We'll keep these people off your back for a wee while.'

Dila and I bumped and barged our way down a rough track, and found ourselves in the eerie quiet of the tunnel. 'Are you OK?' I asked, and my voice rebounded from all the surfaces. There was no reply, so I looked over my shoulder. She was fast asleep (or dead).

We followed Seamus' instructions, and began a cautious journey along the tunnel. It was extremely dark in there, and the ground was strewn with shovels and other devices. We progressed towards a pale shaft of light, some way further down. The experience was uncanny. I cycled along in strange silence, yet I knew that the Orangemen and their bands were directly above us, marching along this stretch of the Ormeau Road for the very last time. Next year, the sound-proofed tunnel would be complete and all those bowler hats would be down here instead. I had no time, however, to contemplate this prospect. With some difficulty, I cleared a path through the next makeshift entry-point, using some of the tools that the workmen had left behind. I then pow-ered my way up and out in the lowest of my twenty-four gears. We emerged once more into the light of day, and zag-zigged hurriedly through the red-brick terraces of the Markets before regaining the riverside toe-path once more. Thankfully, there was no sign of our pursuers at the next roadbridge, and we made it down to the Waterfront Hall without further *confrontación*.

Begoña and the others were waiting, but they had problems of their own. It was obvious that the usefulness of Mrs. Naughtie was now quite exhausted.

'Poor woman,' said Bego, 'she drove the car into a concrete barrier, and now there's something wrong with the brakes. She is finished.'

It seemed an accurate description, for the dear lady had clearly spent her penny. She was leaning against a huge statue of a blue fish, her large mouth opening and closing at regular intervals.

Begoña took my hand.

'I think we must go home and confront our critics,' she said. 'You haven't done anything truly terrible, so I'm sure we can sort it all out. Today has been mysterious and exciting, but it's *un poco loco*.[72] What do you say?'

My dander was still up, though I must concede that it was somewhat lower than it had been twenty minutes previously.

'Perhaps you are right,' I said. 'In any case, our bucket of options is empty. Damn it. It was going to be fun.'

('You must get away for the Twelfth Fortnight,' insisted a disembodied voice in my head.)

"Where were you taking us, anyway?" asked Bego.

There now seemed to be little point in withholding this information.

'To a magical island in the ocean,' I said. 'I thought we might spend a little of your money, and fly to Tahiti or Hawaii, somewhere far away, just for a week or two. There

---

[72] A little crazy.

would be sunshine *without* showers, and nobody to bother us.'

On hearing this, Dila awoke and her sisters became almost engagingly enthusiastic.

'An island in the sea! Let's go! Come on, Mamá, it'll be good crack!'

'No,' I said firmly, 'your mother is right for once. It is time to meet the music face-to-face.'

At this moment, a smart blue car drew up alongside us. The window opened with an automated hum, and I saw that the driver was a woman of what you would call the middle ages. She presented a creditable cleavage, but her skin was orange and unnaturally taut across the cheekbones. Her clothes were new, but they too looked painfully tight. Her recently-styled hair was dyed an improbable purplish colour, and there was something vaguely familiar about her eyes. The ensemble was clearly feminine, yet her voice was deep and rough, even manly.

'Bout ye, big lad?' she asked, to the bemusement of us all.[73] 'Would yuus be looking for a lift?'

I peered more closely at her face. A penny dropped on my head, and I paused in shock while it sank in.

'Connor, is that you? What in the name of holy fock have you done to yourself?'

Now the accent changed, becoming more like one of those Australian 'Neighbours' from the television. The new voice was also disturbingly womanish.

'I think you're mixing me up with someone else? My name's

---

[73] This means, approximately, 'How are you, my fine friend?'

Maureen Charles, and I'm from Melbourne? I'm just over here for the world line-dancing championships next week?'

His flippant demeanour needled my haystack, and I retaliated with two questions that were both as angry and pointed as spears.

'Is life just one big joke for you?' I asked. 'Do you really exist at all?'

'Aw, don't be like that? You can tell I'm a genuine Aussie because my voice rises at the end of every sentence, whether it's a question or an incredibly decisive statement? You see, it's irrefutable? The only time I don't do it is when it actually is a question? Now, how about that lift.'

Bego looked doubtful, and I could tell that she wanted no truck with him. She hissed an old Spanish proverb straight into my ear.

'*Ni amigo reconciliado, ni asado recalentado.*'[74]

Conchi and her sisters, in contrast, had already clambered into the car and were busy belting one another up. 'Connor to the rescue!' they chanted.

I told him of our destination, but he laughed and said in his more familiar voice, 'Ock, don't be such an eejit, Jayzo. If I drop you at the airport, they'll be onto you in minutes. I didn't get where I am today by going to an airport at a moment like this. I've a much better idea. It's an island, but far more mysterious and exotic.'

'Is it tropical?' I asked.

'Well, sub-tropical. You'll love it. You've often talked of it. What do you say, girls?'

---

[74] You would say, 'Neither a reconciled friend, nor a re-heated stew.'

Predictably, they cheered.

Effectively, we were captive once more and we soon found ourselves bound and gagged for the little port of Ballycastle at the other end of County Antrim. We felt guilty about Mrs. Naughtie, but Bego had tranquillized her before we left and Connor had given her the phone number of a "wee man" who would come to her assistance. Now, in Connor's vehicle, a large blanket of silence fell upon the group. I had many things to say, but I could not articulate a single thought. I stared blankly through the window as we passed by a sign welcoming us to the charming little town of Ballybilly, 'Officially Twinned with the Rock of Gibraltar since AD 2001.' My dander was now completely down and it quivered pitifully at my feet while the rest of us looked on in wordless wonderment. It was Concepción, a born talker, who eventually stuck her head through the ice.

'Are you going to steal our money now, Mr. Walrus?'

Connor laughed uneasily, and answered, 'No, I'm not, and I'm truly sorry to have misled you. I would never hurt any of yous.'

Another period of silence ensued.

'And what is your real name?' I asked.

'Ock, it's been so long since I used it – I honestly can't remember. It's something like Brian Smith. Dead boring, really.'

Now Begoña spoke for the first time.

'Do you think you might have a disordered personality?'

'Not at all. I'm just restless, mischievous and work-shy.

Anyhow, it's time for me to settle down. Getting to know all of yous has made me think I should maybe try something more conventional.'

'Yes, we are conventional, aren't we?' I agreed.

'Well, sort of. There are five of you, from two genera-tions, and you live together in a house. And sometimes you tell the truth. It's nice. I've enjoyed it.'

Purificación now pulled the conversation in another direction.

'So, Connor, where's your treasure hidden?'

'Right at the bottom of the deep blue sea – you'll never find it.'

'Unbelievable,' I murmured.

It was not much of a conversation, but it was a start, or perhaps a finish. He dropped us off at the harbour in Ballycastle with instructions to get on the next ferry for Rathlin Island, of all places. We said our strange goodbyes.

'Thanks for the lift.'

'You're OK.'

'Would you do us one more favour?'

He nodded.

'Please phone *The Orb* newspaper, anonymously of course, and tell them that you glimpsed us at the ferry terminal in Larne, heading for Scotland. It's a little white lie, but I'm sure you're up to it. We just need a few days' peace.'

'Good thinking, it'll throw them off the scent. I'm yer man!'

He looked thoughtful, and said, 'I never lied to you, you know – except about my name and my qualifications. Oh, and the game called whirlyball,[75] of course. But you knew that was a joke, didn't you?'

This was yet another shock to my system, but I said simply, 'Of course I did, yer big bollocks!'

He chuckled, shook his head, and drove off.

---

75 For whirlyball, see above p47.

Chapter 39

Concerning what happened when Jesús and his attendants sought refuge on one of Ireland's sodding islands.

Bego and I were not pleased at the prospect of heading for a miserable sponge of an island with none of the facilities of a major city. A day-trip might have been tolerable, but to live like peasants for an indefinite period in such a desolate place most certainly was not. Had we left Andalusia for this? A little glumpily, I wrapped up Begoña in an old coat to protect her from prying eyes. An evening of drenching showers appeared inevitable, and our hearts were suddenly full of lead. The rush-hour of adrenaline was over and the horrible post-match trough had been tipped on our heads. Conchi also looked depressed, but Puri and Dila continued to float on a cloud of enchantment. Their high spirits grated upon my nerves like old cheese. From the boat, they gasped in glee as porpoises sliced nonchalantly through the waves alongside us and giant white suicide birds crashed into the sea from great heights.[76]

---

[76] In Portrush, there is a multi-million pound visitor centre devoted exclusively to these creatures. Go to the town centre and follow signs for 'Planet Gannet'.

'Do you have to be so relentlessly adaptable?' I asked.

I put my hands over my ears before Puri could answer, and I looked up at the island's forbidding cliffs of chalk and basalt. A bedraggled gaggle of day-trippers stood on the dock in the little drawn-out village, waiting for the ferry to convey them back to Ballycastle. 'Why are there lots of people leaving and only us arriving?' asked Concepción suspiciously.

'Because it is not Tahiti,' Begoña replied.

We were all exceedingly hungry, having eaten nothing since breakfast, and we therefore dragged our paltry belongings round to the island's only café. The staff were closing for the day, but they agreed somewhat resentfully to stoke us up a little. We positioned ourselves beside the window, with a view over the deep grey Atlantic towards Donegal, and we ate some chips and fish. There was, of course, no wine. We treated the girls with ice cream and, when they had finished, we moved into the public house next door in order to do some of your misery-drowning northern alcoholism. Puri and Dila wandered around the room, peering up at the maps and photographs that decorated the walls. They talked incessantly about a gargantuan bull's head, said by the barmaid to be over one hundred years old. 'It was shot by Mr. Gage, the local gent, when it got ideas above its station,' she told them.

When Begoña and I were suitably inebriated, we grew a little more cheerful. We fell into a conversation with an ancient man of the island, cosily settled in an enveloping armchair beside the fire. He was a weathered brown colour, broad of shoulder, his hair a shock of creamy white. There was a pint of stout in his hand, and it looked for all the world like his dwarf twin brother. He surprised us by recognising Bego, but tapped his bulbous nose sympathetically when we expressed our desire to remain hidden from the wicked world beyond the island for a few days.

'If it's peace and quiet ye are after,' he said, 'you'll not be short of it on Rathlin.'

He introduced himself as Micky McCurdy, and he answered our questions with willing warmth.

'I'll tell ye of a place you can camp — up on my cousin's land, along the road to Rue Point. There's a ruined cottage there'll give ye some help gainst the wind. It was Rosie McCormack's place before she went to New York.'

His tone was nostalgic, dreamy, vacant.

'Did she leave quite recently?' asked Bego.

'Ay, she did,' came the reply. 'After the famine. 1853. It's sheltered there, and this cousin o'mine'll not give ye any bother at all.'

Mr. McCurdy was a voluminous fountain of colourful information about the island, and his habit of coughing up throat-phlegm, then spitting it onto the floor, only added to his overpowering air of authenticity. We let it all wash over us, and in our state of drunken exhaustion we half-learned many things. He told us that Rathlin had once produced state-of-the-art prehistoric tools, but that the economy had been in a slump ever since the porcellanite axe market dried up at the end of the Stone Age. We also heard of three famous visitors to the island: "Robert the Bruce", a medieval Scottish king who could speak spider-language; "Marconi the Mast", a gifted pioneer of intercourse

318

on the radio; and "Francis the Drake", some sort of pet water-bird.

After a while, we were joined at the table by a bronzed American gentleman in his swinging sixties who evidently knew Micky already.

'Allow me to introduce myself,' he said. 'I'm staying on the island for a few days. It's where my father was born. The name is Red Black.'

I chortled, Begoña frowned, and Micky McCurdy belched.

'It's true,' said Micky, 'Black's an oul island name. I knew his father, before he left us. Don't know where the Red bit comes from, but. He's a yank.'

Red Black told us his story, which I will summarise succinctly for you: Black Senior left Rathlin to seek his fortune in America, but found only alcoholic melancholy; his son, in contrast, grew immensely wealthy in the beef business; but then his wife left him and he replaced her with a hot-air balloon; he decided to float solo around the world, calling in on the people of Rathlin to nourish his roots and proclaim his prosperity.

'I've been showing him his da's place,' said Micky.

'Get this!' said Red. 'It's smaller than my capsule. Can you believe that?'

We all looked astonished.

'You know, back home,' he went on, 'I can get into my car in the morning, drive for the whole day, and still be on my own land at nightfall.'

'Ock, aye,' said Micky, 'I had a car like that once meself.'

This caused some mirth, and Micky looked thoroughly pleased with himself. He spent the next two hours lurching from one doggy-shag story to another while we poured drink after drink down his interminable gullet. He also told us where to go and what to do (but he did not tell us why). He drew particular attention to the cliff-stacks at the western end of the island, where thousands of entertaining seabirds nested, including "guillemots", "puffins" and a mean-sounding one called "Razor Bill".

'You can catch Lusty's bus,' he suggested. 'He takes all the visitors back and forth. But go soon, for the birds are starting to leave. They spend most of the year at sea. Lusty does tours of the whole island too. If he's at himself, he might even show you where those new birds are nesting this year, up in the reeds around Ushet Lough. We've had a lot of twitchers. What d'you call them, now? Red phalarope is it? Something like that.'

I felt a curious fluttering in my guttering, and an inane grin spread over my face like soft butter. Perhaps there was, after all, pattern and poetry in the universe.

Begoña looked at me and said sternly, 'If you see one, duck.'

'Och no, it's not a duck,' Micky corrected her. 'It's a wee wading bird I believe, and very rare to see.'

We still had a campsite to establish, and so we took our leave. I bought Micky and Red a double whiskey each, and Bego said, 'Thank you for being so kind to a couple of strangers.'

Micky leaned over towards her.

'Shall I tell ye a wee secret?' he asked.

'By all means.'

'The landlord gives me free drink and crisps to sit here blathering during the summer – he says it's good for the tourists.'

We gathered our girls and our luggage, then made our way haltingly up towards our designated camping spot. Puri and Dila insisted on taking a detour in order to explore the white pebble beach. Even Conchi was now irritatingly enthusiastic and prone to giggling. We established our headquarters at Rosie McCormack's dejected and deserted cottage in the overgrown field overlooking Kinkeel Lough. It had no roof and no doors, but the shape of the small house – walls and gables – was clearly visible in rough uncemented stone. It was all too easy to imagine a large nineteenth-century family clustered around the fireplace on a cold evening with no fridge, no oven and absolutely no fockin' satellite television at all. We had some clearing and trampling to do, but we managed to pitch up the tents and lay out the sleeping bags before the sun sank behind the hill without so much as an apology for its rank inadequacy. As darkness descended, we lay there listening to the splatter-splitter of the rain, while the girls chattered excitedly next door like cold teeth. This got my goat, and my annoyance did not dissipate when they laughed at me for offering, with the patience of several saints, to sing them an alibi.

Eventually, they found their way into the dusky domain of dreams, but neither Bego nor I could follow, despite our extreme fatigue.

'This is miserable,' she said, 'I want to go home to where it is warm and cosy.'

'And where is that?' I asked.

At this point, there was an unusual pause, but eventually she replied, 'To Belfast, of course.'

'Yes, Bego, I want that too. But for now we are like maroon pirates. I think we must devise a survival policy – to keep misery out of harm's length.'

'And what do you suggest?'

You will not be surprised to learn that my head was steaming with ideas.

'Well, so far we're sulky, and it will not do us any good. Do you remember when we came up this way before, during our first week in Belfast? And how we dribbled over all the scenery, like real urban tourists?'

'Of course, but we had a car and a lovely new home waiting for us. Look at us now.'

'But don't you understand? We must recapture that mood. Think of it like this: we are on a rustic adventure weekend with our concrete metropolitan offspring, and then we are going home. It is no more than an idyllic Stone Age inter-lude in our modern and successful lives. Regard it as a game. We will seek out all the amusements of Arcadia!'

Bego was inexplicably unconvinced.

'Do you know what Dilatación said to me today?' she asked.

'I dread to think.'

'She said, 'You know, Mamá, Vog *always* gets her man.' Do you know what that meant?'

'I have no idea. Some childish fancy, I'll warrant. Don't change the subject, Bego. What do you think of my suggestion?'

'OK,' she said reluctantly, 'I'll try anything once. Oh, Mother Mary, however did we end up in such a curious position?'

This gave me a romantic notion, and so I closed the day with an unprecedented and skilful piece of what I like to call oneupmanship.

Chapter 40

In which Jesús is initially enthused but ultimately confused by prehistoric living.

During the next few days, we roamed the island in an exhilarating search for food, fuel and shelter. For fear of recognition, we gave birth to wide tourists and phalaropes, but we wandered the more remote corners of the island in the ever-refreshing rain, soaking up everything that Rathlin had to offer. We found towering rock-stacks block-a-chock with auks. The sight and sound of these densely packed seabird-cities dazed and amazed us, and the stench of the *guano* was the icing on our sensory cake. Puri in particular breathed deeply and dreamily, and put her arm on her little sister's shoulder. This encouraged Dila to ask a question.

'I like it here. Do you like it here?'

'I think I can make myself throw up,' Puri said, by way of an answer.

Our diet was peculiar, but delectably organic. From time to time, we returned to the café, but during the daytime there were rather too many people there and we did not wish to run over the risk of discovery. The quaint island shop provided basics such as milk, eggs and *pains au chocolat*, but not much else. We therefore lived off nature's wondrous bounty. Our vegetable intake was limited to seaweed and a few wild mushrooms. This, as you say, kept us regular (and at times continuous). Micky gave me an old fishing rod and some advice on catching eels in the island's loughs. The girls managed to land several of these slippery creatures, and Conchi beheaded them by the loughside using a prehistoric axe-head that she had tumbled across inside a cave. It was truly idyllic. Eels are extraordinary animals and they somehow cling onto life even after decapitation. We could well learn from their example. To our delight, their bodies would continue to squirm for some minutes following severance, while their heads looked on in frank disbelief.

An old woman added to our joy by bringing us two freshly killed rabbits. She was astonished when Bego explained that she knew how to complete their preparation. Purificación assembled some shellfish, and we attempted to boil them alive over an open fire made from damp driftwood. We ate more winkles than you could swing a cat at, but the rubbery limpets proved a crustacean too far. I even endeavoured to hunt and kill a seal as it lay quietly on the rocks. I crept up on it from a position down-wind, and managed to draw very close without arousing its suspicion. Then, in a flash, I grabbed a boulder and bashed it upon the head with all my might. Only now did I realize that my victim was already dead, somewhat rotten and largely inedible. My, how I laughed!

We also spent some time with Micky McCurdy, while Red Black was kind enough to let us penetrate his capsule. The balloon itself was deflated and pinned to the ground in an adjacent field, but we were nevertheless excited to finger his control panels and visualise ourselves in the clouds. He explained to us the purpose of every button and dial, but when I asked if I could pump him up and make a maiden fly, he said, 'Over my dead body!' This was not particularly stimulating at the time, but it may acquire a certain piquancy on page 337.

At the end of our four-day sojourn, we decided to stay another week, then another, then another. This was partly because we were having such a blissful time, and partly because we had no choice. We telephoned Mrs. Naughtie, and she said there were still a number of persecutors in the lane, though one or two of them had now departed for Scotland. Bego's agent advised her to lie down with her head low for the time being while desperate efforts mere made to salvage the perfume contract. In the end, we lived this energising Neolithic life for just over a month. I was very good at pretending to be contented, but I grew confused, and thus somewhat dejected, when it dawned on me that my good humour was becoming dangerously genuine. Can you even begin to imagine, dear reader, what it feels like to be made sad by one's own happiness? I was simply too convincing, and, strangely, I actually began to enjoy the sensation of living with my ear close to the earth. For the first time in months I began to dream lyrically of oranges and lemons and *las bellas de Andalucía*. Needless to say, I was embarrassed by my condition, and I kept it very much to myself. Bego, I knew, was anxious to return to Belfast, though she too was making the best brave fist of it, superficially at least. She would manage to smile as she chopped up rabbits or split hares. But I knew that, deep in her prize-winning marrow, she was aching to recommence her exciting and competitive life as the new Mrs. Decade. I worried that our circumstances and our differing responses to them were once again inserting the thin end of a wedgie between us.

Chapter 41

Here, you will learn how Purificación and a Policeman –
unlikely bedfellows – joined forces to suck the wind out of
Jesús' once billowing sails.

Ultimately, the difficult decisions that faced us were pinched
right out of our noses by the red hand of fate. In the first
place, Mrs. Naughtie became, if anything, even less encouraging when we snatched phonecalls from her in idle
moments. The local television station had disseminated a
report in which a policeman suggested that the missing
Sánchez Venturas might actually be 'holed up' within
Northern Ireland rather than without, as had previously
been presumed. More disturbingly, we learned that our
house had been searched by a specially-trained team of wildlife invaginators. Mrs. Naughtie had probed one of them
with her persuasive tongue, and had eventually been
informed that I was suspected of cooking and consuming
a number of endangered animals.

'As you will know,' he said, 'the man tried to trap a rare
wader in County Mayo, and I'm sorry to have to tell you,
off the record, that we have found the bones of several
medium-sized birds in his bin. These remains are currently
undergoing analysis. I'm sorry to say that your neighbour

is a depraved individual, and must be stopped. He's Spanish, you know.'

Mrs. Naughtie then asked him if she and her husband were in any immediate danger, at which point he bent down, thus lowering his voice, and whispered, 'Och, no. I think you're OK, love. We've just heard from the RSPB that a bird of the same species has been spotted north of here – I can't say where exactly – and we're looking at the possibility that he may have gone after it. It's some sort of dirty dietary vendetta, I'm afraid.'

As you can imagine, this information set all my alarming bells dangling at once and made it difficult for us to plot a route back to our house and garden.

Secondly, one of Purificación's pork pies fell off her trolley when it broke down with a screw loose, leaving us with little alternative but to abandon the picnic. She took to wandering off alone and spending large swathes of each day in what seemed to us indecent solicitude. She would sit behind an old wall near our hovel, and mutter to herself for hours at a time. She would often laugh, sometimes almost hysterically as if being pickled, but would fall immediately silent and secretive should any one of us approach her. Puri also mystified us by deploying a wide array of peculiar phrases in her daily discourse. Her Belfast tones and expressions were swiftly being displaced by something even more incomprehensible. She made old Micky McCurdy sound like Sir John Bitumen, the famous poet whose work covers the highways and byways of England so durably. She referred to the island as 'Rackery', and declared – if ever we set her a task – 'This is wild thirsty work for a wain.' When I reported to Bego that the island priest was planning to retire, Puri said, 'Well, that's a noggin and spoon for someone else.' She also claimed to have seen a hare only a few feet away, and when I asked why it had not run away, she said, 'We were behind the wall, and we got a squink through a vent.'[77]

This 'we' surprised me, so I asked which of her sisters had been with her. Puri grew coy, and said she had actually been alone. I pressed a little harder, sensing the possibility of *una revelación significativa*, and she eventually admitted that she had been with her 'friend'.

'Who's that?'

'I'm not allowed to say. Would ye everr leave me be? Ye are not allowed into my brain.'

'Why can't you say?'

'He told me. You're cruel and you're upsetting me. Your heart would'na make a rattle for the inside of a stone-checker's egg! Go clod the tangle, why don't you?'[78]

Puri was beginning to cry, but her resistance was infuriating me so much that dropping the subject was simply nat an aption. I gave her the third-degree burns, and eventually she began to crackle under the pressure.

'He's just a wee man who talks to me by the wall and other places. He's my friend and you cannae have him.'

Begoña had now joined the inquisitorial committee.

'What's he called, Puri?' she asked soothingly.

---

[77] I have attempted to translate some of these expressions in my glossary. If you are not satisfied, I suggest that you visit the island in person and ask for old Micky McCurdy.

[78] I refer the reader respectfully to footnote number 77.

'Not telling, he said I shouldn't.'

'What's his name, *chiquita*?'

She whimpered through her tears, then said 'Mr. Gro-og-ug, I think. But he's very shy and you have to leave him alone.'

'What does he look like?' I asked.

'He's wee small, not even as big as me. And he has no clothes on, but he's hairy all over.'

'*Santísima Virgen!*' said Bego, 'I think we must meet this Mr Gro-og-ug.'

Next morning, Begoña and I crept up to the wall while Puri sat on the other side. She was chatting away, as if in conversation. We tried to stay hidden, but eventually we grew impatient and looked over the parapet in what you quite rightly call a fit of peek. She was completely alone, and it was therefore strange that she called out, 'Why are you going?' and watched as if she were witnessing some-body's hasty departure. We made our way back towards the cottage, and Bego whispered, 'Well, better an imaginary friend than *un pequeño nudista rechoncho y peludo del norte*.[79] Perhaps she will leave him behind when we get out of here. I suppose it must be time to think of this?'

'We will burn that bridge when we come to it,' I replied effortlessly.

She sighed, cleverly mimicking the feigned reluctance to depart that is so characteristic of city trippers out in the wilderness for an uplifting frill.

I visited the pub that evening, and drifted in and out

---

[79] A little squat hairy northern nudist.

of another conversation with Micky McCurdy and Red Black as they slurped oysters from the fireside armchairs. Red was preparing to float off into the clouds, and he had already begun to inflate the balloon with his own supply of hot air. He was complaining that there were not only pins, but needles too, in his shoulder, and he looked decidedly unwell as he attempted to persuade Micky to accompany him to France. Predictably, the idea of 'gallivanting among the continentals' was treated with scorn.

'That sure is a pity,' said Red. 'I get awful lonely up there sometimes.'

Micky considered the matter closed, and I could tell that he was about to start telling me something about puffins (he had an unfortunate habit of ramming them down one's throat). I headed him off by encouraging him to think seriously about Red's offer.

'You should try it, Micky. You could go anywhere. The oyster is your world!'

Derisively, he scoffed, coughed, slurped and burped. Then he told me that, in his opinion, the world was a huge red herring. This sounded suspiciously like a food chain, and I sensed that the puffins were next up. I therefore took deflective action once more by presenting him with a short rasping report on Puri's curious conduct.

'I do not suppose that you have been talking to her, Micky?' I asked at the end. 'She has been using some most peculiar expressions.'

'What manner of expressions?' he asked.

I regurgitated a number of Puri's choice cuts, and Micky

stared into his drink with a thoughtful frown upon his brow. He sat like this for some minutes.

'That's a queer business, so it is,' he said at last. 'Them's old island expressions – there's not many as calls the place Rackery now, though once they all did.'

'Didn't she say who she's been talking to?' gasped Red.

'Indeed, she did,' I replied. 'But it makes no sense. She says she has befriended a little hairy man called Mr Groog-ug or some such. I don't suppose you know him?'

This was intended as a facetious remark, but Micky's eyes were on fire, set aglow by something that, for once, was neither amusement nor whiskey.

'The Grogock,' muttered Micky. 'Your wee girl has been talking to the Grogock. Would you fetch me another drink?'

I filled his glass, and sat stupefied in the gloomy room as he proceeded to illuminate me. The Grogock, according to Rathlin legend, was a small hairy man who once in a while appeared 'buck naked' to selected islanders. He was almost always benevolent, offering various forms of charitable assistance to those whom he visited. When the recipients of his favour presented clothes, however, he invariably pronounced them too big and promptly turned them down, often becoming rather decomposed in the process.

'He can't take anything back to his own world, you see,' said Micky, 'but nobody rightly knows why.'

He added further detail to the portrait.

'They say he can withstand great heat and cold, and some have seen him sunbathing out on the cliffs. But there's been never a bit of word of him for fifty year.'

'It sounds as if your girl is kinda special,' wheezed Red thoughtfully.

Micky slurped from his pint, and wiped the froth from his leathery lips with the back of his hand.

'You mustn't take her away.'

This thought rebounded like one of your squashed balls from the gleaming white walls of my mind as I walked back to the cottage. Of course, I did not really give two hooters about the future of Puri's friendship with the Grogock, but I did feel almost genuinely torn up at the prospect of leaving my little island heaven by the sea.

Chapter 42

This begins with Begoña's surprisingly wet dream but then rather goes downhill in a curious sky-machine.

That night, it rained. I was strangely aroused in the little hours by the unmistakable sound of water driplets invading our tent and striking my wife's forehead with a delicate series of successful splashes. To my surprise, they made no impression upon her. She continued to sleep, and then she began to dream. I should tell you at this juncture that when Bego fantasises in the night, there is sure to be quite a flower-show. She bangs and bashes, threshes and thrashes, and puts herself through torture; she laughs and sings and reveals secret things that can light one's passage to the future (if one is lucky). I therefore booked a front seat and asked the barmaiden if I could pre-ordain my interval drink. Initially, Bego spoke only nonsense, deploying a sultry French voice to ask somebody for a cucumber sandwich. As she did this, she seemed to press her pelvis into the bowels of Mother Earth, and I was frankly dumb-plussed. Then, however, she abruptly changed her tune and the main act began. The language she chose – interestingly enough – was Spanish, and for your pleasure, I will extract her snippets in recognisable form: 'Run, Pedro of the Mountains, run – go like the clap, my baby!' and 'May St. Roland himself mount you and inject you with speed!' and 'Do this for me, and I will be Queen, oh yes, I will be Queen!' She even began to give off the faint scent of oranges as she lay there squirming. Of course, I knew in a jiffy that she was dreaming of Picazón del Moro and the yearly Contest of the Rodents. My Begoña was back in Andalusia on a parched summer's day, and planning her victory speech. She had gone all the way home inside her head, and suddenly the future appeared clearer. It had been a long, arduous journey, but now, at last, we were nearing the end of the plank.

It is at this point that my tale begins to droop towards an anticlimax, and I fear that you will be disappointed that I cannot waggle it more energetically at its terminus. It is something of a non-eventity. Our closing episode was like the final, quiet drink of a pleasurable evening out with friends. Of course, in Spain we are in the habit at such moments of consuming either a glass of *agua ardiente* or a small thin cup of big thick coffee, and the effect is invariably to re-stimulate us for further nocturnal escapades (the last drink is never the last drink, as we like to say). For you, however, I suppose the beverage in question would have to be a mug of so-called 'Horlicks' (incapable, despite its auspicious name, of inducing anything other than sleep). On second thoughts, perhaps you will not after all feel let down by my warm milky ending.

I will not weigh you down with a heavy handbag of details, but will instead place them all in a convenient nut-case for you: we stole Red Black's balloon of hot air and went home to Spain. There was no other course of action open to us, and I hope you will not be censorious. We could not simply serve ourselves up to the so-called authorities like caramelised pears, for we had our honour and our dignity (although it is difficult to be dignified when, after several weeks on an island, one looks like a filthy sea urchin and stinks like a polecat in high heaven). In any case, those authorities would probably have interpreted any attempt at an apology or explanation as too little too late, like bolting the stable door after the horse has already locked it. Whatever I did, I knew that my name would be Lady Mud on the streets of Belfast.

In the morning, therefore, Bego and I exchanged words and were as one. While I summoned our forces, she sidled over to the balloon pod in order to establish that Red was not in residence. I received from her a signal that was pregnant with urgency, and I therefore sent my largest daughters over to join her. Next, I scooped up Dilatación and galloped across the field like a gypsy's donkey with quicksilver in its ear. After a certain period of swearing and mild violence, we managed to complete the inflation procedure and off we wafted. At first, we were carried north, and Bego screamed, 'Hell, no! It's even colder that way!' Then, by divine providence, the breeze turned itself inside out and we found ourselves heading in a vaguely southerly direction. It was a great crack, and we took to the air like ducks to the manor born.

There was only one genuine hiccup, which was fortunate because hiccups usually operate in teams. Red was not in fact tucked away in the pub with old Micky, as we had imagined. Instead, lonely old Red was stone-cold dead in his fold-out bed. This was tremendously sad for him, but he was quite old and every dog must have its day. We surmised that his heart had been attacked in the night. The situation was not ideal for us, either, but we proved more than capable of paddling our own canoe. Puri said she wanted to eat him, but the notion proved to be no more than a piece of puffed-up childish blister and she soon spat it out. So, for several days, Red just lay there, as if quietly contemplating his future. For the most part, our altitude was good and the low temperature of the high air dissuaded him from fuming unpleasantly (which was a mercy). Over central France, however, we began to lose height steadily and could not manipulate the controls in such a way as to regain it. There was no alternative, and after a short prayer we therefore jettisoned Mr. Red Black over a small village in the region known as Provence. He was quite a weight: bad news for the market trader who thoughtfully broke his fall, but good news for the Sánchez Venturas.

The remains of our voyage passed over smoothly enough. Of course, the children bickered and drove me towards lunacy by singing evangelical northern Protestant songs that they had learned in school. Our new vehicle, in merciful contrast, was surprisingly easy to fly, and we became so proficient that, eventually, we overshot the Sierra Nevada and landed in the Mediterranean, just off the beach in Malaga. We made quite a splash as we descended amongst all the lobster-pink northern tourists with our girls chanting 'The Son of God is Shining in Me, I will be his Bicycle Light' at a hysterical pitch.

As we made our way ashore, we half expected to be

arrested and extradited for our various alleged misdemeanours, but to our relief we found that a peculiar alliance of the saints in heaven and the governors of Spain was watching benevolently over us. The authorities in Northern Ireland later heard of our whereabouts, and they strove to reclaim us. It so happened, however, that the British and Spanish governments were, at that very moment, locked in one of their periodic quarrels over the status of Gibraltar. A group of Spanish customs ladies had developed the amusing habit of strip-searching all of the young men with British passports who tried to cross from the Rock to the mainland. It was their harmless way of saying, 'This piece of land is ours.' The British government complained, even though the men did not, and so Spain suspended the relevant extradition treaty. We were home and dry.

Postcript

In which some at least of Jesús' loose ends are tied up after a fashion.

Of course, I would like to tell you that fortune's wheel had by this time been fully revolutionised and that everything in my life settled thereafter into a new-old equilibrium. I would like to say that my year in the province is remembered only as some fantastical aberration, a period during which I fell off the horse of happiness before re-mounting it with a triumphant cry of 'Hooray Henry!' It would be pleasant to report that nothing consolidates one's true identity or one's sense of belonging more than a spell in some appallingly damp northern wasteland. To find one's home one must first lose it. I would like to tell you all this. But I cannot.

I had, of course, been lucky in a number of respects. Neither I nor Bego was prosecuted, and the relatives of Dead Red did not even want his balloon back (we donated it to the Sisters of Sorrow in Granada, and sometimes they still wave to us as they drift over our land on one of their aerial retreats). I had found a new friend in Micky McCurdy and I vowed to stay in touch with each and every one of him. Audrey was a different matter, and I heard nothing from her. Connor's latest identity and location remained mysterious, though I did receive a curious self-promoting card from a woman in Galway called Mrs. May McAloran, described as an award-winning estate agent and the guardian of two poor little Lithuanian orphans whom she had painstakingly adapted.

In most respects, however, I was no better off than I had been at the outset, while in some ways my condition had actually deteriorated. The fundamental problem was not the sensation of rejection. Mother Ulster had chewed on my flesh for a while, and then she had blown me off and thrown me up. But I was an adult, and I understood that this was Mother Ulster's choice. More potently, the following realisation formed itself within my mind: once a man has lived in a throbbing city and watched Brazilian ladies' football on a large flat-screen television built into the door of his three-metre high fridge/freezer unit, it is difficult for him to return to the life of a humble fruit-farmer. We transported the fridge to Spain at great expense, but there was insufficient electricity to feed its habit. For months, it sat in our courtyard as a monument to our dissatisfaction. Andalusia was still dry, hot and mainly brown. Somehow the land continued to cough up the occasional fruit, but there are only so many figs that a man can reasonably be expected to hold down. Unfortunately, I found that the perpetually shining sun got inside my head and fried my brain. Half of the time, there was no water in the taps because the foreigners had discharged it all into their swimming pools. When these people were not swimming, they were chasing flies around the country with their little electric swatting bats, as if it were possible to exterminate all of the insects in Andalusia. This, at least, offered me some light relief, but it was merely a sticky plaster and did not cure my disease. The children, as usual, resettled contentedly, but their happiness only served to emphasise the disappointed cravings of my heart.

Begoña returned to her rural life with reasonably good grace. She cooked and cleaned and trained her pet rats for the *Concurso*. She did not appear unduly bitter when some twig-legged Norwegian became Mrs. Decade in her place. She sold her businesses and we were therefore more than comfortable, economically if not psychologically. Sometimes, however, she was rather more assertive than I would have wished, and I was painfully aware that she had tasted the sweet 'n' sour fruit of your northern feminism. There were too many occasions, for example, upon which she contradicted me in front of my fellow members of *El Sindicato de Cultivadores de Naranjas*, and this caused me considerable annoyance.[80]

Our love-making was not quite what it had once been, but on the hole we rubbed along reasonably well. Begoña, in particular, pined for "Jumping Jack: the Spermicidal Maniac", and she strove in vain to locate a local supplier.[81] Strangely, our most successful acts of love occurred during the performances of a little Ulster role-play in which we indulged from time to time. We would replicate Northern

---

[80] The institution to which I refer is The Union of Orange Growers.

[81] We eventually learned that JJ had been taken off the market after an American consumer developed a sexual condition known as Perpetual Numbness Disorder (PND).

Irish conditions in the relative privacy of our olive terraces, and both of us found this activity quite engaging. When the water supply was willing, I would situate my special sprinkling hosepipe on a suitable terrace in such a way that it sprayed synthetic rain continuously onto the one below. I would then place thick black plastic sheeting in the surrounding trees, thus blocking out the sun or, if we were intent upon *una cópula nocturna*, the stars. Next, by way of foreplay, I would call loudly, 'Is thur a womman roiynd aboiyt here whuuus in the muud fra gud fock?' Invariably, Bego would come running, and she would reply, 'I wudden say no, so I wudden' or 'I always like my fur shurr, so I duu.' To this, I would respond, 'Och, that's dead orn, love,' and we would make moderately pleasing love in the drizzle, occasionally shivering slightly. I must tell you, however, that in the depths of our intimacy I was frequently unable to evict from my mind unsettling memories of Audrey in the woods and the most exhilarating sexual experience of my life, bar nun.

Glossary of previously inexplicable expressions

Since completing my memoir, I have undertaken further scholarly research into the curious speech habits of the Ulster people. Here is a list of terms, designed particularly for the enlightenment of strangers to that portion of the planet. In each case, I have endeavoured to provide an alternative expression that is both accessible and applicable.

Ackaway with yuu: you are undoubtedly mistaken and it would be better for us all if you went somewhere else for a short while.

It was boggin, so it was: it was dirty beyond belief, and I wish to emphasise that fact.

Yurra wee fockin' chancer: I regard you as a small and disreputable opportunist.

If he's at himself: if he is in a happy mood, and not drunk, depressed or deranged.

You binlid, [also dirtbird, blirt, girney gub, scut, skite-the-gutter, galeeried gunterpace, thundergrub, spoon and sponge]: you stupid, idiotic, filthy or irritating person.

He's a blethercumskite: this individual talks in a ridiculous fashion.

The sticks are fur <u>camogie</u>: these implements are designed for use in a competitive game played by stout Catholic ladies with balls and sticks.

A <u>canty</u> wee thing: an object that is small and neat.

<u>Catch</u> yourself orn: come to terms with it and take immediate control of your destiny, you silly person.

Thassa <u>clinker</u> (also cracker): that is a particularly fine representative of its type.

Go <u>clod the tangle</u>: please proceed to gather the kelp or seaweed for processing (archaic).

A bit of <u>crack</u> and a wee blather: some sociable fun and a light-hearted conversation.

Ay's a <u>dacent spud</u>, so ay is: he is a good potato, yes indeed.

That's <u>dead orn</u>: that is just right, perhaps even perfect.

You're a wee <u>dote</u>: you are an unusually small but sweet-natured person.

You've a <u>face like a Lurgan spade</u>: you do not look particularly happy today.

He's a queer <u>hallion</u>: he is an uncommonly irresponsible person.

Have a <u>hoke</u> around in it: why not search my container, a little roughly if you must, with your bare hands?

It's a <u>nockin shap</u>: this building is habitually used for sexual intercourse.

A <u>noggin and spoon</u> for someone else: a pleasant opportunity, perhaps created by the timely death or departure of a colleague (archaic).

It gives me the <u>nyrps</u>: it induces in me certain depressing thoughts.

He's a <u>raker</u>: that man is a loveable rogue and/or a competent gardener.

I need to get my head <u>sharred</u>: I require some peace and quiet in order to regain my natural composure; alternatively, I need to wash my hair, for it is boggin [see above].

<u>Shiramoanlycoddin</u>: calm yourself down – it was intended as a harmless joke.

Your heart would'na make a rattle for the inside of a <u>stonechecker's egg</u>: the organ that drives your blood is so small and shrivelled that it would not even produce an audible sound were it to be placed inside the empty egg of a tiny bird called a stonechat and shaken.

We got a <u>squink through a vent</u>: we were able to peer through a gap.

Stop <u>takin the hand</u> out of him: kindly refrain from teasing him – you can see he is upset.

Ay's a fockin' <u>Taig</u>: he is a Roman Catholic, and I do not care for him one bit.

You're a <u>tube</u>: I consider you to be either a cultural conduit or an idiot.

Let's have an <u>Ulster fry</u>: shall we consume an enormous and potentially fatal meal of fried eggs, bacon, soda bread etc?

I've to look after the <u>wains</u>: unfortunately, I have no choice but to tend to my troublesome offspring.

Menciones

I must close this book with a thump by expressing my gratitude to the following kind-hearted citizens of Belfast and other places: Paul Bew, Janice Carruthers, Mark Carruthers, John Curran, Richard English, Tamsin Griffiths, Katherine Josselyn, Jonathan and Lucy Kelly, Jonathan Marsh, Katie Marsh, Michael and Linda Montgomery, Laura Morris, Mícheál Ó Mainnín, Ian Parsley, Simon Petherick, Nini Rodgers, Catherine Skully and Isabel Torres. I also wish to acknowledge my debt to each and every one of the generous reviewers and to the prominent persons who dared to puff up their blurbs for my benefit (please examine the front end of this volume for evidence). It is thanks to them that this unquestionably laughable volume has been flying off the shelves like hot potatoes.

May all their doings savour of success and may none of their droppings return to haunt them!

For the pleasure of these and all other humans, I have taken the liberty of concealing an ancient Spanish coin at or near a cold northern location that has featured in my chronicle. Please know that this small and now slightly curved piece of booty was not purchased from one of the grubby street traders near the cathedral in Granada. No, indeed, it was once the personal property of my ancestor of famous memory, the medieval adventurer named José del Antojo Repentino. Part of his story is told on p. 223, and here, on p. 352, is another small segment of him: when José eventually reached the New World during the early sixteenth century, he did so with the coin of which I speak safely in his pocket. He came to treasure it over the ensuing years, for its evident magic preserved him from a plethora of perils (he was regularly picked on by native gods and pecked at by native birds – and sometimes the two groups doubled up). Now perhaps you can understand from whence derives my itchy travel-sickness! The hard-working disc returned to Spain with José's great-grandson, and has been passed about in the family ever since, looming large among the heirs of both men. It is thus a cherished hand-me-down with verifiable pick-me-up qualities to boot. Sadly, the experiences that are documented in this book have left me unconvinced of the coin's protective qualities. And thus I leave it willingly into the care of the reader who proves clever enough to find it.

It was not easy to secrete such a valuable metal item, I can tell you. Begoña strove to dissuade me, but I put my foot down and returned alone to my former stamping grounds. You will of course understand that I must take care not to reveal myself too nakedly in any part of Ireland these days, but under cover of the moist murk that blankets it more often than not I accomplished my task (I wore one of your Frog Man costumes and travelled mainly by water, just to be on the safe side – perhaps you will find a clue in this revelation).

If you are fortunate enough to locate the token, you are instructed to take it forthwith to the Conor Café on the Stranmillis Road in Belfast. Here, the upright staff will inspect your find and, if it appears to be the genuine article, they will proceed to take a booking for a delicious evening meal to be consumed by two persons. As the last morsels of this refreshment descend your flexible gullet, the lovely waiting people with their shiny and tasteful trays will again advance upon you. Do not flinch an inch! Their purpose is merely to present you with an exceptionally fine old bottle of single malt whiskey from the celebrated Bushmills distillery. If you wish, you may drink this on the spot, but please remember not to drive home afterwards or the fockin' Peelers will stick their points on your licence as sure as $x = x$.

I will even provide you with a verse-riddle, just in case you prove unable to locate the treasure without such a crutch. These words arrived in my mind one night, during a characteristically wet dream of Ulster:

A coin stored ('twixt rhyme and reason) by doctor in sea

> *Thrifty wife with clean Portaloo,*
> *Licks the leaven of heaven,*
> And upward points at a seam of red,
> With openings from one and seven.
> (Where poacher and gamekeeper live as neighbours,
> They rarely do each other favours).

If and when the token is taken and the whiskey won, the momentous news will be posted on the Beautiful Books website in order to put all the disgruntled also-rans out of their misery as humanely as possible.

★ ★ ★

**Beautiful
Books**